THE MANY

ALSO BY SYLVAIN NEUVEL

Take Them to the Stars
A History of What Comes Next
Until the Last of Me
For the First Time, Again

The Themis Files
Sleeping Giants
Waking Gods
Only Human

The Test

THE MANY

SYLVAIN NEUVEL

SOLARIS

First published 2026 by Solaris
an imprint of Rebellion Publishing Ltd,
Riverside House, Osney Mead,
Oxford, OX2 0ES, UK

www.solarisbooks.com

ISBN: 978-1-83786-689-2

10 9 8 7 6 5 4 3 2 1

A CIP catalogue record for this book is available from the British Library.

Designed & typeset by Rebellion Publishing

Printed in Denmark

MIX
Paper | Supporting responsible forestry
FSC® C104608

“Pray, don’t find fault with the man that limps,
Or stumbles along the road.
Unless you have worn the moccasins he wears,
Or stumbled beneath the same load.”

‘Judge Softly’
by Mary T. Lathrap (1895)

INTRODUCTION

On October 4 of the year 2014, an object originating from the far edge of the galaxy collided with another body inside the asteroid belt. A small chunk of the visitor broke off and hurtled towards Earth at 74,000 kilometers per hour. Most of the meteor, the size of a grapefruit, burned up in the atmosphere, but a small part, about the size of a grain of rice, crashed in the woods near Marquette, Michigan. The tiny meteorite shattered on impact. Inside it was a small cluster of amino acids and hydrocarbons, which would soon come into contact with the most unlikely of creatures.

PART 1

SPILLOVER

1
TICK

THE TICK WAS… existing, doing tick things in a tick world, unaware that he was a tick, or that he even *was*. His life was simple, to say the least, more akin to that of a smoke detector than to anything we'd consider sentient. Stimulus. Response. Stimulus. Response.

Hunger

Hunger

Hunger

Heat

The tick let himself fall onto whatever was there and tried to bite into it. Nothing. Whatever this was, it was not satisfying, and the tick continued its slow voyage in search of warmth. The tick had done this a thousand times, climbed up and fallen on whatever it could eat from, but as it walked across the mossy ground, it felt something… different, something very strange, something it had never experienced before.

Hunger

Hunger

…

I. Hunger.

2
BOOKER

Booker was in deep trouble, and he knew it. He was supposed to pick up his child and be at the doctor's office at five. It was now 5:45 and he was pulling up the driveway. It wasn't his fault, not really. He'd made a custom cake for little Betsy Lane's birthday—Blossom from *The Powerpuff Girls* in red velvet cake with buttercream frosting—and her mom couldn't make it to the bakery before 4:45. Then that asshole cop stopped him on the way home. 'License and registration.' 'Keep your hands where I can see them, sir.' Booker was always amazed at how much disrespect and condescension one could pack into a well-timed 'sir.' He'd gone through the same routine last month, and the month before. Same cop, of course. Big man, out of shape. Booker wasn't sure what was worse, the spit bubble that formed every time he opened his mouth, or the stupid grin that replaced it when he kept it shut. One thing was certain, that guy was an asshole through and through—you could smell the bigotry on his breath. Just another racist bully who got himself the perfect job and savored every bit of power over others that it gave him. Ironically, the police force was probably the only place that would hire this troglodyte.

He wouldn't last a day at the bakery, and Booker couldn't imagine anyone willingly subjecting themselves to that man's presence in an office or anywhere else. Irony or not, he'd wasted another fifteen minutes on that bullshit traffic stop and Layla would be extra pissed. They were already mad at him when he left for work, and he knew that doctor's appointment meant a lot to them. He took a deep breath before coming in. He could deal with the anger, but being a disappointment left a deeper wound every time.

—Dad! What the hell?

—I'm so sorry, kiddo. I got pulled over on the way back.

—Again?

—Mm-hmm. You remember when we talked about that, right?

—Yes. Hands on the dash. Don't reach for anything.

—Don't speak unless they—

—Wait, why are you taking your coat off? We gotta go!

—Oh, it's too late now. I'm sorry.

—No! You promised!

—We're an hour late, Layla. What do you want me to do? We'll go some other time.

—You said that a month ago. I've been waiting for this! You know it!

—I know, but what's the rush? I thought we'd agreed you'd wait a bit before doing anything… drastic.

—I know, Dad, but… you know.

—What?

—Boobs! We talked about this!

—Oh, that. But what if it's dangerous? You don't know what these… blocker things'll do to you.

—That's why we were going to see the doctor! So she can explain it! I told you all this, you just weren't listening.

—I was, and we'll go.

—When?

—Soon.

—*When?*

—I don't know! I'll make another appointment tomorrow. Okay?

—What if she won't see us because we didn't show?

—It'll be fine, Layla! Trust me. I'm here for you, always.

—You keep saying that, but I know you don't want this.

—What do you mean? Are you still mad at me because of your friend? I told her you were my daughter, let's not make a big deal out of it.

—You do it all the time.

—No! I use your pronouns, just like you asked. There's just no gender-neutral kinship terms.

—Child.

—True, but that sounds weird. And sometimes people, older people mostly, they get confused, and then I have to explain and…

—I have to explain too, Dad.

—I know. That's not what I meant. It's just—

—You said you understood. You said—

—I know what I said, but you're eleven, Layla! I just don't want you to do anything you'll end up regretting, that's all.

—Forget it.

—Layla! Come back…

Booker didn't mean it. He didn't want Layla to come back. All he wanted was a cold beer to chase down the lies and a hot shower to wash away the shame. His plea for Layla to come back wasn't the only thing he didn't mean. He never wanted to go to that doctor's office. He didn't want Layla to transition. He'd reluctantly learned to live with non-binary Layla. Boy Layla, whatever his name would be, was a different story altogether. Booker had it all figured out, once. He had a good marriage, a gorgeous daughter. The rest was already written. Layla would get an MBA, have children, take over the business and visit him twice a week so he could play with his grandson. Then his wife met someone and moved to Portugal. His little girl went from *her* to *they*, and now wanted to be *he*. He felt he'd lost control of his life, every single part of it. He'd failed as a husband, he was failing as a father. Worst of all, he never saw any of it coming. He'd been angry for a long time, blamed his ex-wife for everything, but he'd slowly come to accept the truth: it had been there the whole time for him to see. He'd just never paid enough attention to the people he loved to realize how unhappy they were.

Folks say understanding the problem is half the solution. Booker promised himself he would listen, and he did, to the best of his ability. It worked, to some extent. He now fully realized how unhappy Layla was. That half a solution didn't make him feel any better, though. The other half, well… he was still looking for the other half. She—Damnit!—*they* wanted something he just didn't understand. He'd always thought of himself as open-minded, but his open-mindedness was from the '90s and showing obvious signs of arthritis. It's hard to see yourself as the stiff old man when you were once the wild kid during wild times. He'd been to Burning Man! It doesn't really matter how 'cool' one is, or rather, has been; at some point, everyone's take on the world hardens like cement. After that, even if you *know* you're biased, it's impossible to tell where that bias begins or ends. Everything Booker did made sense to him, or he wouldn't have done it. Layla was eleven. It was his job as a father to set limits. No sleepovers on school nights. Bedtime at 9:30. No soda except on special occasions. Not once, however, not for a second, had Booker given even the smallest thought to puberty blockers until Layla brought them up. He didn't even know these things *existed*. Layla said he should just trust them. He wished it were so easy, but they couldn't be trusted with *cake!* Whenever Booker brought home something from the shop, he'd have to hide it, or Layla would tear through it like it was their last meal. Layla needed an adult who knew what was best for them. He had the adult part going for him, but how the hell was he supposed to know what to do about hormone blockers? How was *any* father supposed to know? Booker had no one to talk to, not about this. He rarely missed his wife but, at that moment, he wished she'd come back, just for this. 'Dad, I—' 'Ask your mom, okay, kiddo? The Packers are at the goal line.'

3
CAROLE

CAROLE GOT WHISTLED at by road workers on the way to the bus stop. Nondescript assholes in nondescript work clothes. 'Take it as a compliment!' the mailman had half-heartedly said as he and an angry Carole passed each other. She knew better. Carole was well aware that she wasn't particularly attractive, not in the magazine or TV sense of the word. She was in her mid-forties, short and a little chubby, 'well-rounded' as her husband called it. There was nothing notably unique or endearing about her physique. Brown hair, brown eyes. She had a semi-flat nose and a semi-weak chin. She'd have made the perfect movie extra, never drawing attention away from the leads. No, the catcalling was never about desire, it was about *power,* the power to make her feel like an object: small, consumable, disposable. That's not what made Carole angry, though. She was mad because it had worked. She felt small and consumable, like a ham sandwich. She'd feel like lunch all the way to work, where the feeling would gradually dissipate and be replaced by one of inadequacy and insignificance. Carole was good at her job, and she knew it. She'd gone back to school after her divorce. She finished first in her class at Michigan State before she moved back to the Upper Peninsula and found a job at an ad agency. Today, they would pitch her campaign to the U.P. Health System, the agency's biggest client. *They* would pitch it, not Carole. She wasn't 'the sales type,' they'd told her many times. What they meant was that she wasn't young enough, thin enough, assertive enough, et cetera, et cetera. She'd learned to live with it, though. Carole wasn't enough for her first boyfriend, her first husband, she wasn't enough for her job. The jury was still out on husband number two, and it would likely stay that way. It hurt too much the first time around, she wouldn't let anyone else catch her by surprise.

—Hey Carole! Today's the big day, ain't it?

Carole was startled. The voice was that of Lana Lannister, Carole's neighbor and the newest addition to the town police force. She was sitting on the passenger side of her patrol car, waiting for her partner to come out of Booker's Bakery. Carole never liked Lana, and always hated herself for it. Lana was younger, and taller, and always happy, and every other thing Carole was constantly reminded she wasn't. Lana would definitely have pitched the ad campaign. Her first husband had left her for a Lana. Her second probably would, given the chance. Carole felt petty for resenting her, which was still better than just resenting her and not feeling bad about it.

Carole nodded and smiled. The smile part took some effort, but she thought it was an acceptable grin, at least better than the one she'd given Lana the night before. They often ran into each other in the driveway—Lana lived across the street. Lana wanted to be a 'good neighbor,' and brought food or small gifts over at least once a month. She also made small talk with everyone on the street every chance she got. That's how she knew about Carole's work life, and her personal life, and—

—Go get 'em, girl!

Gawd, the giddiness. Like nails on a chalkboard. Carole wasn't a happy person. She had discussed the matter with her therapist, who suggested she find activities that bring her joy, like a hobby. That seemed easy enough, but days went by, then weeks, then months, and Carole couldn't think of a single thing. Carole just didn't like being Carole; not in this universe, anyway. She'd have been happy being someone else, or perhaps being Carole someplace else, some place far, far away. She wasn't depressed, just permanently hovering between various states of mild displeasure. If life were a restaurant, her meal was something like egg salad with tiny bits of eggshell in it, or fried halloumi that's been sitting for an hour: something that *could* have been great, but wasn't. She wished she could talk to the manager, but she didn't believe in a higher power. It was one thing for the world to suck all on its own, but an all-powerful being creating the universe from scratch and coming up with *this? Nah, I don't think so.*

Carole had all sorts of strengths and talents. She was smart, and fair, and loyal, and a bunch of other things people didn't seem to appreciate, or even care about. She was a fish in a tree-climbing contest. 'Everyone is a genius. But if you judge a fish by its ability to climb a tree, it will live its whole life believing that it is stupid.' Was that from someone famous? She didn't know. It could have been one of those inspirational quotes on the office calendar. Carole always wondered why people bought those. They couldn't possibly believe it would make a difference in anyone's life. Who knows, maybe they really thought the quotes were deep and wanted others to share in their amazement at cheap metaphors. Life is like a rollercoaster, a rainbow, an onion, a box of chocolates, a mirror. Life is like riding a bicycle or eating an elephant. The tree-climbing fish thing wasn't that much better. It was also plain wrong. Not everyone was a genius at something. She knew plenty of people who had no special talents, no brains, no social skills, no outstanding qualities whatsoever. What's more, all these folks seemed happy; happier than she was, anyway. Granted, that was a low bar to clear, but…

Maybe it was just a low bar to clear.

Carole realized she was getting lost in her thoughts again. She daydreamed a lot. Did that count as a hobby? She imagined herself a little taller, looking a little better, wearing that Chanel suit Victoria Abril wears in *High Heels*. She'd step into the conference room at her own agency to meet some billionaire client who'd flown halfway across the globe just for her. Would she really want that, though? Probably not. She'd picked advertising after her divorce because it seemed more attainable, but young Carole Veilleux had wanted to be a doctor. She'd have been good at it, maybe. She had the grades, she liked being in school. The only thing she liked more was her boyfriend, a semi-pro hockey player who doubled as a poet. He was reasonably good at both, and said he owed it all to Carole. She was his muse, on the ice and on the page. As flattering as that was, it came with a small caveat. Muses, as she would soon learn, needed to be around all the time or the magic wouldn't happen. They couldn't be at work all day, or out with friends, or even in school. So instead of being a doctor, Carole became a wife and travelled with the Flint Bulldogs until her husband broke his leg and the team moved to Utica. Oh, well. What is it they say again? Hindsight is 20/20? Shivansh, the new husband, would have been more than happy to support her while she went back to school, but it was too late for that and the last thing she wanted was to be dependent on another—

A car drove by and hit a puddle of water near the sidewalk, splashing Carole from foot to waist. This wouldn't be a great day. She winced as her wet pants stuck to her thighs like a hungry leech. There wasn't enough time to go back home and change. Not that it would make a difference, she was going to spend the day alone, hidden in her office, kept away from anything and anyone that mattered. Carole peeled her pants away from her legs, then stepped closer to the curb as the Shopper Route bus drew near. She was about to climb on board when she felt a *slight* sting on the back of her neck.

4

LANA

LANA SAT AT her desk, coffee in hand. She glanced at the framed picture of Al Pacino sitting next to her computer before reorganizing her pens and supplies. She recognized the effort the janitor made to leave things the way he found them, but important details still escaped him, like the immutable fact that the blue pen should be closest to the hand, followed by other colors based on frequency of use. Every object on that desk had a purpose which, in turn, determined its preferred location: the pens, the paperclips, the phone, even the framed picture of Al Pacino.

Her first day on the force, Lana was invited for drinks with her new colleagues. She'd once dreaded all forms of social interaction, but a friend in therapy had changed all that with three simple rules for her to follow.

1. Show interest. Always begin a conversation with something about the other person.
2. Smile a lot. Happiness, even when faked, is highly contagious.
3. Never sound smarter than the person you're talking to.

Lana had despised putting on that bubbly act at first, but found that people seemed to like her staged self a hell of a lot more than the genuine article. She entered the local cop bar armed with a large smile and a modicum of rule-induced confidence. The evening went reasonably well, enough for her to allow herself two drinks instead of her usual one. She was returning from an extra trip to the restroom when Frank, a man twenty years her elder and her freshly assigned partner, pushed her against the wall, stuck his hand inside her shirt and forcibly kissed her. Lana fought him off and left. The next morning, Frank and three other officers presented Lana with a picture of Al Pacino. They told her how much they admired his acting work, and that he deserved an Oscar for his portrayal of Serpico, the New York cop who was shot in the face for being a rat. They told her to look at the picture every day, and that she was forbidden to get rid of it. Like every other object on Lana's desk, the picture of Al Pacino had a purpose.

Most people would have quit on the spot, but Lana's autism made her particularly good at compartmentalizing. Though she loathed a good portion of the department, she found the job itself rewarding. She was helping people. True, she could have been helping people doing something else. Electricians helped people, so did cashiers, hairdressers, pharmacists, and so on, but she offered help in more dire situations. It wasn't necessarily better help—she also gave parking tickets, while, say, pharmacists provided life-saving medication—but the feeling of accomplishment was generally greater than what she'd experienced in her previous job as a cashier. As for Frank, she spent about six hours alone with him every shift, which, in a twenty-four-hour day, meant that nearly sixty-one percent of her time was Frank-free. He also didn't like getting out of the car for anything other than food, and he seemed content letting Lana handle every mundane thing on her own. He would take pleasure in scaring some poor kid every now and then, order her around in public to reassert his manhood, but, objectively, he was more of a chauffeur to her than anything else. She hated him, profoundly, but that was a separate thing, and she'd have hated him the same if she were off the force.

Lana stared at her coffee, tapping her foot impatiently. She liked hers black. That meant it was still too hot to drink when she got to her desk. Those seven to eight minutes of waiting—depending on how long Frank talked to the cashier before coming back to the car—were excruciating. Every morning, she considered the possibility of altering her coffee habits. Adding milk would no doubt shorten the waiting period, perhaps reduce it to zero. But no. Altering habits was not Lana's forte. People said it was the autism that made her rigid that way, but she wasn't sure. There were, objectively, serious advantages to a well-established routine. Decision-making is time-consuming. Saving four minutes of pondering every day gave one a whole twenty-four hours of extra time per year, a couple months over their lifetime. Performing the same activities repeatedly also made people better at them, which resulted in improved performance and fewer accidents, not to mention stress reduction and all the health benefits that came with it. Granted, drinking coffee with milk would soon become a habit of its own, but once that door was open, there was no telling where the changes would stop.

Lana noticed a blinking red light on her phone. Someone had turned down the ringer volume when she was out on patrol, as they often did. She readjusted the volume to a proper level before answering. It was Billy, the part-time cashier at Booker's Bakery. Lana immediately thought about the fake birthday cake in the front window. She wasn't a hundred percent sure it was fake, but it had been sitting there for as long as she could remember. Whether it was real or not, Lana had vivid dreams about that cake. Her diabetes was relatively easy to keep under control, but she could never allow herself to eat that delicious-looking pink frosting.

—Billy! How are you? You must be excited to finish college. It's your last year, isn't it?

—Euh, yeah, sure, but you gotta come down. Some lady went berserk at the store and bit Booker.

—I'm sorry, did you say someone bit him?

—She tried to chew his arm off, like, for real. He's bleeding pretty bad. Just come get her, okay?

—Does he need an ambulance?

—BOOKER! Do you need an ambulance?… He says no doctors. He'll be fine.

—Okay, I'm on my way. Why didn't you call 911?

—Booker said to call you. He said you know her.

—Me? Who is it?

—I think her name's Carole.

Carole Veilleux. Lana was surprised. Carole and her husband—what was his name? something… foreign—both looked like they were on the verge of a breakdown, but neither seemed like the type of person who would terrorize a donut shop. When she first met them, Lana thought they might have had marital problems, which would have explained the constant look of frustration on Carole Veilleux's face. Lana made an effort to visit every few weeks, bring over some cookies or flowers, just to make sure everything was okay. It was, they were fine. In fact, the only time she'd seen Carole laugh was with her husband. He, on the other hand—*what was his name?*—never laughed. It was like his facial muscles were all severed in a freak accident. He seemed… content, though. Then again, Lana couldn't read people well and it was at least possible that she'd gotten them all wrong.

Lana decided not to tell the chief right away. He might decide a violent act in a public place required a bigger response and Lana didn't want to needlessly escalate the situation. Carole was a friend and neighbor, and there might still be a way to resolve the issue without an arrest. She was ready to go, but she had to find her partner first. Frank's chair was empty, which wasn't unusual: he liked roaming around the office making inappropriate jokes or startling the receptionist from behind. She grabbed her jacket and began looking for him, visiting his usual spots in decreasing order of probability.

5
CAROLE–TICK

Carole wasn't feeling well by the time she got to work. She tried her usual, ibuprofen and a double espresso, but no luck. By eleven, she was shivering in her chair and her boss told her she should leave, just to make sure she didn't spread whatever she had to the entire office. Carole wanted to stay. Their big client was coming at 1:00 and there were plenty of things only she knew about the project. Sure, she wouldn't be the one presenting to them, but she could help answer questions. Her boss reminded her of that time everyone got gastroenteritis and told her they would call if they needed anything. Carole *did* feel like crap, and there was always a chance her husband would stop working long enough for them to watch *When Harry Met Sally*. He always liked watching movies he'd seen a million times. Carole put her coat on and walked to the bus stop. The ride back home felt like it lasted two days. The sun was too bright, the road too bumpy. The entire bus smelled like a gym locker. She'd stood next to smelly people before, but this was more intense than anything she'd ever experienced, and it was *everyone*. Dozens of smells swarmed the odor receptors in Carole's nostrils, each person with their own recognizable aroma. The teenage boy reeked of alcohol. The old woman's sweat had a hint of green tea in it, which Carole found oddly attractive. The man next to her smelled a lot sweeter, like burnt sugar or maple syrup. Carole was profoundly repulsed by it. She moved as far away from him as she could, only to find herself standing next to a woman who stank like she'd been dipped in vinegar. Carole thought she might throw up right there and then, but her gagging was interrupted when she started seeing things. They weren't really *things* in the sense of discrete objects, so much as a shapeless blur of color and texture. Flesh-colored and bumpy, like human skin seen through an out-of-focus microscope.

Thankfully, her stop was next and Carole rushed off the bus to get some fresh air. She looked at the big 'Booker's' sign over the door in front of her and suddenly she was *hungry!* HUNGRY! She needed food like she needed to breathe. There was no fighting it, she had to eat *now*, as if her life depended on it. Maybe it did. She rushed in, cut in front of the three people standing in line and put both hands on the glass display. She wanted it all: donuts, croissants, a birthday cake for someone named Susan. Carole was *hungry!* Customers behind her started protesting, Billy the part-time cashier refused to serve her, but none of it mattered except the hunger. Carole jumped belly-first on the counter and reached for the food herself. She'd completely stopped thinking by then. Her body had turned into one big eating machine and was acting on its own. She'd have jumped into a volcano for those donuts, fought a grizzly bear, anything.

Booker, who was working in the kitchen, heard the ruckus and rushed to poor Billy's rescue.

—Carole? What the hell? Get your ass off the counter right now!

Maybe it was Booker's deep voice, maybe it was hearing her name, but Carole stopped moving immediately. For a moment, she looked puzzled, as if trying to remember why she was there in the first place. Everyone around her calmed down, thinking the worst was over, but Carole was simply coming to terms with a new realization. Booker was standing right there, and he smelled *really, really* good. Suddenly, she wasn't hungry for donuts, or for croissants, not even for Susan's birthday cake. She didn't want to eat *at* Booker's, she wanted to eat Booker himself. She wanted to bite deep into him and suck on his blood until she was so full that she'd explode. It was a disturbing thought—Carole knew full well it was wrong to eat people—but one so clear and profound she simply could not ignore it. Carole lunged at Booker and stuck her teeth deep into the inside of his forearm as he tried to stop her. When the skin punctured, the blood rushed into her mouth, overloading her taste buds with the tang of iron. Carole sucked in as much blood as she could, then bit deeper to get a taste of Booker's flesh. The flavor was underwhelming: rather bland, like pork, maybe a bit more sour. The texture, on the other hand, was to die for. Booker's arm was firm but buttery. It melted in the mouth like raw tuna from that fancy Japanese place where she and Shivansh ate when they went to New York for Easter. Carole wanted to stay there forever, jaw clenched, sucking blood and tasting human sashimi. It took Billy and all three customers to get her to let go. There was nothing in the shop to restrain her, no duct tape, no rope, so they pushed her into the bathroom and locked her in from the outside.

Carole was seeing things that made no sense, surreal things: A Daliesque tongue with barbs sticking out of the side. White veins on a red background, something halfway between steak and a Jackson Pollock. She managed to regain focus after a minute or two and looked at herself in the bathroom mirror. She was horrified by the blood covering her from her mouth to her chest. She tried to replay the events of the last few minutes in her head, but it was all hazy, distorted, like she was looking at life through an empty glass jar. She flipped the seat cover down and sunk onto the toilet to think. She really needed to think. She'd just done something awful, that much was clear, but she didn't fully understand what or why. The most puzzling thing was that she didn't feel bad about it. To the contrary, she felt content, fulfilled in a way she'd never experienced. As weird as it was, sucking on Booker's blood felt really fucking good. It also calmed her down. She didn't feel hungry anymore, or sick for that matter. For the first time ever, at least for as long as she could remember, Carole was... happy. She got up from the toilet, eager to tell everyone about it.

—Hello?

She changed her mind when she heard Billy calling the police. Perhaps these weren't the people she should be talking to, especially Booker, who might not appreciate hearing how great it was to chew on him. No, she had to go home and tell her husband. Could she, though? She couldn't leave right away—the bathroom door was locked, and the cops were on their way—but then what? She *was* in trouble, but she hadn't killed anyone, at least she didn't think she did. She'd never heard of anyone going to prison for biting people, but there were a lot of people in prison and she'd never heard about most of them. Still, this didn't feel like a life sentence type of thing. She'd once TP-ed a house as a teenager. She'd been scared shitless when the owner ran out, but in hindsight, there was only so much he could have done to her. This was sort of the same. They could arrest her, but at *some* point, they'd have to let her go. Then she could go home and be with her husband. That's what she wanted now, more than anything, to go home and share her newfound happiness with Shivansh.

She started singing to herself to pass the time while waiting for someone to let her out. She'd never done that before and found it quite soothing. She went through her favorite songs from *The Sound of Music*, adding a few lyrics of her own to 'My Favorite Things':

—Sprinkles on donuts and cheddar on croissants
Bright yellow letters on a round cake with fondant
Sucking on blood like vampires with wings
These are a few of—

Oh! Carole heard the bell over the front door ring. The police had arrived.

6

SOFTY

His real name was William Willoughby, but no one had called him that in ages. Softy had lived on the street for a good five years now. Shelters in winter, parks in the summer. He was in a small, poorly-organized Nazi punk gang and he mostly dressed the part. Shaved head, white power bullshit on T-shirts two sizes too small. He'd done all but one of his tattoos himself, most of them uneven shwastickas—swastikas? Something-stikas. Softy wasn't good with big words. His right knuckles sported a greenish F.T.W. with the F pointing to the left instead of the right. It's hard to write things upside down. For real, though. *You* try! Anyway, Softy was racist as fuck, but really, he hated everyone, every single person on the planet. He called himself a self-taught man. His mother had taught him to hate the Jews, the Blacks and the gays, and the rest he'd learned to hate all on his own. He hated them personally, one by one. They were to blame for absolutely everything, including the weather. His life sucked not because of the system, but because of that guy, and that one, and her, and him, and them…

Despite the Monica—the nickname, whatever—Softy was tough, real tough. His stepdad beat the crap out of him before he ran away, but Softy got into all kinds of fights long before that asshole came along. He *loved* getting into fights. The rush of adrenaline made him feel alive more than anything else. He didn't want long-drawn-out fights, rolling on the ground like those wrestlers in girly tights. What he liked were hyper-vicious, thirty-punches-in-ten-seconds bouts. *Bam! Bam! Bam! Bam!* Pure, an-adult-rated violence. He liked it even when he lost. Sure, there was more pain involved, but he felt alive just the same. Softy beat someone up almost on a daily basis. His favorite spot was on the lakeshore. Lake Superior was like an ocean. He knew it wasn't a real ocean, but it had big waves and shit. He found the sound of the waves hitting the rocks inspiring, a reminder that nature itself is prone to violence. Softy didn't need to be provoked to get into a fight; often he'd pick a random guy on the sidewalk and kick his teeth in before stealing his wallet. That was his thing, and people respected him for it. He didn't have a lot of friends, but men moved out of the way when he walked by and when he stared, no one dared look back. That was respect. He was a bit lonely at times, but all kings are, and Softy was definitely a king in his own little world. He got a big rush out of it. Softy didn't do drugs, he blacked out too easily and hated losing control, but he spent every dime he had betting on sports games. Always the long shots. He lost most of the time, obviously. Someday, though, he'd win big and leave this shithole behind. Despite his profound hatred for the entire world, Softy was a firm believer in the American dream.

Most days, Softy would steal a few things at Target and sell them to buy food. On that particular day, however, he'd decided to rob Booker's Bakery. If he'd been asked why, he'd have said it was because you can't have a black man selling donuts to kids. It normalizes things. Next thing you know, you have a black president and the whole country's gone to shit. Mostly, though, he needed the money. He'd gambled on the wrong team and owed the wrong people. Softy was king, but these guys were king-er. One of the few bigger fish in Softy's very small pond. There was no real plan for this robbery other than wearing a mask, walking in with a crowbar, maybe a baseball bat, and swinging at anything that came near. All he needed now was a crowbar, or a baseball bat. Oh, and a mask.

The mask he got from Target, as usual. The store was close by the park where he slept, and he already knew where everything was on the shelves. Anyone who ever went to a different supermarket would know how much time that saved. The crowbar was a problem, though. He'd sold his leather jacket to some dude called Spades—Spades promised to sell it back when Softy had the money—and stealing a crowbar wearing shorts and a T-shirt seemed like too big of a risk. Getting caught for a small crime was count her productive to committing a bigger one, that was basic logic. Logic, however, wouldn't provide a weapon and Softy was left wandering the streets in search of something long and heavy. That could have taken all day. It did not.

He hadn't even walked two blocks when he spotted three kids in baseball uniform leaving the park with their gear. That was a sign, a stroke of Sir and Dipitty the likes of which he'd never seen. The whole thing would be easy as pie, now. Softy could take the kids with no trouble, but odds were he wouldn't even have to. Ten-year-olds don't pick fights with grown men. They just don't. Softy needed the baseball bat for practical purposes, but there was no reason not to have a little fun at the same time. He ran to the street corner and hid behind a delivery truck. When the kids crossed the street, he jumped out in front of them, yelling 'Boo!' just to give them a good scare. That *was* funny. The kids all ran, but not before one of them threw his bat at Softy. He jumped quickly to move out of the way. The bat hit him in the shin and after some truly… not graceful acrobatics, Softy fell backwards onto the sidewalk. He heard a snap when his neck hit the curb—like when someone cracks their knuckles before a fight. He didn't make much of it at first, then he tried to get up and—What the fuck? What the actual *fuck?*

Panicking sounds like something people do in their head, but it's not. Most of it is physical. Muscles tensing, trembling, shallow breathing, rapid heartbeat, that tightening feeling in your stomach. Softy had none of that. He'd have killed for shallow breathing, actually. He had no breathing. Zero… Shit! That's no fucking way to die! All of it because of a black man selling donuts. It was his fault, and Spades's. If Spades hadn't taken his leather jacket, he'd have just stolen the crowbar and none of it would have happened. *Fuck!* Softy, like most thugs, had very high hopes for his death. He'd envisioned a knife fight, being shot a hundred times by a hundred cops, all sorts of scenarios worthy of a Hollywood blockbuster. Tripping on a baseball bat was most definitely not it. Softy was scared, and angry. He was good at being angry. Scared was another story. He'd spent his whole life trying to feel bigger and stronger. Now he was small, puny, a weakling. He just couldn't stand the fear. He wanted it to end, even if it meant all of him had to end with it.

7
LANA

LANA FOUND FRANK in the break room, eating peanuts. Of all of Frank's snacking habits, peanuts were the one Lana found most annoying. Frank didn't like the skin, yet insisted on buying the ones *with* skin—something about blanched peanuts not tasting the same. Lana was reasonably sure the only difference in flavor came from the skin, which Frank didn't eat. Even if she were wrong, the difference still wouldn't justify leaving brown bits of peanut skin everywhere, on the table, on the floor. Lana explained the situation as best she could—the one at Booker's, not the peanut thing. Frank didn't grumble about getting up, which was unusual in the presence of food. Lana thought it was the prospect of violence that had him excited. Whatever the reason, she was glad to skip the usual argument and chose to walk behind him all the way to the car, as he had once requested. He returned the favor and stayed silent during the ride, except once to whine about an unfixed pothole. A legitimate grievance. They arrived at Booker's a few minutes later.

Because they might need to restrain Carole, it seemed best to take everyone's statement before freeing her from the bathroom. Booker went first.

—Can we make this quick? I have a whole batch of baguettes to make.

—You're still bleeding. Are you sure you don't want to go to the hospital? I can take you.

—I told you already. No doctors. I'm not selling the shop to pay for stitch tape and disinfectant I can get for ten bucks at Walgreens.

—It's your call. Now can you tell me what happened?

—Carole came in and she tried to steal some food—maybe she'd have paid for it, I don't know, but she tried to grab it and then she jumped on the counter—

—On her feet?

—No, belly-first. Why? Does it matter?

—No, it's just… The counter's very high and—Please continue.

—Then I came and I told her to stop and she just lost it.

—What does that mean?

—She lunged at me like a… like a wild cheetah and she bit me. Real fucking deep too, do you wanna see?

Lana shivered uncontrollably. She could barely handle a tap on the shoulder, couldn't stand a hug or even a handshake. Booker had had someone put their mouth on him, their teeth *inside* his arm and—Okay, let's think about something else!

—Oh, God, stop! Did she say anything before she attacked you?

—Nope.

—Did she look disturbed, or angry?

—Other than the biting thing?

—I meant when she walked in.

—I was in the back. I wouldn't have known anyway. It's not like we're best friends. She buys a sandwich once a week on Friday and that's it. I only know she's your neighbor. That's why I called you.

—Do you want to press charges against her?

—Hell no! Last thing I need is to waste a day in court. I just want her out of my shop.

—Okay. Thank you.

That last part made Lana feel better. There was a chance this could end without anyone getting arrested. She talked to Billy next—his shift had ended an hour before and he had homework to do—then to the other customers. The whole thing took about twenty minutes. They all had little to say other than that Carole had gone crazy and attacked Booker unprovoked, like a feral animal.

Lana approached the bathroom and knocked gently before unlocking the door. Frank unsnapped his holster, took his pistol out and aimed forward, ready to fire at the beast when it lunged at them. He must have been disappointed. They found Carole sitting on the toilet seat, perfectly calm. It was hard to tell with all the blood on her face, but Lana thought she might have been smiling. Carole recognized Lana right away and followed her of her own free will. She didn't even object when Frank put the cuffs on her, over Lana's protest. Lana made her agree to it three times, just to make sure they wouldn't get in trouble. All they could do without a warrant was to ask Carole to accompany them, and they couldn't keep her in Booker's bathroom for hours until a judge signed the papers. Assault and battery—that was the infraction, unless one counted teeth as a deadly weapon—was a misdemeanor offense and didn't allow for a warrantless arrest unless an officer was present during the commission of the crime. Frank was never a big stickler for rules and procedures. It was always up to Lana to fix things and make sure all their work didn't get thrown out in court. Voluntarily going to the police station wearing cuffs was a bit of a stretch, but seven people had witnessed Carole saying yes. That would have to do.

They had to stop along the way to take a statement from a jogger who'd found some neo-Nazi unconscious on the street. The paramedics who were on the scene said he probably wouldn't make it. That meant they could soon be looking at a series of crimes. Assuming the victim had been hit by a car, the driver could be charged with vehicular homicide, leaving the scene, et cetera, et cetera. That was rather a big deal, by Marquette PD standards, and Lana didn't want to let Frank mess it all up from the start.

Carole spent the whole time alone in the back of the patrol car. Nearly an hour had passed when she finally sat in the interrogation room. Lana asked the chief if she could talk to her alone; Carole was more likely to openly confess to someone she knew. The chief acquiesced and Lana sat in front of Carole before centering her yellow notepad on the square desk between them. Lana knew her three rules didn't apply to police matters, but Carole was her friend and neighbor, and she was unsure how to approach the conversation. Carole did look like she had come straight from the set of a horror movie and Lana ultimately decided platitudes would, under the circumstances, be less than appropriate.

—Can you tell me what happened, Carole?

—I'm not sure. I think I hurt Booker.

—You did. You bit him hard. Can you tell me why?

—…

—Carole?

—It felt like I had to? Does that make any sense?

—Not really, no.

—…

—Let's start from the beginning, okay? What were you doing at Booker's?

—I was hungry.

—I mean, what were you doing there in the first place? Weren't you working today? I thought you had your big presentation.

—I wasn't feeling well. Can I go home now? I want to see Shivansh.

Lana probed as best she could for another twenty minutes. All she could get out of Carole was that she wanted to go home to her husband. She said it over and over again, as if it were the only thing that mattered to her. Booker had refused to press charges, but Lana wanted to make sure Carole was fine and posed no threat to anyone before she let her go. Carole always seemed moderately depressed, but she was never aggressive or belligerent. More to the point, people generally didn't feel they 'had to' chew on other people without something being wrong with them. The best explanation she could think of was rabies. She asked Carole to wait and left the room to go tell the chief. The chief wasn't impressed. Carole was completely calm, anything but rabid. Most importantly, taking Carole to the hospital involved a lot of paperwork and procedures, which meant a lot of desk time, which meant his budget would suffer. Lana suggested going to Dr. Schlapp's, who was Carole's family doctor. If Carole agreed, it would simply appear as a regular visit. The chief looked mildly annoyed, but did not respond, which could be taken, as Lana had learned over time, as a tentative yes. Lana called Dr. Schlapp at the clinic and asked if she could bring Carole over, while Frank stared at her incredulously. Lana finished her call and returned to the interrogation room.

—Carole? I'd like you to come with me to Dr. Schlapp's office, just to make sure you're okay. Okay?

—*No!* I want to see my husband! You need to take me home to Shivansh!

—I'm sorry, Carole. I don't think it's a good idea for you to go home before we know if there's anything wrong with you.

—I WANT TO GO HOME TO SHIVANSH!

Carole was getting agitated. She didn't want to go to Dr. Schlapp's office, she wanted Shivansh. And so she lunged over the table and tried to bite Lana's face off. Fortunately, Carole was still in cuffs and Lana was quick enough to get out of the way. Carole landed awkwardly, face-first onto the floor, cutting her chin open in the process. Half a dozen officers stormed the interrogation room and helped restrain Carole before throwing her in a cell. Lana understood they had to book her—Carole had assaulted an officer in front of everyone—but asked the chief to send her to Dr. Schlapp first. When he predictably refused, Lana reminded him Carole might be contagious. The rabies theory did make a lot more sense now, and while the chief couldn't have cared less about Carole, the prospect of a hundred prisoners attacking each other at the county jail made him reconsider. He told Frank and Lana to make it quick and bring her back before five. The last thing this place needed, he said, was more overtime. Frank grumbled plenty this time around.

The next twenty minutes were spent trying to put a coat on Carole, but she was in no mood to get dressed. Finally, they threw a blanket over her shoulders and dragged her to the car. Her toes dragged against the pavement the whole way and Lana had to retrace their steps to find Carole's missing shoe before they could leave.

8
LAYLA

LAYLA WAS A great many things. They were eleven. They were black. They were wicked smart, except for math. They weren't bad at it or anything, just not as good as with the other stuff. They were an author. They'd written two books—well, they *were* writing two books. They'd started the first one, about a preteen girl going through some stuff, but that got awkward real quick, so they began writing another novel, space fantasy this time. It was kinda like that show Dad made them watch, *Farscape*, except that none of the characters were human, or gendered. Some of them were just, like, geometric shapes that spoke through telepathy. Sphere was gentler, Cube was very rigid and all about rules, Pyramid was the fighter, 'cause of the pointy end… It was much better than it sounded, you really had to read the whole thing. Anyway, that one was going well, and they thought it was pretty good, even if no one would ever read a single word of it. Where were we? Oh, yeah. Layla was many things. They were sensitive—they cried a lot during movies, it was kind of embarrassing, really. They had a sweet tooth. It's hard not to when your dad makes desserts for a living. They were… well, many, many, many things, some more complicated than others.

There were also a great many things Layla *wasn't*. They weren't a girl; they knew that pretty early on. They liked girls, though. Girls are pretty. They weren't in a relationship or anything like that 'cause that would mean telling people and, well, they weren't telling people. But when they *imagined* being in a romantic thing, it was with another girl. One other girl, mostly. We're not saying who, though. Layla wasn't like other kids their age. Their mom used to call them 'dark.' They weren't dark! Just, like... Okay, so you talk about death a few times when you're five and suddenly you're 'dark.' But like, you're alive and you have all these thoughts and suddenly you're not alive. What happens then? Do you still have thoughts? Is there still a you? And if there isn't, what does that mean for, like, right now? Is there really a you now? Right? All legitimate questions.

Layla wasn't exactly happy with the world the way it was, but who would have been? There was racism to deal with, and sexism, and every other -ism you can think of. There was climate change, and chicken pumped full of antibiotics. People were still dying in Afghanistan. Mr. Humfrey, the science teacher, was super rude and, like, *wrong*, all the time! Elizabeth Kwan had laughed in their face in front of *all* her friends, which wouldn't have hurt so much if Layla didn't have a crush on her. Oh, I guess we *are* saying who it was. Anyway, having a crush on someone super popular who mostly ignored them was one thing—Layla could have handled that—but never, ever, being able to *tell* that person, or talk to anyone else about it, that was hard. Layla had friends in school, but they were all nerds and, like, super straight and more into *Littlest Pet Shop* than, say, gender identity and sexual orientation. They didn't *mind* Layla being what they were, but they also didn't really want to hear about it. They definitely didn't want to hear about Liz Kwan unless it was to say she got into a car accident. Liz was always mean to them. All this was to say that there was nothing particularly peachy about Layla's school life.

Things weren't that great at home either. Their mom was gone. *Poof!* Just like that. One minute she was there and the next she was frolicking in Europe with some yoga teacher. He had a ponytail. They weren't getting along with their dad. They used to, though. They'd been *soooo* close! He used to be the one person they could always talk to, the one person who really listened. Life was tough sometimes—kids can be real jerks, especially Liz Kwan—but their dad was always there for them. Since the divorce, though, he'd been… different. It was hard to put into words. Playing for keeps, maybe? It was like he was trying to hold on to all the things he used to have, even if they were already gone. Did that make sense? Maybe it didn't, but people were weird sometimes when they hurt… What else? Layla wasn't really into sports, except for soccer but that wasn't a passion or anything. And they weren't that great at math, but we've said that already.

Another thing Layla wasn't was going to Dr. Schlapp's office to talk about puberty blockers. They'd been trying to get their dad to take them for months and he hadn't and that was, like, just the first step! They needed a referral to see an endo… cri-no-logist? Anyway, some other doctor, and a psychologist, and this all took time and there was no point taking puberty blockers if they'd already finished going through puberty. Right? Right. It shouldn't have been that complicated. Someone on the internet who took them said you could just stop, and your body would just go back to doing its thing. Either way, Layla already felt alien enough in that body of theirs, the last thing they needed was their mom's giant curves. Their dad had said he'd make another appointment today, but he'd come home super late and locked himself into the bathroom without saying a word. That was rude. He'd been in there for almost an hour and Layla was too afraid to ask why. Whatever was going on, it wasn't good news, and it most certainly meant he hadn't called. There was also the small matter of the report card. It was just one bad grade—a B- ain't even that bad—and it's not really their fault Mr. Humfrey couldn't give clear instructions to save his life. Still, Layla's dad had never finished high school and he'd sworn his child would have it better than he had. Layla was going to college, by force if they had to. Anyway, Layla didn't want to get into another argument, not then. Their dad looked like he was about to pass out when he came in, so *his* bad news must have been *really* bad, a lot worse than a B- for sure. Maybe someone had died. Maybe the bakery had burned down, or it'd gone bankrupt. Oh, gawd, they could be homeless. No home to live in and no money for food. They would sleep at a shelter and maybe Child Services would take Layla away and they'd be all alone for real. Also, no food! They were starving *right now!* That was probably normal. It was past seven and they hadn't eaten anything since breakfast. On second thought, maybe going over there to talk to their dad wasn't such a bad idea. Layla was just getting up from the couch when they heard Booker scream like he was dying, or being electrocuted, or something else god awful. They ran to the bathroom and tried to open the door.

—Dad?

—…

—Dad, what's wrong? Say something!

9
DR. SCHLAPP

EVELYN SCHLAPP WAS a God-fearing sixty-one-year-old Jewish woman. She was proud of her heritage but never cared much for its rituals. She didn't keep Shabbat, couldn't imagine life without bacon, and had been saying she should start attending service since Gerald Ford was president. She liked Purim, and Hanukkah. She called it Judaism *à la carte*.

Her fear of God, on the other hand, was anything but casual. She was terrified, all the time. It was only a matter of time before He—God was definitely a *He*—would unleash His wrath on her in the most epic of ways. She would say God and her had 'history.' What she wouldn't say was that she'd been having an affair with a married man for over twenty years. It was true that plenty of people were having affairs and the ground didn't split open under their feet and send them falling into a fiery pit, but hers was with a rabbi. Surely, that called for punishment of more biblical proportions. The constant fear did have its upsides. She lived every day as if it were her last, and gleefully indulged in all manner of cheese and chocolate. She also had the best collection of high-end tequila in all of Marquette.

She was about to leave her office early and enjoy some of that fancy spirit when she received a phone call from Lana Lannister. Evelyn knew most women in Marquette. She was one of two doctors still seeing walk-ins outside the hospital, and the other one had a reputation for both philandering and general assholery. Lana asked if the ficus in her office was getting enough light. Evelyn killed plants on a weekly basis and had no memory of that particular one, but the niceties meant Lana was calling as a cop and not as a patient. Evelyn was quite strict about her office hours, but the thought of Carole Veilleux running riot at the donut shop was too intriguing to pass up. Carole was many things, but a raging maniac was not one of them. She had last come in to ask about getting an IUD, 'just to feel safe,' as she and Shivansh hadn't had sex in years, except for that one time at the Christmas party when they'd both had too much to drink. Carole's outburst likely had nothing to do with her physical condition. Bad news was the trigger for most people: lost job, breakup… affair? She couldn't quite picture Shivansh playing hanky-panky all over town. Then again, she'd been wrong about plenty of people before. Whatever the reason was, it was interesting, from a gossip perspective if not from a medical one. It would take a good twenty minutes for Lana and Carole to arrive, and Evelyn allowed herself a sip of the Maestro Dobel Diamante she kept in her desk drawer for emergencies. This *was* a police matter and thus, by definition, an emergency. Slight sting on the palate at first. Lots of depth. A hint of vanilla, some butterscotch, then… Whoa! A *wallop* of alcohol that flooded the nose on finish. Similar to the Tromba, she thought. She would confirm that assessment when she made it back home.

Carole arrived in cuffs about forty minutes later, flanked by Lana and Frank. Evelyn had seen her fair share of gore, but she was startled enough at the sight of Carole to consider having another shot. Carole was a complete mess. She'd run her hand over her face, dragging blood all the way to her forehead. Her chin was split open, still dripping on her red-soaked shirt like a leaky faucet. You could smell the blood from five feet away. Evelyn grew angry. It wasn't the first time she saw someone bleeding after a run-in with Frank.

—You did this to her?

Frank did his best to look surprised at the suggestion. He was genuinely astounded when Lana came to his defense.

—No! Some of the blood is Booker's. Then she came at me at the station and hit her chin on the floor.

—Well, she looks calm now. Can you take her cuffs off so I can examine her?

—I don't think that's a good idea.

—I need to take off her shirt. I can cut it off, but if she becomes agitated, I'd rather not have a pair of scissors right next to her neck.

—Okay, but only for a minute.

Lana removed Carole's restraints before Frank could object and Carole sat in silence on the examining table. Evelyn began by cleaning her face. She disinfected the wound on her chin and closed it with Steri-Strips before removing her shirt.

—Do you mind if I throw it out? I don't think this is coming off. I'll give you something clean to wear until you go home.

Carole shook her head slowly. Evelyn went through the usual motions while Lana watched intently. Evelyn had always thought Lana would make a good doctor, a surgeon maybe. Her attention to detail was phenomenal. That wasn't unusual for high-functioning autistics, but Lana had the whole package: great hand-eye coordination, photographic memory. She'd even developed relatively decent social skills.

—Can you tell what's wrong with her? I thought she might have rabies.

—Give me a minute, Lana! I've barely had time to look at her.

—Can we put the cuffs back on while you do?

—I said give me a minute! She doesn't have a fever. Her heartbeat's a tad high, but I think that's normal under the circumstan—Wait, what have we got here?

Evelyn had lifted Carole's hair and found a large tick on the back of her neck. She grabbed some tweezers and tried to remove it. That's when Carole lost it. She screeched like a banshee and started swinging at everything and everyone. Evelyn got punched in the arm before she could move out of the way. It probably hurt, but she was so scared she couldn't feel anything. It wasn't the punching—she'd had patients react violently before. It was the scream. Whatever sound came out of Carole's mouth, it was one hundred percent not human. For a moment, Evelyn thought Carole might be possessed. She'd always thought her punishment would come directly from the Almighty, but maybe that was the sort of thing God outsourced to the Devil. She did her best to push the thought out of her head and finished removing the tick while Lana and Frank held the patient down. She dropped the insect in rubbing alcohol and moved out of the way for Lana and Frank to put the cuffs back on. Carole stopped screaming almost immediately. She looked puzzled, as if she didn't understand what had just happened.

—Doctor, do you think the tick could have done this?

Lana had asked a good question. There was clearly something wrong with Carole physically. This wasn't heartbreak or stress. Some kind of intoxication seemed more probable than rabies, but Evelyn was intrigued by the arachnid. Symptoms of Lyme disease wouldn't show this quickly, but it seemed at least possible that a tick could transmit rabies from one host to the next. That was a scary thought to have, since ticks had been migrating north for a while and anyone who'd gone camping in Michigan would tell you the forests were now seventy percent ticks and thirty percent trees.

—I'm not sure. Can you roll up her sleeve so I can draw some blood? Carole, is that okay with you?

—I want to see Shivansh.

—I don't think that's possible right now, but I want to make sure you're not sick, so I'm going to draw your blood and run some tests. Do you have any idea how long you could have had that tick?

—How long?

—Yes. Have you been in the woods, somewhere with lots of trees in the past couple days?

—I don't know. Can I go home now? I want to go home and be with Shivansh.

—That's not up to me, honey. I'm sorry.

Carole seemed to disappear in her thoughts for a minute, then she looked straight at the doctor and smiled gently.

—It's okay, Doctor. I'm already there.

10
SHIVANSH

SHIVANSH HAD A cool-sounding Hindu name. That's what he thought, anyway. Folks in the tiny Wisconsin town where he grew up weren't that impressed. Shivansh had been adopted when he was five, by old dairy farmers who'd never got kids of their own. He was raised Catholic, destined to take over the farm after his parents retired. Shivansh didn't like the farm. He hated cows with a vengeance. The only thing he hated more than cows were the looks he'd get every time he went into the tiny town he was forced to call home, the whispers he heard as he passed by. There was some name calling, of course, but he didn't mind the names. At least these people had the courage to say it to his face, and the slurs were always so idiotic and unoriginal, they were more of an insult to the people saying them than they were to him. Still, the looks, and the whispers, and the cows were enough, and when his parents died, Shivansh left the profuse racism of his tiny, tiny town for the vaguely less profuse racism of a slightly larger one. Shivansh didn't like big cities. He'd never been to New York, or even Detroit, but what he saw on television didn't make it sound that appealing. Still, he wasn't convinced the move would work out, so he'd made a list of increasingly larger places to move to until he found the right balance between traffic and bigotry.

Shivansh did fairly well for himself in Marquette, the very first town on the list. He'd got a job, then a better job, then he'd started his own business. He'd found someone whose company he enjoyed and who didn't want kids. They'd been married within the year. Shivansh had never loved his wife. He liked her very much, which was exactly what Shivansh wanted. He'd been in love before and hated it, profoundly. He understood how some might find the euphoria pleasing but he'd found himself unable to work, or to think about anything else. The relationship hadn't lasted and he'd been miserable the whole time, not to mention before and after. Shivansh believed that the human brain didn't deal well with big emotions, so he sought a life filled with little ones. He'd once told a friend Carole was like an old pair of jeans. Carole had overheard the conversation and reacted poorly, but to Shivansh there was no greater compliment. She was intelligent, independent. She had no discernible sense of humor, so he could take anything she said at face value. She wasn't uncomfortably attractive and never needed gratuitous shows of affection. She was perfect, in the least exciting sense of the term.

Shivansh worked from home. He was, to all who knew him, the quintessential accountant, a living testament to the universe of accounting clichés and stereotypes. He *looked* like an accountant, and not just because of his haircut or the way he dressed. Shivansh had the face of someone impervious to pain or pleasure, joy or sorrow, a face *so* stoic it screamed 'spreadsheet' at first sight. He was, of course, a creature of habit. He woke up every weekday at 5:26, sat at this desk at 5:50 sharp, and worked for two hours before sharing breakfast with his wife. He'd take an hour for lunch, nap for thirty minutes, then work the rest of the day until 5:30, which was right around the time Carole came back from the office unless her bus ran late.

Today was no exception, and when he heard the front door open at 5:37, he came downstairs to ask Carole about her day. To his surprise, it was not Carole waiting for him in the kitchen but a rather large black man with a poorly bandaged arm. For a second, he thought he recognized the man from the bakery up the street. Whoever he was, the man threw himself at Shivansh and gave him a bear hug before trying to kiss him. Shivansh pushed him away as hard as he could, causing the man to bite down on Shivansh's lower lip. Shivansh threw everything in sight at the man until he found a kitchen knife on the counter and began swinging wildly in every direction. When the intruder grabbed Shivansh's hand to stop him, Shivansh rolled into his arm like a salsa dancer and both men fell face-first to the ground.

The fall knocked the wind out of Shivansh and the man on top of him was too heavy to push off, so he waited. For what, he didn't know; maybe for the robber to grab whatever he was looking for and leave. A few seconds passed, and then the man did just that. He left the house running, apparently without taking anything. Shivansh let out a huge sigh of relief. That kind of excitement would have been taxing for anyone, but Shivansh was so exhausted, he thought he was going to pass out. At least he wasn't injured. He wasn't even robbed. Maybe this wasn't a robbery at all, and this man just desperately needed a hug. A huggary? No one would have known it from looking at him, but Shivansh thought that was rather funny.

Shivansh rolled onto his side and looked around to make sure he was truly alone. He was. He was also wet. The air coming in through the open door made his shirt feel cold and Shivansh worried he might have peed himself. No pee. There was, however, a lot of blood and a large knife handle sticking out of his gut. He'd probably fallen on it during the struggle. He didn't feel any pain, but that didn't matter much. What Shivansh had grabbed from the counter was no ordinary knife. It was a Takeshi Saji Rainbow Damascus Gyuto made in the famous Takefu Knife Village in Japan. Half work of art, half kitchen utensil, the ironwood handle coming out of him was attached to a *big fucking* blade engraved with the blacksmith's signature. Shivansh was afraid to cut himself just washing that thing, as he'd seen it cut through meat and bone like butter. Now that it was inside him, he didn't need a medical degree to guess his prognosis. He was going to die. He was going to die *very soon,* judging by the amount of blood on the floor. Maybe he should have stayed in Wisconsin with the cows. There wasn't as much violence in his tiny, tiny town. It was too late now.

Shivansh had never given death much thought other than that one time he and Carole wrote their will. Now the Reaper was staring him in the face and he wasn't ready. He wasn't prepared for this! There were things to do, documents to file, a million things to tell Carole, and he would accomplish none of it. He had spent every moment of every day bringing order to chaos, one decimal at a time, but his life would end in a mess, unfinished, his tasks unaccomplished. Nothing was more terrifying to Shivansh. He started crying like a baby, calling for Carole, his mother, for anyone to make things better.

11
BOOKER–CAROLE–TICK

BILLY BURNED A whole batch of croissants before the shop even opened. They weren't slightly charred, as often happened with the new oven. He *incinerated* them. The fire alarm went off. Booker rushed to call the fire department to stop them from coming. There'd been a false alarm in April already. He'd have to pay an absurd amount of money if it happened a second time: a couple hours of every firefighter's salary, costs for the trucks and equipment being dispatched, plus whatever the Township Board 'deemed reasonably necessary and appropriate.' That could mean just about anything, but most likely it would spell bankruptcy. Booker opened every door and window to let the smoke clear, but the place still smelled like a disaster when the first customer walked in. The barista was leaking water again and they were all out of icing sugar.

So, Booker was already having a rough day when Carole showed up and went all *Night of the Living Dead* on him. Booker was livid. He wasn't just angry at Carole, he was mad at the whole world. There was Layla to deal with. There were bills to pay, more bills to pay than there was money coming in, and that meant finding ways to make money, which probably meant more bills. There was a shitty landlord and the stupid Township Board, and the barista, and burnt croissants and icing sugar, and now there were customers fucking *chewing* on him. It was too much, too much for one person to handle on their own, and Booker wondered what was the point of waking up every morning. He'd thought of giving up before that day, Carole was just the cherry on top. He might have, had it not been for Layla. At the very least, he'd have gotten wasted enough to forget about it all for a few hours. But he couldn't.

After the ruckus, Booker rummaged through the bakery looking for the first aid kit. He didn't have insurance and couldn't afford to spend even a minute at the emergency room. He disinfected his arm and wrapped it as best he could with the *one* roll of cheap white bandage the little box contained. He started feeling sick about an hour after the police left, and asked Billy if he could close the store for him.

Booker was about halfway home when he felt a sudden urge to go… home. Not to his house, but *home* somewhere else, near the bakery. He turned the car around and headed there without thinking. He nearly crashed and had to pull over when images started flashing before his eyes. The backseat of a car. What looked like giant skin pores. The images slowly faded after a few minutes. They weren't gone, but he could see *through* them, like one can see through the reflections on a window. He could focus on the road in front of him, though not without a fair amount of effort. When he got to the house, he couldn't wait another minute to see Shivansh, though he had no idea who that was. Booker ran inside and rushed to kiss his husband when he appeared into view, and then—

Booker was sitting in his car in front of his house, *his* house. How'd he get there? It didn't really matter, because it was a good thing that he had got there, however it had happened. The real question was what had happened *before* he got there. He'd kissed a man, wrestled with a man. That much he remembered. The rest of the evening—it was evening, wasn't it?—was mostly a blur, except for a few flashes. Falling face-first onto the floor. Getting blood drawn by Dr. Schlapp. But he hadn't gone to Dr. Schlapp's, he was sure of it. Blood on the floor, different blood, on a different floor. Some weird-ass spiky monster leg. Ewww, what the fuck *was* that? Whatever, he'd somehow managed to drive himself home. Unfortunately, it was getting late and Layla would be waiting for him.

Booker didn't think he could handle talking to another human just then. He didn't say a word as he walked in and locked himself in the bathroom as fast as he could. Booker looked in the mirror to remember who he was. It was undoubtedly Booker staring back, yet he could have sworn he was a white woman not five seconds before. He felt the weight of his breasts pulling at his chest, and his hands, he clearly remembered, were really fucking white. He *was* a woman. That thought stayed with him for a while—how long had he been a white woman? Did Layla know he was a white woman?—then things got really messed up. Booker's heartbeat shot through the roof, his breathing became shallow, and he started to sweat profusely. He had been afraid before, but this new fear was overwhelming. Booker was afraid to die. He was afraid to die because he was lying on the floor, a knife sticking out of his gut. He could *see* the fucking knife, yet he also knew he was standing in his bathroom, *and* talking to Dr. Schlapp. *And he was fucking hungry for blood*. Wait, what?

Booker had a sudden case of vertigo, as if someone had yanked him up from the ground. The next thing he knew, he was drowning in some chemical. He couldn't breathe. His entire body was burning. Booker screamed at the top of his lungs when he felt himself die. But he didn't die, did he? He was still staring at himself in the mirror, so probably not. Was he still a white woman? Damnit! This made no sense. But after the drowning part, he began to think more clearly. Booker *was* a man. He was at home. He was also a white woman at the doctor's office. That was weird, but okay, sure. He was still afraid to die, though. Why? He was scared of needles, but not *that* much. There was no imminent danger in the bathroom either. Was he anyone else? Oh, shit! He'd forgotten about the knife in his gut. He was another man—the one he'd kissed—slowly bleeding to death on his kitchen floor. Booker took out his cell phone and called an ambulance to Carole's address. Oh, God. He wasn't just a white woman, he was Carole fucking Veilleux and his husband—her husband, whatever—was dying on the floor. He—he heard a knock on the door.

—Dad?

—...

—Dad, what's wrong? Say something!

That voice. It was... Layla. His child. *His* child. Booker had a child, and he was Booker. Why was Layla there? They must have heard him scream. Yes. They had heard him scream and were checking in on him. He had to say something.

—...I'm good. I just... hurt my toe.

That wasn't the best answer, but it was an answer.

—You've been in there for an hour! I'm starving!

Booker wasn't hungry anymore, not for blood or anything else. Layla was, though, and they wouldn't leave him alone without the promise of food.

—What do you say we order in tonight?

—Pizza?

—Whatever you like. Just call. I'll be out in a minute.

That's not what Booker would say, he thought, before wondering what that even meant. He suddenly felt lighter. It took him a second or two to realize he wasn't Carole's husband anymore. His husband was dead. Booker started crying. He cried in the bathroom for another twenty minutes until Shivansh woke up at the hospital. Oh, thank God! Being three people was definitely not good, not to mention creepy as hell, but it was a hell of a lot better than being two people plus a dead one. He still had to do something about being other people—there had to be something he could do, right?—but he was too shook up to think of anything, and smart enough to know that wouldn't change in the next five minutes.

Booker couldn't spend the rest of his life in the bathroom, so he tiptoed his way to the living room and turned the TV on to avoid a conversation. When the seafood pizza arrived, he sat down in front of Layla and started eating. He was relieved when they took out their phone. God, he was tired, so tired. All he wanted was to lie down in his cell at the county jail and sleep—or home, because he was home. He was about to go to bed when the ER doctor walked in and told him the blade had missed all vital organs. He was going to be fine. Booker smiled the biggest smile and grabbed himself another slice of pizza.

PART 2

TRANSMISSION

12
CAROLE–BOOKER–SHIVANSH

CAROLE WOKE UP in jail the next day feeling much better, physically at least. She felt awful for assaulting Booker, and Lana, and Dr. Schlapp, and almost killing her husband, sort of. She was also pissed at Carole—wait, she was Carole—pissed at *herself* for biting into… her arm, and trying to kiss herself and falling onto a knife. Whoa. There was a lot there to unpack.

Her first thought was to meet Booker and Shivansh and discuss what was happening to them. That thought lasted for about half a second until she realized there *was* no one to meet or talk to. She was them. They were her. They had nothing to say to each other. The thought of never talking to her husband again was strange, but she supposed strange things were par for the course when you're married to yourself. Also, Carole was in jail, which significantly limited her social prospects. Whatever. She was three people, one of them was bound to talk to someone at some point. A lot had happened in twenty-four hours.

She thought about taking the day off from the bakery, but she was already there, working. That was weird. It didn't matter. She was taking the day off from advertising because she was in jail, and there would be no accounting done from her hospital bed, so she was *mostly* taking the day off. And she was feeling *so much* better. She should have been terrified of what was happening to her—this was, objectively, scary as shit—but she wasn't. She was mostly... curious. For starters, she wasn't sure how long this would last. It could be permanent, or it could go away after a few days, like a mild case of the common cold. She also had no idea how this happened in the first place. Well, she could be relatively certain that she had brought Booker on board when she bit into his arm, and then Booker had brought *Shivansh* on board when he accidentally bit into Shivansh's lower lip in their kitchen. It was also a good bet that the tick Dr. Schlapp had removed from her neck was to blame for her sudden urges. How the tick got transformed was unknown, but she didn't really care. The real question was whether sharing a mind was the end of this or if there was more in store for them. This could be fatal, they could lose their hair, grow a third arm... The possibilities were endless. Carole chose not to stress out too much about it. As much as she felt bad for what she'd done, she liked whatever this was a whole lot.

Carole had plenty of reason to feel better. Shivansh was alive and getting stronger by the hour. He'd disappeared again for a few hours when they gave him general anesthesia to remove part of his small intestine, but Carole and Booker were sound asleep and neither of them had noticed. And with the tick gone, Carole could resist the urge to do absolutely everything that came through her mind. That mind was also bigger, better. Whoever said two heads are better than one should have kept counting. She was now an accountant, and a business owner on top of everything else. She could speak Spanish! Wait, no, that was her. She'd always spoken Spanish. Still, 187 times 345… 64,515. Wow! Carole had always been smart, but this was a different kind of smart, one she wasn't used to at all. It was more than that, though. She felt better about *everything*. The mere act of existing was more enjoyable than it used to be. She'd just woken up in jail, but she was already at work on a wedding cake. Carole had never made a wedding cake. Or maybe she had. Either way, she was enjoying it immensely.

Whatever happened to her, to them, Carole had learned all sorts of things in the process, more or less instantly. Her husband had never loved her. She loved him very much. Carole couldn't put her finger on how that made her feel. There was some surprise, a bit of shame, awkwardness, perhaps. All these things, mingling and forming unfamiliar shapes, and yet it was… peaceful. There was great kindness in Shivansh's absence of love, lots of respect and devotion. Carole had never wanted children, but she was now a parent, a father no less, filled to the brim with pure, unconditional love.

There wasn't much to do in jail, except to think. Fortunately, Carole had plenty of things to think about. There were Shivansh things. When would the hospital release him? How long would his stomach hurt? Carole things, of course, starting with the question of how much trouble she was in. Assaulting an officer was a misdemeanor offense, just like biting people she didn't know, but if the judge wanted to make an example of her, she was pretty sure she could end up in prison for a couple years. Carole had tons of questions, but the answers would have to wait. Shivansh had already called his attorney from the hospital, but he couldn't see Carole before her arraignment. Then there was work. She'd already missed a couple of days.

Would she still have a job when she got out? Did she care? There was also one important Booker thing to think about. He'd called 911 from his cell phone. It was a prepaid thing, but Booker might have had to fill out a form or something. She couldn't remember if she had. There was a small chance the police would be able to trace the call back to him. They needed to come up with a plausible story or Booker could get in trouble.

The thinking took most of her morning. Lunch was the most amazing pastrami sandwich, or so she thought until they brought her something pretending to be stew. The bad food came with worse news. Judge Shaw had a terrible case of the flu and wouldn't come to court until tomorrow, which meant she'd have to spend another night in her cell before she could post bail. There *was* a TV in Shivansh's hospital room, though. With any luck, there'd be a half-decent movie to watch during the day.

Everything was confusing, but Carole wasn't alone and that made her feel safe. She was grateful, profoundly grateful to share all this with her husband and the man she bought sandwiches from. Okay, technically, she *was* alone, but being three people gives the word a completely different meaning. She had three bodies, three physical presences, each with their own sensations, many of which she'd never experienced or even imagined. Her Booker arms felt very different to hers, so did her Shivansh hair. Each of herself had their own flesh, their own body parts, their scars and imperfections. There was a degree of intimacy there that she, that *no one*, presumably, had ever experienced. They weren't merely close, they were each other. It was exciting, very exciting. It was… kind of arousing. She didn't realize she was touching herself until a guard walked by and started staring at her. She felt awkward for a second, maybe two, then she went right back to it. She was locked inside a beige room with bars and no windows. If her jailers didn't want her to masturbate, they should have provided better entertainment options.

13
LANA

LANA NEVER HAD three cups of coffee. She wouldn't have a third one this morning either, but she thought about it at least twice. Her routine had been seriously disturbed the day before and she'd barely closed an eye. There was the incident at Booker's, Carole attacking her at the police station, her violent outburst at Dr. Schlapp's office. She and Frank had brought Carole to the county jail, then they were called to Carole's house for a stabbing and a B&E. This was as much action as Marquette had seen in months, and all of it was somehow connected to Carole Veilleux. This was a mystery, a puzzle, and there were few things in life Lana found more engrossing than a good puzzle. It was past midnight when Lana made it home and she spent what was left of her night attempting to connect the proverbial dots. By morning, the dots were as disjointed as ever, and Lana wished she had just gone to bed.

Her first order of business was to canvass her neighborhood, which also happened to be Shivansh's, in the unlikely event someone had caught a glimpse of the intruder. Shivansh was obviously in a better position to see his attacker, but trauma makes for bad witnesses. If this case ever made it to court, a prosecutor would likely prefer testimony from someone who wasn't bleeding to death at the time. Lana had drawn a map of the neighborhood, relatively to scale, and ranked every house she would visit by order of interest based on proximity to the scene and the occupant's characteristics. Her first knock was on Billy Joel's door—no connection to the singer, Billy was a bassist. His band had played a dive bar in Harvey the night before and he hadn't come home before five. Second on the list was Martha Smith. Martha was as nosy a neighbor as there had ever been. She called the police on someone at least once a week—usually black people enjoying themselves in the park—and Lana held high hopes for her. If anyone saw anything, it would be Martha.

—Good morning, ma'am. I'm—

—He ruined all my cobbitty daisies.

—I'm sorry, ma'am, what—

—The dog next door pees on the daisies. Every day, he does it. That's why I called.

—Oh. That's not why I'm here. There was an incident last night at Carole and Shivansh's house and I was wondering if you saw anything out of the ordinary, anything suspicious going on between, say, five and six.

—No… I was watching the news. I didn't see anything after Booker stopped by.

—Booker came here?

—No! Across the street. You know Booker, right? Big black man, sells donuts—

—I know who he is. Are you certain it was him?

—It was his car.

—What kind of car does he have?

—I don't know cars. Whatever Booker's car is.

—What color?

—Blue, grey, I don't know. What part of "It was Booker's car" don't you understand?

—Do you know how long he stayed?

—Like I said, I was watching TV.

—Thank you, ma'am. You've been very helpful.

—What about my daisies?

—I'm sure someone will be over soon.

The dots practically connected themselves. Booker had a grievance with either Carole or Shivansh. Carole attacked him, and he took revenge on Shivansh that evening. It seemed out of character for Booker to hurt anyone, but the theory fit the facts. Frank hadn't showed up for work yet, so she got into her patrol car and headed straight to the hospital. Everything was going according to plan. Shivansh was conscious. He would say Booker stabbed him, she would arrest Booker and solve an attempted murder before lunch, all on her own. When she got to the hospital, she found Shivansh in a room with two beds. Next to him was a bald young man staring at the ceiling. Shivansh was watching *The Truman Show* on TV. She recognized the movie immediately—she'd seen it in the theatre when it was released—but couldn't, for the life of her, remember if she liked it or not. That bothered her, somehow, as she prided herself on having near-perfect memory. Maybe her lack of recollection had nothing to do with the movie. Maybe something else, something more important, was on her mind that night. It didn't matter. Well, it did matter, but it didn't matter *then*. She was doing *real* detective work, even if she wasn't 'officially' a detective.

—Good morning, Shivansh. Glad to hear you're feeling better.

—Thank you.

—I need to ask you a few questions, if you don't mind.

—Sure. Go ahead.

—Was Booker at your house yesterday?

—No, I don't think so. I was waiting for him. He was supposed to come over to talk about a cake for Carole's birthday. It's next month and I wanted something special. He never showed up.

—Are you sure?

—Am I sure? Well, I guess he could have come while I was unconscious, but…

—Okay, then do you know who it was that stabbed you?

—Stabbed me? Wait, what? You think Booker stabbed me?

—I don't know, but if it wasn't him, then who was it?

—No one! I picked up the knife to put it in the drawer and I slipped. Silly, I know. I kind of wish I'd been stabbed. It would hurt the same, but this is so… humiliating. I haven't told Carole yet.

Poof. All the neatly connected dots came loose again. Nothing made sense. Why did Carole attack Booker? Why would Booker, or anyone else for that matter, do house calls for a *cake?* Lana was about to leave when she noticed some blood on Shivansh's lower lip.

—What happened there?

—Oh, that. I must have bit my lip when I fell.

That made sense, it did, which only served to highlight how much the rest of Shivansh's story didn't. Lana left the hospital with more questions than she had walking in.

One thing was certain, there was more going on here than Shivansh was letting on and she was more determined than ever to find out what it was. The next step was to talk to Booker. He was involved in all of it, whatever *it* was. She would do it now so they wouldn't have time to get their stories straight. She thought about the fake birthday cake in the shop window and reminded herself to look the other way when she walked in. She didn't want to be distracted while questioning her suspect. This was good detective work. If she managed to catch Booker in a lie, any lie, maybe she could get him to talk, and this mystery would start to unravel.

14
SOFTY

EIGHTY-SEVEN. EIGHTY-EIGHT. EIGHTY-NINE. Softy lost his train of thought when a woman came into the room to talk to the patient next to him. One ceiling tile. Two ceiling tiles. Nah, he didn't feel like counting anymore. He didn't feel like doing anything. He didn't *feel* anything. Some Pakistani-looking doctor had come in the night before to give him the bad news. Fracture of the C2 verta… Hangman's fracture, that sounded kind of badass at first. It wasn't. He'd lost the use of his legs and arms. He needed a respirator to breathe, a catheter to pee. There was no treatment. He'd be like that for the rest of his life. 'I'll be back to check on you later,' and that was it. The whole thing took less than five minutes. The doctor had said all of that very matter-of-factly, like someone ordering food at a restaurant, then she left and never came back. Softy figured it had something to do with the swas—with the cross thing and the white power tattoos the hospital gown didn't cover. At least, he thought he was wearing a hospital gown, he assumed he was, but he couldn't see. He wished someone would sit him at an angle so he could watch TV. *The Truman Show* was on. He'd seen it before, but he couldn't remember a single thing about it.

Softy hadn't cried when the doctor told him everything. In hindsight, he wasn't sure he *could* cry, but he didn't. He'd have laughed if he'd had time to think about it. That was funny, in a very dark, I'll-never-walk-again sort of way. He'd fought God knows how many people before, three-hundred-pound men, folks with black belts in *I'll fuck you up nicely*. He'd fought three men at once, once, but in the end, it was some ten-year-old white kid in a Padres uniform who got him for good. It had taken Softy most of the night to come to terms with his diagnosis and stop trying to move, but he had by morning. Wait, diagnostic or diagnosis? What was the difference? Anyway, that was his life, now. No sense bitching about it. There was another thing he realized during that time. He didn't hurt. He didn't feel anything good, either, but the pain was gone. Every minute of Softy's existence had hurt until then. A subtle pain, the kind you get used to. He'd forgotten it was there, but now that it was gone… Granted, lying there like a corpse was boring as fuck, but it was calm, simple. He figured the doctors would find a way to get rid of someone like him at some point, but he would take the break while it lasted. There was nothing to do—he *couldn't* do anything. He was… relaxed, for the first time in as long as he could remember. He didn't have to be on guard all the time, or steal shit, or find food or money. His body was gone, for all intensive purposes, but in a weird way, this was a reprieve, a vacation, like those all-inclusive places his stepdad talked about all the time. The doctor *had* mentioned something about denial, and learning to cope with loss, some shit about seeing a grief counsellor. Denial. That too was funny. If anyone was in denial, it was that Paki doctor thinking she could mess with his mind. Hell, no. Softy was coping just fine.

Now, if only someone could sit him at an angle. TV would be good, more vacation-y than counting ceiling tiles, for sure. This was Softy's first day at being paralyzed. What were the odds it would get better with time? Probably very low. He'd find a way, though. What doesn't kill you makes you stronger. He'd repeated that line to himself every time he took a beating, or got arrested and took a beating. Those were different things. Fists had evolved over millions of years—or was it thousands?—so folks could punch each other without doing too much damage, but batons were a whole other story. He remembered pissing blood for a week after that asshole cop busted him for sleeping in a park. Maybe his kidneys *did* grow back stronger after that. This, though, it was harder to see the silver lining. This might be an exception to the rule. There was a growing possibility that what doesn't kill you really wasn't that great, just... slightly better than what *does* kill you. That one line was pretty much Softy's entire life philosophy, so the possibility didn't sit well with him. Could he have been wrong about everything that entire time? No... He had this. He'd survived a lot worse with his simple belief system. Okay, not *a lot* worse. Maybe not *worse*, per say, but he'd survived. That had to count for something. Still, he was feeling less and less enthusiastic about paralysis.

'How can anyone expect me to carry on under these conditions?'

Oh, he remembered that line! He was pretty sure it was Truman's wife who said that.

—Yo! Was that Laura Linney? I can't see.

That's what Softy said, in his head at least. There was a tube in his throat for the mechanical respirator that stopped him from talking. Obviously, no one answered.

No one was talking, period. Softy hadn't noticed, but the woman who came in had already left. As for his roommate, he was watching TV or he'd gone back to sleep. Sleeping sounded pretty good and Softy thought about doing the same. It was either that or counting ceiling tiles. Not true, there was a movie on. He couldn't see it, but he'd already seen the movie so that might just work. Oooooh, Softy had an idea. Maybe none of this was real and he was on a TV show like Truman was. Just then he thought of what to say the next time the nurse came to check on him. 'Good morning, and in case I don't see ya, good afternoon, good evening, and goodnight!' Oh, wait, he couldn't speak. Still, it would be funny in his head.

15
BOOKER–SHIVANSH–CAROLE

BOOKER WOKE UP that morning feeling much better, physically at least. He was still fucking pissed at Carole for chewing on his arm, but he also felt really bad about doing it so maybe that evened things out. He felt like shit for wrestling with Shivansh but that was sort of Carole too and he'd forgiven her but not himself, if that made any sense. Nope. It didn't. His first thought was to meet Carole and Shivansh and discuss what was happening to them. That thought lasted for about half a second until he realized there was no one to meet or talk to. He was only one. *They* were only one. He should have been terrified of what was happening to him—this was, objectively, scary as shit—but he wasn't. He was mostly… curious. And he was feeling *so much* better.

Booker had plenty of reasons to feel that way. Shivansh was alive and getting stronger by the hour. With the tick gone, he could resist the urge to do absolutely everything that came through his mind. That mind was also bigger, better. It was more than that, though. The mere act of existing was more enjoyable than it used to be. He was at the shop working on a wedding cake, something he'd done a hundred times without giving it much thought, but he was enjoying this cake as if it were his first. He marvelled at the smallest thing, the slow rise of the dough, the way fondant can be shaped into anything. Who knows, maybe this *was* his first wedding cake? All that mattered is that he was having the time of his life making it.

He'd learned a ton since yesterday. Shivansh never liked Booker's food. He never loved his wife either. Carole loved her husband very much and she farted in her sleep. Booker knew he should feel awkward just for knowing these things, but he didn't, he felt… It was a strange emotion, impossible to put into words. This would take some getting used to, but it was really cool. It was fucked up, for sure. He'd been attacked. He should have been angry, and part of him was, but he was also kind of glad it had happened. Maybe this was some kind of Stockholm Syndrome thing. After all, he *was* his attacker. There seemed to be no point worrying about it. There was nothing he could do to change things, and he felt better about his life than he had in a *long*, long time.

There was one thing that bugged him, though. He'd called 911 from his cell phone when Shivansh was bleeding to death. It was a prepaid thing he'd bought at Walgreens, but he might have had to fill out a form or something. He couldn't remember. If he had, then the police might be able to trace the call back to him. He needed to come up with a plausible story or he could get in trouble.

Booker was on his lunch break eating his usual pastrami sandwich when he noticed he had an erection and a profound desire to sleep with Carole, or Shivansh. He wasn't quite sure how he felt about that, other than being thankful for not wearing sweatpants that day. Perhaps serendipitously, his erotic thoughts were interrupted when Lana Lannister walked into the shop and asked if they could talk in private.

—Hi, Booker! How's your arm?

—Meh. I think it'll leave a scar, but it's healing alright.

—Good. I see you changed the vinyl on the corner booth. You really keep this place clean.

Booker barely remembered getting that seat cushion fixed. How did she even notice these things?

—I try. What can I do for you, Lana?

—Well, I was just at the hospital talking to Shivansh, Carole's husband?

—Is he okay? I tried to call him after I went to his place, but I got no answer.

—What? So you *did* go to his house last night.

—Oh, yeah. When I got there, I saw the front door was open. I peeked inside and saw some plates and stuff on the floor. Looked like there'd been a struggle or something, so I just called 911 and left.

—You called 911?

—I did—where's my phone? Oh, here. See? I know I should have stayed, but I was afraid whoever robbed the place was still in there. Twenty years ago, I'd have gone in, but I ain't as brave as I used to be. With Layla, you know…

—I understand. What were you doing there? I didn't know you two were close.

—We're not. He wanted to talk about a cake for Carole's birthday. It's next month and he wanted something special.

Booker realized he'd used the same words twice. That was something Lana Lannister wouldn't miss, if she'd noticed the booth vinyl. Then again, what could she do? He couldn't be arrested for a crime when there was no crime. She'd probably think they were hiding something from her, which was fine. They *were* hiding something from her, and as long as they kept hiding it, she'd never know what it was. He was also proud of himself for the 911 thing. The best defense is a good offense. He'd always thought that was a sports thing, but now believed it had something to do with George Washington.

—Funny. That's exactly what Shivansh said.

—Great minds think alike, I guess. What's he doing at the hospital? You never said.

—Knife wound to the stomach.

—What? That's horrible! Did someone stab him?

—He said it was an accident.

—Wow. Like I keep telling Billy, you can never be too careful in the kitchen. What happened with Carole, by the way?

—She's still at County waiting to post bail.

—Why? I said I didn't want to press charges!

—It's… complicated.

—Well, I hope she's feeling better. Anything else I can do for you?

—…No. That's it. Sorry for bothering you during your lunch break.

—It's fine. Have a good one, Lana!

—Okay, bye now.

Booker waved as Lana left the shop. It was done. Shivansh would soon be discharged from the hospital. All that was left was to get Carole out of jail and they would be free to live their new life as they pleased. Booker split the rest of the day between baking with newfound joy and watching *Working Girl* on the hospital TV. Closing time came and he headed home to spend some time with Layla. When he got there, they were standing in the kitchen, tapping their foot on the floor.

—So?

—So… hello to you too? How was your day at school?

—Did you call?

—Did I…

—The doctor. You said you'd call today to make a new appointment!

That took a moment to decipher. There were many doctors, one of them talking to him right now at the hospital. No, that was a different one. Oh shit, *that* doctor.

—I'm sorry, Layla. I forgot.

—You promised you would! Why do you keep lying to me like that?

Had he been lying? Not really, but he hadn't been telling the truth either. Booker looked at Layla and, for the first time, he didn't see his child, not the baby he'd fed and raised or the little girl who'd fallen off her bicycle and came home crying. He saw a beautiful, complex human being who'd struggled through so much to become who they were, who still struggled, day in and day out, to make their place in a world that wasn't made for them. He didn't notice he was crying until a tear tickled his upper lip.

—Oh, Layla, I did forget. I really did. It's… it's been a weird couple of days, but I need to tell you how much I love you, Layla. I never do, I realize that now. And I see you. I know you don't always believe me, but I see you. I can only imagine how hard it's been for you. Everyone, including me, trying to force you into a box you could

> never fit in. I'm so proud of you, Layla. You're stronger and more courageous than anyone I've ever known. And if you say you want to be a boy, I will forever be proud of my son. And if somewhere on that journey you realize that's another box you just can't fit in, I'll be proud of you then, too. I love you, Layla. That'll never change because it's you I love, what you are, not what people think, not what I thought you should be. It took me a long time to figure that out, honey, I know it has, and for that I'm sorry, but I want you to know that I love you and that I do see you… That's… all I wanted to say.

Layla started crying, smiling, and crying, and snorting. Booker realized he'd never seen Layla cry, not like that. They ate dinner in silence, then sat on the couch and fell asleep in each other's arms.

16
SHIVANSH–BOOKER–CAROLE

A WEEK HAD gone by since the tick fell on Carole's neck. She'd posted bail. Shivansh was back at home. They were slowly getting used to their situation. Plenty of things were still confusing. They hated asparagus even though Shivansh used to love it, which seemed to suggest some sort of majority rule, that two people's tastes were negating one rather than averaging it all out. That seemed like a good thing, if the alternative was constant ambivalence about everything. On the other hand, they all liked looking at birds now, a *lot*, and Booker was the only one who'd ever shown any interest in it. Maybe this was like mixing paint colors. In theory, half-blue, half-yellow should make a true green, but certain pigments are stronger than others and the result is rarely what one would expect. Thinking about themselves was very 'meta,' and weird, mostly weird. They were three bodies, but having only one mind meant that the people they were before no longer existed. Yet they still very much felt like Booker. They also felt very much like Carole, and Shivansh. Where it got weird was that it was all the same feeling. One thing was certain, they were happier that way, and for the most part they *kind* of knew who they owed their likes and dislikes to. Memories were a big mess, though. Some memories were easy to identify because they meant a lot or were really detailed, but on the whole, it was like sorting through the laundry pile trying to figure out which black sock belongs to whom. They decided it would be best not to talk about the past with others.

Other rules were established quickly. For one, they couldn't drive at the same time. They were a lot smarter than they were individually but not enough to drive multiple cars at once, as evidenced by the humongous scratch on Shivansh's SUV. Most importantly, they decided not to add anyone to their little circle. 'Not without consent,' they'd promised to themselves. As happy as they were being one, none of them had chosen this. Carole didn't choose to be bitten by the tick. Booker never agreed to have his arm chewed on. Shivansh was completely terrified when Booker tried to kiss him. None of them would go back to the way things were, not in a million years, but this... thing might end up killing them, and they wouldn't force this change on anyone even if the experience had been profoundly enlightening and full of joy. They all wished they could share this new life with their child, but Layla was on their own journey. Shivansh, Carole and Booker had known exactly who they were before all this. That's *why* they were unhappy. Layla, on the other hand, was still searching. It seemed wrong and selfish to rob someone of that discovery. Later, perhaps, if this even lasted, *and* if they found a way to explain it to them without sounding insane.

The past few days had been quite the rollercoaster. Shivansh's appetite for strong emotions was far greater than it used to be. His body, however, was still very much operating on Shivansh's terms. He was exhausted all the time. He'd gone to bed around eight since he'd left the hospital and missed the usual movie nights with Carole. That didn't matter much since he remembered every film in the morning. Him and Carole being the same person meant they had, technically, watched the movie together. Despite spending less time with his wife, he was undoubtedly closer to her than he'd ever been.

Shivansh had taken a much-needed break from the balance sheet of a poorly-run café and had gone to Booker's house for lunch. They were having passionate sex in the kitchen, listening to the latest Against Me! album. They had fought the urge to sleep together for a couple of days but capitulated the moment Carole posted bail. Shivansh was still in a lot of pain, so Carole and Booker did the honors, then Carole and Shivansh, then… It didn't matter who was there, the sex was just… epic. Trumpets blazing, angels singing. They knew *exactly* what they liked, what they all liked. They knew each other's bodies as if they were their own, because they were. They were getting instant feedback from beginning to end. This was, without doubt, the best sex any human being had ever had. No contest. They were nearing their third orgasm when they heard a very heartfelt knock on the front door.

Both men growled a little, frustrated by the interruption. Booker started getting dressed while Shivansh went to look through the peephole. Dr. Schlapp was standing outside, looking like a wet poodle. Shivansh fixed Booker's hair as best he could, grabbed his clothes from the kitchen floor, and ran upstairs to hide. On the way, he noticed Booker had put his shirt on backwards. He heard Dr. Schlapp step in and waited forever for Booker to say anything.

—Shit, where are my manners? Let me get you a towel.

For a second, Shivansh thought he was the one who had said it. He let out a sigh of relief when he recognized Booker's voice. What was Dr. Schlapp doing there, though? She'd examined Carole and run some tests, but she had no reason to come to *this* house. Maybe Layla had taken matters into their own hands and gone to talk to her about puberty blockers. Shivansh wasn't sure if a doctor could talk to a child without informing the parents and wished at least one of them had a modicum of knowledge about the medical profession. Perhaps that's what this visit was about, the doctor informing the parent after talking to the child. That made sense. Shivansh saw no other plausible explanation and let out a second sigh of relief. Oh, crap, not again. Sighs of relief, like guffaws and other spontaneous reactions, were sometimes an issue. The wrong body would often do it and end up looking silly, or worse. This time, Carole had sighed while her boss was giving some sort of pep talk. She'd apologized profusely, but they needed to get that under control ASAP. They also needed new towels. Booker had returned with a large pink rag that looked like it had survived the Revolutionary War.

17

DR. SCHLAPP

THE DOCTOR WAS having a bad day. The rabbi's wife was becoming suspicious of her husband's extracurricular activities and had significantly tightened the leash on him. Evelyn was showing all the symptoms of rabbi withdrawal: absent-mindedness, irritability. To make matters worse, the office above hers had a plumbing leak and her ceiling was dripping on her desk. The office next to hers had a new tenant, an architect by the name of Lopez. That sounded suspiciously Mexican, and Evelyn was always suspicious of Mexicans. She wasn't racist or anything like that. Her father was racist, and she was nothing like him. The woman who did her nails was Mexican and she'd had a Hispanic friend for a very long time—from Guatemala, but still. She just felt… *uncomfortable* around some people who just happened to be from the same place. That was perfectly normal. There was also Lana Lannister to deal with. Lana was becoming obsessed with Carole's case and was now calling twice a day for updates. Evelyn had been assured the plumbing would be taken care of and there was nothing she could do about the rabbi's wife, or the architect's origins. Identifying Carole's mystery condition was the only thing she had any control over, and she dove headfirst into it to keep her mind off everything else.

As it turned out, one *can't* get rabies from a tick bite. Lyme disease, on the other hand, was transmissible by ticks, and was known to cause mood swings and, in some rare cases, outbursts of violence. She even found a study detailing the struggles of fifty people suffering from Lyme disease who committed homicide. Patients experienced recurring violent urges to kill their siblings, parents, wives, et cetera. They also described horrible, vivid nightmares, horror movies playing in their head with more blood and gore than one can imagine. This 'Lyme rage,' as they called it, seemed like a good avenue of investigation, and Evelyn read up on it as much as she could. Carole's blood tests had come back negative for Lyme disease, but it wasn't unusual for patients to receive one or several false negatives before being diagnosed. Obviously, Lyme disease wasn't the only possible explanation. The more she looked for possible causes, the more she was amazed at the many ways nature can turn a normal person into a homicidal maniac. There were other bacteria to consider. She might have had a viral infection. Limbic encephalitis was known to cause aggressive behavior in some cases. There was rabies, of course. Parasites might also be involved. Toxoplasma gondii, a brain parasite that causes toxoplasmosis, has a high incidence in patients with IED, intermittent explosive disorder. It could be a genetic disorder, a neurological condition. Carole's white cell count was also a *bit* low, which could have meant anything. Evelyn requested every test in the book. She also planned on calling Carole back in for an MRI. To cover all her bases, she ordered a whole-genome sequencing, in large part because she'd never done it, and a police matter seemed like the perfect excuse. Unfortunately, it would take weeks to get the results, which meant Evelyn had nothing to do but think about all the things she didn't want to think about.

She opened her desk drawer and stared at her newly acquired bottle of Fortaleza Blanco. She'd heard great things about it: notes of black pepper, earth, olive and butter. Earth and olive seemed like a fine remedy for her uneasiness, and she grabbed herself a clean glass from the shelf. She was about to remove the agave-shaped cork when she mechanically peeked at the clock on the wall. Hmmm, ten to twelve. Evelyn moaned a little as she put the bottle down and closed the drawer. She still congratulated herself for buying that big clock. It was reasonably nice to look at, kept time fairly well, and doubled as Evelyn's conscience from time to time, as it did that morning. Having renounced tequila for at least the next ten minutes, Evelyn started thinking about lunch. That made her think about dessert, which in turn made her think about chocolate. Evelyn's train of thought frequently ended on chocolate, but on that day, she went a couple steps further. From chocolate to cake, and from cake to Booker. Lyme disease is not normally contagious, but Carole had bit the hell out of Booker's arm. Even if it were something else affecting Carole, there was a good chance Booker would end up with it as well. The odds of detecting whatever was affecting Carole would be greatly increased with two people to look at instead of just one. That was a great idea. She could call Booker, explain the situation, then make an appointment at his earliest convenience. That would take time, though, time she'd spend alone in her office, twiddling her thumbs and listening to the ceiling drip while she thought about running her fingers through the rabbi's lush beard. Booker's earliest convenience might also be anything but early, or convenient. Evelyn had never been the most patient person in the world—she told people she was a doctor, not a patient. Most people didn't get the pun, but she kept saying it anyway. Booker's Bakery was only a few blocks from her office, and she decided to go for a walk, thinking some fresh air would do her good anyway.

The air was fresh alright. It started raining as soon as she left the building. Then it started pouring. She was wet and cold when she walked into the bakery, only to be told Booker had gone home for the day. She should have headed back, but she'd left to stop thinking about her lover. Turning around then would only mean thinking about her lover while wet. Evelyn's mood improved a bit, midway to Booker's house, when she reached the point where her clothes and body couldn't absorb more water. Still, by the time she got there, she'd made peace with the fact that she would die of pneumonia, God's long-awaited punishment for her unholy affair. She tried to fix her hair when she got to Booker's house. There was nothing to fix, just random clumps of matted-down hair partially covering her scalp. Okay, so perhaps walking there hadn't been her greatest idea, but she was still right to have come. It was too late to turn back anyway, so she knocked on the door and waited, and waited, and waited.

18

BOOKER–SHIVANSH–CAROLE

BOOKER SAW HIMSELF through Shivansh's eyes as he walked by and realized he'd put his shirt on backwards. He quickly tucked the label inside the collar. Dr. Schlapp had been waiting in the rain for a good minute and a half and he figured she might not notice if she didn't see the Red Wings logo on his back. He was more worried about the whole house smelling like sex. Booker opened the door and let the doctor in, hoping she didn't feel like she'd just walked into a French brothel.

Dr. Schlapp stepped inside and stood in the middle of the doormat, hugging herself. She and Booker stared at each other for a moment while the doctor dripped on the wooden floor like a melting snowman.

—Shit, where are my manners? Let me get you a towel.

Booker went to the bathroom and returned with a large pink towel.

—I… I think your shirt is on backwards.

—What? Oh, you're right. That's funny. Why the house call, Doc? Is anything wrong?

—No, not at all. Well, maybe. You remember what happened with Carole at your shop—of course you remember, you were there. I… I can't talk about my patients, but I guess I won't be revealing much if I say I think there might have been something wrong with her when she attacked you.

—No shit.

—And I was thinking that something might be a virus, or a microbe, or… Anyway, if she broke skin, *and* if it was a bug, then she might have transmitted it to you with her saliva.

—Are you saying I'm gonna start chewing on people for no reason?

—No, I don't think so, but just to be on the safe side, I'd like you to come to the clinic for a blood test. It'll only take a minute.

Three hearts stopped beating for a second. This was bad, way worse than the sex smell. As far as the law was concerned, they were in the clear. Lana Lannister could investigate all she wanted, but without anyone filing a complaint, there was nothing she could do. The doctor was an entirely different story. Whether or not Booker took a blood test, it was now clear Dr. Schlapp hadn't given up and at *some* point, she'd find something, because there had to be something. Three people don't just become one for no reason. They would be discovered, experimented on for the rest of their miserable life, and they'd experience three times the pain and horror all at once. Booker could already see it. The three of them locked in separate padded cells with electrodes sticking out everywhere. Shock one and monitor the reaction in the other two. Starvation, drugs, it wouldn't stop until they were all dead. This was *bad*, with a capital B, and a capital A, and D. Short of committing murder, they couldn't stop the doctor from looking, but they could at least slow her down by refusing to cooperate. There was always a possibility that what had happened to them was temporary, that the effects of whatever it was would wear off before she found anything. 'No' was obviously the right answer to the doctor's question. 'No' was the *only* answer. Booker knew that full well, yet he couldn't bring himself to utter one simple syllable.

The prospect of being lab rats forever was, of course, unappealing, but what really got their one mind spinning was that Dr. Schlapp would eventually find *something*. That simply wasn't the kind of something they were willing to give up on. They needed to know. As happy as they were being one, as terrifying as the answer to the question might be, they had to know what had happened to them. It was just human nature, cubed. They had to do it, and they knew how. The only problem was it meant breaking the single most important rule they had set for themselves. They had to make a choice between upholding their moral principles and satisfying petty curiosity. They had to make that choice right there and then before Dr. Schlapp completely ruined the carpentry.

There comes a time in every person's life when they must rise to the challenge, set aside their own selfish interests to further a just cause or to safeguard the welfare of others. For Booker, Carole and Shivansh, that time would come at a later date. Just this once, they thought. They felt sort of bad about it but, really, there was nothing to feel bad about. They weren't superheroes whose powers came with some sort of moral obligation to do good. At best, they could do hard math. This wouldn't be like Superman robbing a bank with his laser eyes. Their thing was that they shared a mind, and that was precisely what they were planning to do. Just… more. Yes, certain aspects of what they were contemplating would be frowned upon by society, but someone once said that law, morality, religion, were nothing but bourgeois prejudices and—oh, they remembered the full quote!—'behind which lurk in ambush just as many bourgeois interests.' That was by… Oh, crap, they were quoting Karl Marx to themselves now. There was, of course, a very real possibility that what made them share a mind was also messing with their sense of right and wrong… Whatever. Even without the bourgeois thing, they weren't planning to murder anyone. Their goal was somewhat selfish, but in all likelihood, it would make someone else happy, so it couldn't be entirely selfish. Hell yeah. Booker etched a big smile and turned to Dr. Schlapp.

—Sure, Doc! Wanna do it now?

—Now? I was hoping I could get Carole's husband to come as well. That way, I could do both tests and be done with it. We could do it tomorrow. Any day that's convenient for the both of you.

—Well, what do you know, Shivansh is upstairs right now. Shivansh!

A disheveled Shivansh emerged from the staircase, still buttoning up his shirt. They wondered how much the doc could guess from the situation. She might think they were sleeping together. That would be awkward, but inconsequential. The worst she could do was mention it to Carole. She might think they were colluding in some nefarious way, but without knowing what the nefariousness was about, that also didn't mean much. Regardless of what the doctor knew, believed, surmised or suspected, there was no way she could guess everything for now, and now was all that mattered. A couple hours from now, she would know absolutely everything.

19
CAROLE–BOOKER–SHIVANSH

CAROLE WAS ENJOYING the Booker-Shivansh lovemaking from the comfort of her new office chair. The change of furniture wasn't her choice, Carole loved the old chair, but her boss thought it looked outdated and… 'telemarkety' was the word she used. Carole was still adjusting the seat, trying to find the optimal long-distance roll-in-the-hay setting, when the good doctor knocked on Booker's door. Her annoyance at the interruption soon turned to curiosity, then to panic when their morally questionable plan took shape almost instantly. She rushed out of the office without a jacket or an explanation. This was an all-hands-on-deck operation if there was ever one and she had to get there quick.

She had no hope of hailing a cab in the pouring rain, so she ran to the bus stop as fast as her body would let her. She was beginning to slow down when she saw the bus turn the corner and head towards the stop. She tried to catch it, but she had no run left in her. Carole screamed and flailed like a cat in water to get the bus driver's attention. Too late. Now, even if she ran the whole way, not that she could, she'd never make it to the doctor's office in time. Booker was about to start the car. Shivansh was struggling with the seatbelt on the back seat. Dr. Schlapp was riding shotgun and apologizing profusely for getting the seat wet. They would be at the doc's office in about five minutes, unless... Maybe Booker could fake the car breaking down. How, though, while driving? Just turning off the engine at a red light seemed a little obvious. Dr. Schlapp was sitting right next to—

—Carole! Get in!

Whoa. Where did that voice come from? Booker's car? No, Booker's car was halfway across town, and the voice said Carole's name, so it made more sense for it to have been near Carole. Oh, behind her! Carole turned and saw a patrol car pull over on the side of the road, Lana Lannister's face smiling through the rolled-down window. That was... ironic, in the most Alanis sense of the word. Ten thousand spoons when—was it knives? Carole could never remember. Seriously, what were the odds in a town of twenty thousand people, probably a good twenty square miles for the city proper, that a neighbor would run into Carole at that very moment? More to the point, what were the odds of a *cop* neighbor running into her when she was on her way to break the law? Carole was still in shock when the passenger door opened, and she climbed in the front seat without thinking. Lana was... a problem, for sure, but the car itself offered a welcome reprieve from the rain. It was also a car, and as such *could* get Carole to Dr. Schlapp's office in the nick of time. It was, in fact, difficult not to see Lana's timely arrival as some form of providence, divine or otherwise. Carole could simply get out when they got there, and Lana would continue on her merry way towards... wherever Lana was going. Nonetheless, voluntarily bringing a cop to the scene of the crime you are about to commit seemed like the kind of story you laugh about endlessly with your murderer cellmate, and Carole chose to lure Lana as far away from Dr. Schlapp's office as she could. She was going to sit this one out. Shivansh and Booker could, hopefully, handle things on their own.

—Thank you, Lana. Where's your partner?

—Frank's on his lunch break. I'm just getting batteries for the TV remote at the police station. It's been stuck on ESPN for a week. Poor thing, you're soaking wet! Where can I take you?

—Oh, home… You can just take me home.

—But… Your home's that way. You were waiting for the Shopper Shuttle, weren't you? Where were you going? I'll take you there.

—I don't want to be a bother.

—It's no problem! Seriously.

The great John Lennon once said: 'There's nowhere you can be that isn't where you're meant to be.' Okay, that was utter nonsense, but sometimes, you just gotta go with the flow. Lemons make lemonade, and when life hands you a free ride inside a cop car…

—O… kay… I was going to drop by Dr. Schlapp's office.

—Is everything alright?

—Oh, yeah. It's just…

—Sorry. It's none of my business.

—It's fine. Just wanted to talk to her about HRT. I think I might be menopausing. It's early, I know, but I've been having—

—It's okay. I understand.

To Carole's relief, hot flashes ranked well above Lana's threshold for polite chit-chat, and she stopped talking immediately. That was a good thing, because Carole nearly had a heart attack a block away from her destination. Whether or not what they had envisioned qualified as a plan, things were not going according to it, at all. Carole needed to be there more than ever, and Lana needed to be anywhere else even more. Seven interminable seconds later, the patrol car pulled in behind Booker's car in front of Dr. Schlapp's office and Carole opened the door before the car even stopped.

—Here we are! Thank you so much, Lana!

—Say hi to the doctor for me.

—Will do. Bye!

One. Two. Three. Three seconds. That's how long it takes to… well, to count to three somewhat slowly, to open a beer bottle with your shirt, to close the bread bag with the little plastic thingy. It's how long it takes for a penny to hit the ground if you drop it from the tenth floor, the average length of those whistle farts Carole made when she slept. If they'd gotten to the doctor's office just three seconds earlier, everything would have worked out fine, *might* have worked out fine. Carole would have gotten out of the car, Lana would have left and turned the corner before anything happened. *One* fewer red light, one more mile per hour. If they'd gotten there three seconds earlier, Lana wouldn't have seen Dr. Schlapp run out of the building screaming for dear life.

—HEEEEELP! SOMEBODY HELP!

20
SHIVANSH–BOOKER–CAROLE

SHIVANSH SAT IN the back of Booker's car. He could have taken his own, but the fewer moving parts this plan had, the better he liked it. Carole was already on her way from work. She would get there long before they were done with the blood tests. It was pouring outside. There would be no passersby, making the situation that much easier to manage. Things were looking good, for about ten seconds. Dr. Schlapp was giving unnecessary directions when Shivansh saw the bus leave before Carole could get in. There was no way she'd get a taxi in that weather. That meant she wouldn't make it in time. This was now a two-person job. Still doable, but they had to make some adjustments. They would forego watching the outside of the doctor's office. In theory, they wouldn't need to leave until she was one of them. Shivansh would stand guard in the office lobby while Booker did the deed. Dr. Schlapp was tiny and frail; she would be relatively easy to subdue—

Wow. That plan of theirs sounded way more evil now than it had when they'd come up with it.

It *was* bad, no question, but they'd only need to keep the doctor still for an hour or so until she merged with them. All in all, it still seemed like a good plan. It was simple enough and required as little violence as possible, considering it involved biting someone.

They were barely out of the driveway when Lana Lannister yelled for Carole to get in. Booker nearly had a heart attack and hit the brakes out of reflex. The only excuse he could come up with was a cramp in his right foot. That seemed harmless enough, but the doctor was adamant about running more tests because of it. Something about his electrolytes and potassium levels.

—Did you know foot cramps can be an early sign of something more serious?

Now they knew. They also knew more tests would take more time. They didn't know how much time, but they could guesstimate. Five minutes if it was a blood test? That wasn't much, and Booker was the only one with a foot problem, so it was only one test. She'd also said something about electrolytes, so there was a chance that required its own thing. If Booker asked a lot of questions, they could easily get fifteen minutes out of this. That potassium thing was exactly what they needed. They thought about it for a second or two, then—with Lana Lannister insisting—they decided Carole should join them. They were back to plan A, or maybe this was plan C, which was only coincidentally identical to plan A. Either way, while Lana's presence in the vicinity might seem like it was throwing a wrench in the works, the original plan called for three people for a reason. As Shivansh always said (or was it Booker?): "Always stick to the plan."

The ride to the doctor's office was a festival of insincere niceties. Dr. Schlapp pretended she was doing this for purely altruistic reasons, and not to satisfy her own curiosity.

Booker pretended to be thankful for her concern. Shivansh didn't want to repeat everything Booker said, so he just smiled the whole way without saying a thing. Shivansh smiling was a rare event, and he wasn't very good at it. He looked like he was sucking on something sour more than anything else. Had the doctor paid attention, she might have figured out he was up to something. Luckily, he was sitting in the back and the doctor was too busy telling Booker how fast to drive and where to turn.

They arrived at Dr. Schlapp's office in no time. Booker, Shivansh and the doctor ran to the building entrance under the rain after they parked the car. Shivansh went in with them, then stopped about halfway up the stairs. Carole was about a minute away and he would watch the outside until she arrived as planned. Always stick to the plan.

—Oh, I'm sorry. I forgot my wallet in the car.

—Leave it, Shivansh. I'm not charging you for this.

—Well, no, it's a… I need it for… something. I'll be right back.

Sure, that was clumsy, but Booker could just change the subject if she said anything. They had a singular advantage over the doctor. There was absolutely no way she would suspect what they were planning. She was more likely to think they would spontaneously combust or remove a rubber mask to reveal their villain faces like they did in *Scooby-Doo* than she was to suspect they were a small hive mind trying to absorb her by biting into her flesh. It sounded absurd even to them. Shivansh went back outside and hid from the rain under the porch waiting for Carole to show up.

Lana and Carole were still half a mile away. The silence in that car was so awkward that Shivansh didn't know what to do with himself and he wasn't even there. He was also nervous as hell, so he started thinking about a recipe for kouign-amann, but that made him hungry, so he switched to itemized deductions for a client who sold Tupperware out of her home. They'd decided not to expense part of the mortgage to keep her home sale exclusion intact, but she could still claim a percentage of utilities, maybe some—Oh, shit.

Oh, shit!

Oh, shit!

The best laid schemes o' mice an' men gang aft agley—What was it with them and all those quotes? Shivansh seriously doubted there was a Scots poem for how fucked up the situation was, or how fast their plan had gone to hell. He rushed back inside before another quote came to mind. He tripped on his way upstairs and cut his shin pretty bad on the metal stairs. The pain was almost unbearable, but it didn't matter, he had to stop her befo—*BOOM*. Oh, God. Shivansh fell backwards and watched the world spin through a few turns before he passed out.

21
BOOKER–SHIVANSH–CAROLE

SHIVANSH'S EXCUSE TO stay behind sounded so contrived, Booker did what he could to steer the conversation elsewhere while he and Dr. Schlapp walked up the stairs.

—Before I forget, I need to talk to you about Layla.

—You made an appointment for them, didn't you?
Are they thinking about transitioning?

Booker was just trying to distract the doctor, but that answer genuinely stunned him. He hadn't been to Dr. Schlapp's office in at least a decade. Layla had gone… a few years back when they hurt their knee during soccer practice? But… how the hell did she know Layla's pronouns?

—I… How?

—How do I know? Well, it's a small town. There
isn't much happening in Marquette that I don't
hear about sooner or later. Also, I play bridge
with one of Layla's teachers.

—Oh! So, yeah, they want to talk to you about
these—

—Puberty blockers, I assume.

Booker felt a strange whirl of emotions: envy, jealousy. Shame. He'd missed so much of what was happening with his child, right under his nose. The doctor, who hadn't seen Layla in years, was more aware of things than he was. She also knew about these blocker things and—Gosh, it would have been so much easier if he'd been the doctor. He'd have known what to say, how to say it. He wouldn't have wrecked everything the way he had. Whatever doubts Booker had about doing this evaporated in an instant. This was the right thing to do. It was meant to be. Booker felt empowered, like this was somehow ordained by a higher pow—

As they reached the top of the stairs, Booker noticed wet boot marks on the olive-green carpet in the corridor and lost his train of thought. The steps stopped right in front of the door with the doctor's name on it. As if the wet footmarks weren't a big enough clue, two pairs of wet leather boots were neatly aligned on the rubber doormat.

—Were you expecting anyone, doc?

—Well, I have a one-thirty with—Oh, dear, they're here already! I guess I forgot to lock, and they let themselves in. Don't worry, I'll tell them to wait. I'm booked all afternoon after that.

Crap. There were people *inside* the doctor's office, which was precisely what Shivansh and Carole were supposed to prevent from happening. That was the only part of their plan that actually resembled a plan. The smart thing to do was to abort, find an excuse to leave and try again some other time.

—I don't want to mess up your whole schedule. We'll just come back another day.

—No! No! Least I can do is not waste more of your time for this. There's a good chance I brought you here for nothing anyway.

Booker's options were narrowing rapidly. He could leave anyway. That would be rude, but who cared about rudeness? He could do the test and go home, but that would just be stupid. Dr. Schlapp might find something before they came back and, well, the whole reason for being there was to prevent that from happening. Abort and leave. That was the reasonable thing to do, and they were very reasonable people, except... They were already there, and they were extremely on edge. Shivansh was physically exhausted. Carole was sitting next to a cop inside a police car. They didn't know if they'd find the courage to do this again and they were worried Carole's blood test could be enough to ruin their lives. Booker, Carole and Shivansh had a moment of... something—courage, panic, weakness, desperation, whatever—and the bazillion things going through their mind gave way to a single, all-powerful thought: Fuck it.

Booker put his hand over Dr. Schlapp's mouth and bit down on her shoulder as hard as he could. Gawd, that was a bad idea, but at least it was done. All he had to do now was find a hiding place, a closet, anything, and keep the doctor quiet for an hour or so. That shouldn't prove too difficult. After all, Dr. Schlapp was tiny and frail and would be relatively easy to subdue.

She wasn't. Evelyn Schlapp was a God-fearing Jewish woman, but she didn't just fear God. She was afraid of street gangs, and muggers, and Mexicans, and Asians, and young black men, and—all in all, a significant percentage of the population. Evelyn thought of herself as progressive. She'd marched for women's rights since the '60s, then gay rights—she was in Detroit in 1972 for their first Pride event—but her father was as racist as they came and, as much as she hated the man, he'd rubbed off on her more than she cared to admit. As a result of that constant fear, she'd been taking Krav Maga classes twice a week for eighteen years. Booker never knew what hit him. His wrist was broken in an instant, then his nose. Fuck, that hurt! He was coming up the stairs to help himself when Dr. Schlapp rammed him down so hard he lost Shivansh-consciousness immediately. Booker tried to get up, but he was too dizzy; he fell back to the floor.

With Shivansh out of the equation, Carole was the only one who could catch up to the doctor before she called for help—they were pretty much screwed if that happened. The doctor would soon be one of them, but a bunch of people biting folks for no reason was going to get them all locked up and get a lot more doctors interested in what was happening to them. Booker felt an ounce of relief when he saw the clinic approaching from Carole's point of view, but that didn't last long. Carole was coming, but she wasn't alone.

Dr. Schlapp didn't even need to call for help. Help was already on its way.

22
LANA

THE PATROL CAR pulled up behind Booker's car in front of Dr. Schlapp's office, and Carole opened the door before the car even stopped.

—Here we are! Thank you so much, Lana!

—Say hi to the doctor for me.

—Will do. Bye!

That's when Dr. Schlapp stormed out of the building, screaming. All signs pointed to an assault. She was attempting to flee. Her right shoulder was bleeding through her white blouse.

—Stay in the car, Carole!

Lana called for backup, stormed out of the car and pulled out her weapon. She could feel the butterflies taking over. It was the first time she'd unholstered that thing, except at home in front of the mirror.

Dr. Schlapp had twisted her ankle and fallen on wet grass in the front yard. She was crawling towards the patrol car, wheezing and coughing. Lana's first instinct was to run over and help her. Her training told her to wait for backup. Decisions, decisions. She could be a good human being, or she could be a good cop. She chose the latter. She couldn't help Dr. Schlapp with her gun drawn and whoever attacked her might come out of the building shooting. She crouched behind her car door and aimed her weapon at the door.

—Lana! I can go and help her!

—I said stay!

Lana wasn't confident Carole would stay. If she left the safety of the car, Lana would have to deal with her *and* Dr. Schlapp. She also didn't trust her. Carole had attacked her, *twice*. She'd attacked Booker. She'd chosen this exact moment to go to Dr. Schlapp's office. That had to mean something. Carole was up to no good, and Lana didn't want to let her out of her sight. For the first time since she'd joined the force, Lana wished Frank was there with her.

The rain was pouring even harder and getting into her eyes. In a few seconds, she'd be blind as a bat, easy prey for whoever had assaulted the doctor. Training or not, she couldn't wait any longer. She stepped away from the car and walked towards Dr. Schlapp, weapon drawn.

—I'm coming, Doctor.

—Heeelp, he—

He. This was indeed an assault, but *he* who? Before she could even begin to guess, Shivansh emerged from the door, limping, his right leg bloodied from knee to toe. Lana stopped dead in her tracks and aimed her gun at his chest. She didn't recognize him at first. Her eyes were half shut, swollen by the rain. She squinted hard to see if he was holding anything. She couldn't see a weapon, but there was no way to be sure.

—DO. NOT. MOVE. Stay right where you are!

—What? Lana, it's me, Shivansh! You know me.

Carole's husband?

Now she recognized him, but that did nothing to reassure her. Shivansh was exactly who he said he was, Carole's husband, the same Carole sitting in Lana's patrol car not ten feet behind. He was the one who'd lied about his injury, the one Booker had likely stabbed for whatever reason. Lana was in danger; she could feel it in her bones. She needed to cuff him or she could lose control of the situation. She could be injured, killed even. Shivansh could run, and she didn't want that, not when she was this close to getting the answers she was looking for.

—Keep your hands where I can see them, Shivansh.

—Dr. Schlapp is hurt! I was going to help her!

Help her? Shivansh could have been telling the truth. He was bleeding like she was. It was entirely possible that whoever injured the doctor had also attacked him. It was also entirely possible he was the one who'd assaulted Dr. Schlapp and that she'd fought back. Lana's gut told her it was the latter, but she rarely trusted her gut. She trusted her brain, though, and her brain was screaming danger at her. Bad news followed Carole and Shivansh wherever they went. They were like Angela Lansbury in *Murder, She Wrote*: people got hurt the minute they stepped out of their houses. People got hurt *inside* their houses. Hell, no. She didn't believe a word coming out of Shivansh's mouth.

—*Stop right there and let me see your hands!* I mean it, Shivansh, don't make me hurt you.

—Okay! Okay!

Lana didn't know if she'd have shot him or not. Shivansh must have believed she would have, because he stopped moving right away. Lana took her handcuffs off her belt with one hand and slowly moved closer.

—Now put both hands forward so I can cuff you.

—WHAT? I COULDN'T HEAR YOU. WHAT IS IT YOU WANT ME TO DO?

Why was Shivansh screaming? The rain was loud, but Lana was standing five feet away from Shivansh. There was no way he didn't hear her. Nevertheless, she repeated, louder this time.

—I said, PUT BOTH HANDS IN FRONT OF YOU so I can cuff you.

—CUFF ME? WHAT THE HELL IS WRONG WITH YOU? I'M JUST TRYING TO HELP!

With the rain and all the yelling, she didn't hear the car door closing behind her. She didn't hear the engine roaring. She heard the tires screeching, but by then it was too late. Lana turned to look. Headlights shining like suns in the pouring rain. Sharp pain in her legs. Her head hit the windshield hard enough to break the glass and then... Weightlessness, a sinking feeling in her stomach, the inner ear messing with her brain. For a second, Lana was flying, then gravity stepped in.

Everything went quiet after she hit the ground. She couldn't hear anything, not the rain, not the car. She couldn't remember what she was worried about a moment before, but she didn't care. It was calm and quiet, so peaceful. Everything was... perfect. Lana just lay there, face up, watching the raindrops fall over her. She wanted that feeling to last forever. Then the sky got darker, the rain brighter. It looked like the *Millennium Falcon* jumping to light speed. For a brief moment, she thought it was nightfall, but the darkness was setting in too fast; it wasn't the sun, it was her. She was going to pass out.

23
CAROLE

CAROLE WAS ALONE, weak and alone. Shivansh was unconscious at the bottom of the stairs, Booker too dizzy to contribute. Carole was Carole again. It hadn't been that long, but she'd forgotten what it meant to be just *her*. It wasn't good. She felt empty, incomplete, as if someone had cut off half her limbs. She felt… small, like a child, powerless. The rain hitting the windshield was as loud as a jackhammer, the wipers sounded like nails on a chalkboard. Being in that car, in this situation, that was simply too *big* for her. There was a cop standing not three feet away. More cops were coming. Dr. Schlapp was still crawling towards them. They were all screwed, and there was absolutely nothing she could do to fix it.

—Stay in the car, Carole!

—Lana! I can go and help her!

—I said stay!

Carole stayed. She closed her door and stayed in the car. She knew she should have done something, anything, but she couldn't move at all. She watched Lana get out and stand in the rain, desperate for someone to come and help her. Someone did. Help came from inside the building, one floor up. Just as Lana stepped away from the car, Booker slowly regained his footing. Carole-Booker saw things a lot more clearly than Carole alone, but they still weren't sure of what to do. They'd all thought *Fuck it* a minute before and attacked the doctor. It hadn't turned out that great, but it wasn't over. They knew there were risks to what they were doing, and maybe, just maybe, 'fuck it' was still the way to go. It was either that or surrender to the cops and tell them everything. Hell, Carole didn't even have to do anything, she was already sitting in a police car. What would happen to them if they did surrender? There was no guarantee they would be discovered. They'd be in trouble with the law, for sure—a third of them would be, at least. Carole and Shivansh could take care of Layla if Booker went to jail. Carole had been in jail and it hadn't been so bad with her other two bodies still on the outside. Maybe they could—

Suddenly, Carole saw the front door of the building. She saw it from the *inside*. Shivansh was awake at the bottom of the stairwell. Oh, yeah, they were whole again. God, that felt good. They were three and they knew exactly what to do… Fuck it. Definitely, fuck it.

Carole scooted over to the driver's side and closed the door before putting the car in reverse. She backed away slowly, then shifted gears and hit the gas pedal as hard as she could. The wheels spun for a second, then Carole was pushed back into the seat. The car jumped the curb just as Lana turned around. It hit her right in the legs. Lana's head smashed the windshield and Carole hit the brakes.

She'd done it. Up until then, she wasn't sure she could. Carole turned the engine off and got out of the car. There was this loud silence, nothing but the rain. What now? They'd fixed one problem, at least temporarily, but they weren't done yet. Carole took a deep breath and turned to the doctor.

—Doctor, you're gonna need to come with us.

—Please, Carole, don't hurt me! Please!

—No one's going to hurt you, but you need to come with us.

—HEEEEELLLLPP!

Okay, so the doctor wouldn't come voluntarily. Booker came out of the building to help, but couldn't do much with his broken wrist. Carole and Shivansh hauled Dr. Schlapp all the way to Booker's car while she screamed for help. They shoved her into the trunk and closed it. Wait, her fingers! No, she was fine, but they could now add kidnapping to the list of their criminal activities. They'd already committed assault when they attacked the doctor, but even assault *and* kidnapping were small potatoes compared to killing a cop—*Maybe* killing a cop? Lana sure *looked* dead. She was lying on her back, the rain slowly washing the blood from her face. Booker leaned down and felt her neck for a pulse with his good hand. Nothing. Oh! Maybe. No, nothing. Looking for a pulse on someone's neck wasn't as easy as it looked on television. Booker moved his fingers about like fifty times, until—*Poom poom, poom poom. Yes!* Definitely a pulse. Fuck yeah, Lana was alive. Carole felt the weight of the world fall off her shoulders. The DA would probably call what they had done attempted murder, but attempted murder sounded a lot better than murder from a legal perspective. More than anything, it meant they hadn't killed anyone.

They almost had, though. That thought was disturbing. This plan was violent from the start. They'd chosen to attack the doctor, thinking she wouldn't mind once she merged with them. That might have been true, but they knew there was nothing altruistic about their intentions. They'd run over Lana, someone they knew—didn't like, but knew—to save their ass without giving it a second thought. Was the merging of their minds affecting them in ways they didn't understand? Was it really their choice to attack the doctor, or had they been pushed to do it by whatever changed them? More likely, the truth was that they had always had it in them to hurt someone. They wondered if it was in all of them or just one. As important as these questions were, answering them would have to wait. They had to decide what to do with Lana. They could leave her there and hope she didn't die from her injuries. Could she drown in the falling rain? Probably not, but she could still die. They could drop her in front of the hospital like they do in movies. They'd surely be seen, though. Booker even knew the security guard standing at the door. Whatever choice they made, they had to make it quick. It had been a good two minutes since Lana had called for backup. Marquette police had a reputation for being inefficient, but the station was five blocks away. They'd be there soon even if they hitched a ride with a toddler on a tricycle. The upside to that was that Lana would quickly get medical help. They chose to leave her behind and drove back to Booker's place like a bat out of hell… (Why would bats want to dart out of hell? Carole never quite got that one. Maybe they'd want to avoid the light coming from the fires, but wouldn't it still be brighter outside? That really made no sense.)

They chose to leave Lana behind and drove back to Booker's place like greased lightning. There. Much better.

24
LAYLA

MR. HUMFREY HAD a heart attack, in class! They said it was angina, but it looked like a heart attack anyway. Like, one minute he was talking about planets, and the next he was doing the bacon dance on the floor. Layla hated Mr. Humfrey with gusto, but not enough to be happy about him suffering like that. It looked *really* painful. Even Liz Kwan felt sorry for him, and Liz Kwan never felt sorry for anyone. Layla was sort of touched at first, then realized this was some sort of Jedi mind trick only Liz Kwan could pull off. Setting the bar so low by acting like a jerk all the time, then when you show an ounce of compassion people think you're Gandhi. Anyway, since that was a semi-traumatizing incident, and probably because they couldn't find a substitute at the last minute, they'd decided to send the kids home early. That, Layla was happy about. They were allowed to be. Yeah, the angina thing was bad, that's for sure, but getting home early was objectively good, even if it was because of a bad thing. It's like if your aunt dies and you find a hundred bucks on the ground, you'll be super sad that your aunt died, but it's not like you're gonna say: 'Them damn hundred-dollar bills lying everywhere!

Someone needs to do something about that!' Right? Right. Layla was happy and that was okay.

It was raining cats and dogs when they walked out of school. Kids were running in every direction with their bags over their heads. Not Layla. They never cared much about fashion, or what other people thought, so they'd asked their dad for one of these yellow ponchos that fold into a smallish pouch. That thing was as big as a parachute when you spread it open, and they could walk home even on rainy days. Yeah, their feet would get wet, but changing socks was a small price to pay to avoid a crowded bus full of wet smelly people. The poncho also made the rain so loud, no other sound could get through. Layla liked walking in a bubble away from the world. It was the perfect time to think about stuff. This time, they were thinking about mac-and-cheese, and Booker.

Layla's dad had been… There were no words to do it justice. Different? Better? Everything Layla wished he could be? He was there, for starters. He'd stopped coming home late every day. He was happy. He was listening. Even around others, he wasn't trying to be the manly man, the tough guy that nothing ever bothers. He was kind, to everyone. It wasn't fake kindness either, the what-can-I-get-out-of-it kindness. That was a rare thing in this world and Layla felt lucky to be around it. Oh, and he'd finally made that appointment with Dr. Schlapp. They thought they could return the favor by making dinner that evening. Layla didn't cook much, but their dad's favorite meal was mac-and-cheese. How hard could mac-and-cheese be? There was a full box of macaroni in the pantry. It'd been sitting there for ages, but Layla didn't think pasta could go bad. Add some cheese. Cream, maybe? Boom, mac-and-cheese.

It wouldn't be a surprise—Layla didn't have the money to buy cheese, or cream if there was cream in it—but Booker would be happy. Layla was sure of that.

They smiled when they saw their dad's car in the driveway. Booker had stopped coming home late, but he rarely came home early. What were the odds that both of them would be home by 2:30? This could be the perfect day. They could play games together all afternoon, go buy cheese, and maybe cream, and watch a movie after dinner. Oh. My. God. Layla'd forgotten it was Friday. They could watch *two* movies, make popcorn. They didn't have any, but they had to go to the store anyway. This was going to be so much fun. Layla opened the door and tripped on a pair of shoes they didn't recognize. Booker didn't have many friends, certainly none that came over. Whoever these shoes belonged to, it must have been a stranger, the plumber, or—Wow, there were all *kinds* of shoes. Maybe Booker *did* have friends over. That would be a first since Layla's mom had left. *She'd* had friends over all the time.

—Dad? You home? I finished schoo—AAAHHH!

What the fuck? What the actual fuck?

—Language, Layla.

—Are you kidding me?!

Booker was sitting in the kitchen, his nose bent sideways, and his wet shirt completely covered in blood. He was holding a gun in one hand. The other hand was on the table, bent backwards and dangling like a rag do—OH MY FUCKING GOD WAS THAT A BONE?! Eww, Layla couldn't look, so she turned to Dr. Schlapp, who was sitting across from Booker with duct tape over her mouth. Her hands were tied behind her back, her feet taped to the chair legs. She looked absolutely terrified. Layla sympathized;

they were scared shitless, and they weren't even covered with tape. As if the scene wasn't weird enough, there were two strangers on the couch: a dude with a bloody leg, and a short white woman looking half naked in her wet white blouse. The woman was sporting the most fake smile Layla had ever seen. The man was… they weren't sure. He looked like he was sucking on a lemon. Layla was in shock. Mr. Humfrey rolling on the floor was bad, but this was seriously fucked up. Their mind was spinning like a flywheel in a hurricane. They almost had a heart attack themselves when the woman on the couch stood up and started talking.

—Layla, we don't have much time but—

—Who the hell are you?

That was a bit rude, but Layla thought it was appropriate under the circumstances. The woman seemed to agree, and she sat back down without saying a word. Booker laid the gun down on the table, stood up, and put his good hand on Layla's shoulder.

—Layla, we don't have much time. There's… something you need to know.

—What's going on, Dad? What's happening? Why do you have a gun?

—I took it off a cop.

—You *what?*

—I know! This looks bad. It kind of is, but there's something else I need to tell you.

—What?

—It's going to be difficult for you to understand. Hell, I'm not sure I understand it myself.

—What? What? Just say it!

Booker took a deep breath. He held it for a second, then exhaled like he'd given up.

—This is…

—DAD! Please! Just tell me!

—Okay, okay.

Booker took another deep breath and told Layla everything.

PART 3
MUTATION

25
LAYLA

LAYLA LISTENED TO Booker talk about Carole's tick and the day she'd attacked him at the bakery. His eyes filled with tears as he described in touching detail the fulfilling warmth of minds merging together, the newfound strength and understanding that came with being more than one. Booker's speech was as wholehearted, as passionate as they came. Had Shivansh and Carole not been him, they would have been profoundly stirred. As for Layla…

—Dad, are you on drugs?

—No. I know how this sounds, Layla.

—No, you don't. You're scaring me right now.

—It's true, kiddo. I don't know what else to tell you. How about you just ask them something?

—Ask who what?

—Ask Shivansh anything, or Carole, something only you and I know.

—You mean them?

Layla turned to the two strangers in the living room. They were still staring, but they'd gotten rid of the creepy smiles. They looked almost normal, if you ignored the blood, and the wet blouse, and the kidnapped doctor moaning in the background. Both were tapping their fingers on their legs. Layla eeny-meeny-miney-mo'ed between them, then cheated and added 'not' at the end when they realized they would end on Shivansh. He looked *really* unfriendly. They moved closer to the couch and peered deep into Carole's eyes, searching for a glimmer of Bookerness, something unique and authentic they would immediately recognize as their dad. The staring got awkward real fast, and Layla was unexpectedly relieved when Carole opened her mouth.

—What are you doing, Layla?

—I—I'm seeing if I can recognize my dad.

—In my face, Carole's face.

—Yes.

—But it's my face. I've always had that face. Why would it look anything like Booker's?

—I don't know! You said—

—I never said anything about a staring contest. I told you to ask me a question.

—What do you want me to ask?

—It's up to you, kiddo. You can ask me about your life, your dad's life. You can ask about your mom.

—You know my mom?

—Well, we were married for fifteen years, but I—me, Carole—have never met her.

—This is weird. And how do I know that's true? Like, you could have been friends in college or something.

—Ask me about something else, then, something you did with m—with your father.

—…

—Come on, Layla! We don't have all day.

—I'm thinking! Okay, I got it. Me and my dad went to Chicago for spring break last year and—

—That was two years ago, I was sick as a dog last year, remember? But yeah, we took the long way there to stop by my sister's in Lakewood, the one you don't like. We never made it to Chicago. The car broke down in the middle of nowhere before we got to Green Bay. We spent the night there. I don't remember the name of the town, but we ended up going to the Hamburger Hall of Fame or whatever it's called. You took a picture next to the hamburger guy.

—Hamburger Charlie.

—That's the one. Isn't that where we bought that ugly... weird doll with the long legs?

Layla started crying. Granted, it didn't take much to make Layla cry, but they'd loved that trip. It was the first time they did anything together after the breakup, first time in months they felt like a family, not just the broken pieces of one.

—Groovy Girl.

—What?

—The doll's name is Groovy Girl. And it's not ugly.

—That thing is creepy as hell.

—But how? How do—

—It's like I said—like Booker said. I'm... your dad, sort of. So is Shivansh. And your dad's me, and... that's it.

That's it? Layla remembered how shaken they were when their mom said she was leaving. They didn't think anyone would ever be able to top that, and yet, here they were. In terms of shock value, 'We're getting a divorce' wasn't even in the same league as 'I'm your dad' coming from the white woman on the couch. Layla took it pretty well, considering. They were still scared as hell, but the whole thing was so fucking weird, it was hard not to be curious about it.

—Can you see what they're seeing?

—Yeah, kind of.

—What does that mean, kind of?

—It's fuzzy, but—

—How many fingers am I holding up?

—Three.

—Whoa.

—We're still getting used to it. Now I'd like you to go to your room and lock the door behind you, okay, kiddo?

—Why?

—Just in case the cops come in shooting.

Okay, that was bad. The white woman might have been her dad, but Layla needed to hear it from the real thing and they turned to Booker.

—Dad?

—I'm afraid so.

—Because you kidnapped Dr. Schlapp?

—Mm-hmm. I'm sorry.

Strangely, the doctor hadn't come up in the conversation until then. The mind-merge thing was hard enough to accept that Layla never thought to ask. Now they wanted to know, but they were scared of the answer. They'd almost forgotten about their dad holding a gun. 'I took it from a cop,' he'd said. The story was quickly taking shape in Layla's mind. They were missing some details, for sure, but duct-taped doctor plus gun plus blood everywhere could only equal one thing. The cops *were* coming.

—What happened?

—It's… complicated. But there was a cop there that got hurt pretty bad. She was unconscious when we left. They'll take her to the hospital, and I'm sure she'll be fine, but whenever she wakes up, she'll tell them that Shivansh kidnapped Dr. Schlapp and that Carole tried to kill her, something like that.

—Is she the one who busted your nose?

—No, the doctor did that. I don't think the cop ever saw me.

—Then why would they come to our house?

—My car was parked up front.

—Maybe she didn't notice.

—Oh, she noticed. She notices everything. It doesn't matter, they'll come here at some point, Layla. Trust me.

—When?

—Depends on when she wakes up, I guess. Could be hours, could be—

Layla heard the sirens approaching and went to the front window. One car, two cars, three, four. They just kept coming. It was just like that scene in *Terminator 2* when Sarah Connor asks how many cops are outside, and John says: 'Uh, all of them, I think.' It was surreal, and scary, but not as surreal or scary as their dad's face and the wrist thing—*oh, gawd,* she'd looked at it again—or the part about sharing a mind and that the white lady was also her dad. Layla was going through a lot of shit. The entire police force showing up at their house didn't faze them a whole lot more. They closed the window blinds and locked the front door like they'd seen people do in movies.

—Dad, what about the gun?

—Oh. Good thinking.

Booker picked up Lana's gun and threw it in the garbage bin under the sink.

—Dad! They're gonna find it!

—Yeah, but they won't shoot us all if they don't see it. At least, I hope they won't. Can you untie Dr. Schlapp before you run upstairs? I can't do it with one hand.

—But she'll tell them everything!

—It's okay, Layla. She's one of us now.

Oh, great, they had *four* dads now. Layla freed Dr. Schlapp's hands and pulled the tape off her mouth. The doctor looked at Layla with gentle eyes and smiled. That was… too much too soon, and Layla ran up to their room.

26
LANA

—YOUR HONOR, AT this time I move to dismiss all charges.

—No! She's lying! You know she's lying!

Lana was never one to let emotions get the best of her and she surprised herself when she spoke out loud. Still, how could the judge not see it? Lana remembered every detail from her course on detecting deception and *all* the signs were there, every single one of them. Gesturing after they finished talking instead of while they spoke—because the mind was too busy making up things. Scratching, fidgeting, tilting their head to the side. Grooming behavior—the doctor kept fixing her hair the whole time. Rolling back the lips, dry mouth, sudden increases in volume. Dr. Schlapp's testimony was a masterclass in looking like a liar. Lana didn't know exactly what the truth was, but peer-reviewed research from the UCLA psychology department strongly indicated that this was not it. Lana was never fully at ease with the social sciences because their conclusions were hard to quantify, but she guessed the odds of the doctor lying to be around ninety percent. Ninety-two. There was some sort of conspiracy going on between Shivansh, Booker, Carole, and now Dr. Schlapp.

Shivansh was charged with assault causing bodily harm, Booker with aiding and abetting. The prosecutor had sought a plea bargain, but they'd all refused. Carole was who they really wanted, attempted murder on a police officer. They'd all pleaded not guilty, of course. Layla was over ten years old and legally allowed to stay home alone, but Booker's attorney had requested a speedy preliminary hearing and the judge had granted it. It had been less than a week since Lana was run over. Both her legs were broken, and the doctor wasn't sure when she'd walk again, but none of that mattered to Lana. What she wanted was justice. No, that wasn't true. What Lana wanted was the *truth*. She had been obsessed with Carole's case from the start and every event added a new layer of mystery to it. She'd been sidelined from the case for obvious reasons and couldn't talk to any of the accused. She'd testified first about what she'd seen. She'd kept trying to come back to Carole's attack on Booker and her outburst at the station, but the judge wouldn't allow it. Booker was sitting there the whole time with his nose bandaged, along with Shivansh and Carole. They'd stared at the floor the whole time. They didn't speak, didn't react in any way. They never even looked in Lana's direction.

After her testimony, Lana waited for Dr. Schlapp to take the stand and seal the case. Then she waited some more. There was no space reserved for wheelchairs in the courtroom and the bailiff had rolled Lana to a corner like a child in timeout. From there she could see the DA and his assistant arguing over something, but she couldn't hear what they were saying. After uttering some curse words even Lana could hear, the DA waved his hands at the judge. The defense attorney immediately stood up and called Evelyn Schlapp to the stand. The *defense* did.

Dr. Schlapp said she was walking up to her office when a tall, skinny white man grabbed her from behind, bit her on the shoulder when she resisted, and then stole her purse. She told the judge that Booker and Shivansh tried to stop the man before being knocked out and pushed down the stairs.

—What happened then, Doctor?

—I went outside to get help. I saw Lana—Officer Lannister—and I ran towards her. It was pouring that day and I slid on the wet grass. I twisted my ankle. It's okay now, but it really hurt at the time. That's when I saw the man come out from behind Booker's car. I tried to say something, but I was out of breath. I'm sixty-one, you know.

—I can only imagine how you felt. What did the man do after he came out of hiding?

—He went straight to the patrol car. The door was open. He sat behind the wheel and hit the gas pedal. I could see Carole struggling with him. I saw her grab the wheel. She tried to steer the car away from Lana but… Well, you know the rest. It happened exactly like Lana said.

—You must have been so scared.

—I was. The man got out of the car and ran away. Maybe I should have run after him, but with my ankle…

—Doctor, please. No one expected you to risk your life to stop a criminal from fleeing. Officer Lannister intervened and she's lucky to be alive. I have one more question, then I'll let you go. You didn't tell the police what happened until this morning. Why is that?

—I… thought I had. It all happened so fast. I was probably in shock. I'd be lying if I said I don't forget a few things every now and then.

—I understand. Thank you very much for your time, Doctor… Your honor, at this time I move to dismiss all charges.

And that was when Lana shouted. The judge admonished Lana for her outburst and blamed this entire fiasco on shoddy police work. He never mentioned Lana by name, but everyone in the courtroom was staring at her. It was Frank who'd taken Dr. Schlapp's statement. Lana wasn't even conscious when it happened. It didn't matter. The DA even apologized to the defendants. Lana was furious. She moved her wheelchair to block Dr. Schlapp's way as she exited the courtroom.

—Why? Why did you lie in front of everyone? Did Carole threaten you?

—Threaten me? Lana, I know how confusing this must be for you, but she tried to help. She tried to save you!

—She attacked me! She bit Booker! Now you're saying it's pure coincidence she and Booker were there when you were attacked in the exact same way?

—It was Lyme disease that made her lose control back then. It's not that uncommon.

—Lyme disease?

—Yes. Didn't I tell you?

—No. You did not.

—I'm sorry. It must have slipped my mind.

She was lying. It was so obvious! And her testimony was the most convoluted cockamamie story Lana had ever heard.

No one in their right mind should have bought it, and yet the judge... Deep breath. Lana was angry, she was aware of that. She was also very good at compartmentalizing. As crazy as it sounded, Dr. Schlapp's story *did* fit the facts. There was nothing Lana had seen or heard that directly contradicted what the doctor had said on the stand. It was at least *technically* possible everything had happened as she said. Still, every fiber in Lana's body told her it didn't. There had to be a way to prove it.

—We should do a bite-mark comparison.

—What?

—Bite marks. I want to check if Carole's teeth match your wound, or Booker's, or—

—Or if they match someone whose teeth we've never seen? That's not how it works. Besides, my wound's healed up nicely since then.

—We have to do it.

—Why? Don't you think you've put Carole through enough already? She was accused of attempted murder, Lana. Murder! You can't put her through this again. It's time to let it go.

The doctor was right. Not about letting it go, but it was true that Lana couldn't do this to Carole. She couldn't do anything to Carole. It wasn't even Lana's case. It never had been, and she'd now been specifically forbidden to work on it. To push this any further would jeopardize her career, assuming she even had one left. Compartmentalize. The smart thing to do was to put all her doubts, her questions, her obsession with Carole in a box somewhere and concentrate on something else she had control over, like learning to walk again.

27

EVELYN–BOOKER–CAROLE–SHIVANSH

Evelyn wasn't afraid. She wasn't scared of everyone who didn't look or think like her. Being a pansexual, brown-skinned, white, black man and woman will do that to people. The confidence that came with being *four* was also hard to describe. She sure as shit wasn't afraid of God anymore. For one, her faith had been obliterated in the merge, but she'd also stopped feeling guilty for simply wanting companionship.

She was still remorseful for attacking herself, but ever grateful for the change. It wasn't all rosy; some of what she'd learned about herself was hard to accept. Aside from her work, her old self felt small and shabby viewed through other people's eyes. She wondered how she'd managed not to see it for so long. She just hadn't wanted to see, she supposed. Few people do, because that takes courage and humility—both noble qualities, but really the All-Bran in the quality pantry. Cowardice, pettiness, spitefulness, they don't sound so great, but *that's* where you get the sugar rush. 'It's my fault, I'm sorry' is a hard thing to say. It's also boring. You can't make a blockbuster movie with 'I'm sorry.' It needs to be *their* fault. Then you can make them pay, make them suffer. *That's* a movie.

Evelyn was always an epicurean, and she'd found comfort in that sugar rush her whole life until now. The hefty dose of humility she'd been given wasn't easy to swallow—no one wants to see themselves in a bad light—but it *was* worth it. For the first time in her life, she really liked herself. Who wouldn't? She was a doctor, a baker, an accountant, an ad manager, and she was smarter than everyone she had ever met. And while she might never be the best person in the world, she was trying really hard to be a decent one. That felt… good.

She'd also stopped missing the rabbi. She wasn't as desperate for affection as she had once been, and the sex she was getting with herself was leaps and bounds above rabbi nookie. There was no guesswork involved; satisfaction was guaranteed. If she wanted sex in a particular way, then the other her also wanted sex the same way because, well, she wanted sex that way. Technically, what they were doing fit the definition of masturbation, but whoever added that to the dictionary had never experienced quadruple simultaneous orgasms at once. They were sex pioneers. The English language just hadn't caught up with them.

It wasn't just sex. They were the first to experience all sorts of things. Evelyn thought they needed to coin new words to describe their reality, like European explorers running into fauna they'd never seen before. That sounded a bit colonialist. She would find a better metaphor, but she was quite excited about the vocabulary thing. They could call it *Glossary of the Gestalt*. Maybe not.

They would find the perfect title some other time. Layla had come to the office to talk about puberty blockers. They'd had an appointment scheduled the week before but thought it best to wait until after the trial. Of course, Layla could have just stayed home and talked to Booker—he was also the doctor—but that was just too weird for everyone involved.

—So...

—So, this is what blockers do. I think we covered everything.

—But should I take them? I mean, you're the doctor.

—I'm also your—

—Don't say it!

—You'll still need to talk to a psychologist, and an endocrinologist, but for people with gender dysphoria, suppressing puberty will often help with mental health and social interactions, especially if you want to present as male or non-binary.

—You're making a face.

—There's no face.

—There was a "but" coming, right?

—No... Yes. But you can be whoever you want to be even without the pills. You're still young. You don't have to make a decision right now.

—That's my father talking, ain't it?

—It's not like we take turns... Okay, he might have something to do with it.

—But I could take the blockers while I wait till I'm older. That's what they're for, right?

—Yes.

—And if later I decide to transition, then I just keep taking them?

—No. If you transition and you want more masculine traits, then you'll have to take hormones. They're two very different things. The blockers won't change your body, they just delay things for a while.

—What happens if I stop taking them?

—Your body will go through puberty like it would have without the blockers. Your breasts will develop, your hips will widen, et cetera, et cetera.

—...

—You just think about it and let me know if you want to see the psychologist.

—...

—I really thought you'd have more questions, Layla. Now's the time if you do.

—How does it feel?

—Side effects are not that common. Headaches, fati—

—Not that. How does it feel to be... like you? Like my dad?

—It's... difficult to explain.

—That's not an answer.

—I was getting there. It's just hard to put it into words. You know how you play soccer on weekends?

—Sure.

—I used to play too.

—You played soccer?

—Carole did. And when she first started, the field looked enormous! Endless. She played defense, but she couldn't stop anyone, there was just too much space to cover. But the more she played, the smaller it felt, and after a while, it was really tough to get past her. That's sort of how it feels, like the field got smaller. A *lot* smaller.

—I wanna do it. I wanna be like you.

—Layla… Okay, first, you wouldn't be *like* me. You'd *be* me, and your dad, and Carole, and Shivansh, and we'd all be you. Most importantly, though, being all of us means you'd also be less you. We want you to be you, one hundred percent you.

—But you're happy about it, right? You said you liked the change.

—I am, but that's the four of us, now, being happy. I have no idea if the old Evelyn would like it. She might want to go back.

—Okay, then what about Carole, or my dad?

—What about them?

—They're glad it happened, right?

—Yes.

Then it's a good thing.

—Maybe. Maybe not.

—What's that supposed to mean?

—It means none of us ever agreed to it. We never had a choice. Yes, we're happy, but there's no way to know if it's real or… or if this is like a disease that's making us *think* we're happy. Before the docto—before I merged with them, Carole, Shivansh and your dad swore they wouldn't do this to anyone else without their consent.

—*Before* you merged with them?

—They… made an exception…

—Okay, then I consent.

—What? You can't—

—You said not without their consent and… and I consent!

—I'm sorry, Layla, but we're not doing it.

—That's my father talking again.

—This is all of us.

—It's so unfair! You said—

—I know what I said. And maybe it is unfair… Actually, no, I don't think it is. We have no idea what this is doing to us, Layla. For all we know, we could be dead in a week. We could explode or turn into goo. We could go mad and start hurting people. We've kind of hurt people already. We're not doing this to anyone else until we understand it, and we're definitely not doing it to you.

28
SOFTY

THE PAKISTANI DOCTOR had Softy fed through a tube. That was her vengeance, he thought. She'd keep him alive for fucking ever, make him suffer because of the tattoos, or some shit he hadn't even done. Softy knew he wasn't a good guy—he'd done plenty of bad things to plenty of people—but he'd never even seen that doctor before he got to the hospital. She had no reason to be pissed at him specifically. No, this was for the cause, one more step on the way to white replacement. Maybe he deserved it, but like Inspector Harry said, deserve's got nothing to do with it. Lots of folks die for no good reason, why couldn't he? There was a machine breathing for him, a machine feeding him. There were machines for just about everything, except changing his diapers. That meant he couldn't just *not* do something and die, he had to do the deed. Granted, his options were greatly limited, because he couldn't move a muscle, but he hadn't even tried. He didn't have the balls.

According to the Kibble-something, Kübler something?—according to some German-sounding name Softy had heard about from the shrink—the five stages of grief were denial, anger, bargaining, depression, and acceptance. It sounded like bullshit at first, but it did have a German name, so Softy paid attention. Denial, he'd done really well. Then he'd skipped anger and bargaining and gone straight to depression. Well, he'd skipped bargaining, at least. He'd been angry all his life, so it was possible he'd done that one and never noticed. Acceptance, as far as Softy was concerned, was pushing it a little. Who the hell would accept being stuck in the same room without moving for the rest of their lives? They *had* inclined the bed so he could watch TV, but the hospital didn't even have HBO, and there wasn't enough on network TV to sustain a person's will to live.

The shrink—she, too, was an immigrant, by the way, which anyone with half a brain would know wasn't a coincidence—had suggested he use his free time to make something creative, write a memoir or some shit like that. They were all in co-hoots and out to get him, obviously, but they played the caring part real fucking well. They'd gotten him a computer, with some gizmo that tracked eye movement so he could write. He did, if 'FUCK YOU' counts. Seriously, what was he going to write about? He'd dropped out of school before he could drive and really sucked at it before then. Writing just wasn't a skill he possessed. That was a really depressing thought to have, because in hindsight, there weren't really *any* skills he possessed. He used the rig the hospital gave him to play sudoku. He'd never heard of it—that was another thing the shrink told him about while pretending to be nice. He only did the beginner ones, but he felt kind of smart when he got them. That was nice. The computer was also his only means of communication, so he couldn't complain too much about it. Yes, being able to talk to another human being was an improvement. No, he wouldn't say thank you. Yeah, yeah, that was rude and all, but there was a really good reason for it.

Softy was aware there was a possibility, however remote, that the people taking care of him actually meant well. If that were the case, then he *would* owe them some gratitude, and maybe, just maybe, he could take what happened to him as an opportunity to reevaluate his belief system. The only problem was, *what fucking good would that do?* He was as close as one gets to being an inanimate object, a brain stuck on top of a mannequin. The machine next to him was Darth Vadering all day, pumping air in and out of him like a fuck doll. He ate through a tube, peed through a tube. He needed another adult to change his diapers. They had to check first, because he couldn't even tell whether he'd shit himself or not. He would never walk again, never hold anything in his hand, never feel sand under his feet, or someone's knuckles dig deep into his ribs. He'd probably never go outside, ever. He couldn't even jerk off and he was too much of a wimp to commit suicide. That's who he was. Was that acceptance? Anyway, the point was, he could be all that. *Or* he could be all that *and* a fucking racist asshole who was wrong about everything his whole life. Tempting, but no thank you.

He was going to live, breathe through a pump, shit himself, play sudoku and hate every last one of these motherfuckers until the day he died. With any luck, that would come soon. His body could just give up, but there were tons of other ways it could happen. An earthquake, a giant meteorite, an orderly who got trashed the night before and fed him the wrong shit. Ebola, bird flu, flesh-eating bacteria, Legionnaire's disease, spoiled medicine, a big air bubble in the needle. The list went on and on. When you thought about it, it was a wonder anyone survived *at all* in a hospital. At some point, his turn would come, and he'd leave this shit life behind giving everyone the middle finger—in his head, because he couldn't move his fucking fingers.

29
BOOKER–CAROLE–SHIVANSH–EVELYN

BOOKER'S NOSE WAS healing slowly. It didn't hurt much but he still had trouble breathing through it. He'd never given much thought to his nose, or noses in general. Up until then, it had just been a hole—two holes, really—for air to get in. It turned out noses were really complex structures. There was bone, cartilage, soft tissue. The thing didn't just let air in either, it had to warm it, humidify it, filter it. Being a doctor had endowed Booker with newfound respect for the facial protuberance. He hadn't been breathing through his since Evelyn knocked him out and he had to drink water a billion times a day because his mouth felt like he'd been snacking on Kleenex.

Booker was coming back from the plumbing supplies store in Negaunee when he reached for his sports bottle between the seats. He had a hard time lifting the cap and for about half a second, he took his eyes off the road. The car must have swerved a little, because as soon as he looked up, he saw flashing red lights in his rearview mirror. Booker pulled over and waited for the cop to come out of the car, praying it wouldn't be Frank.

It was Frank. Booker rolled down the window, then put his hands on the dashboard like he always did.

—I need to see your license and registration.

Booker had gone through this routine more times than he could count. He had 'the talk' with Layla about how to react every few months. The first rule in an encounter with law enforcement was easy: make sure you're still alive when it ends. Simple as that. It didn't matter how absurd the arrest was, no justice would be served by getting shot three times in the chest. Booker knew all that. He knew what to do. But Booker wasn't just Booker anymore. He was an accountant with friends on the city council, he was a white woman, he was an old Jewish lady who didn't take shit from anyone, let alone a half-witted thug like Frank.

—Is there a problem, Officer?

Frank had barely paid any attention to Booker until then. He was just looking around like a bored child waiting for his subject to bow and kiss the ring.

—What? Just give me your license, will you?

Frank was obviously annoyed. How dare this little man waste *his* precious time by asking why he was being stopped!

—I just want to know why you pulled me over.

—Really? You were doing fifty-five in a forty zone and driving dangerously. How's that?

—No, I wasn't!

—You were if I say you were.

—No!

—What did you just say?

—I said—

—Get the fuck out of the car.

Frank took out his gun. He opened the car door, dragged Booker out and shoved him face-first against the burning hood. He checked for a weapon, then tried to cuff Booker's hands behind him, but the handcuffs wouldn't fit over his cast. He walked Booker to the other side of the car, opened the passenger door and took some zip tie cuffs out of the glove compartment before tightening them on Booker's wrists. Frank looked around to make sure no one was watching, then tripped Booker, sending him to the ground. Booker fell on his side and dislocated his shoulder.

—I'm gonna have your badge for this! You have no right—

—I have every fucking right! You wanna know what rights I have? I'mma show you what rights I have, you piece of shit.

Booker rolled on his stomach to protect his face when Frank started kicking him. He felt a rib break, then another. The kicking went on for a good ten seconds, then it stopped. For a moment, Booker thought the worst was over. It wasn't. Frank's knee landed in the middle of Booker's back and knocked the wind out of him. He'd have screamed if he could, but it would have made no difference. Frank grabbed him by the hair and hit his face on the pavement, again, and again…

Booker couldn't breathe, or yell, or move. All he could see was the bloodstain on the asphalt getting larger and larger. Then he couldn't see anything at all. Booker didn't know where he was. Some place dark, and big, really big. One could easily get lost in a place like that. He'd had that feeling before, when he'd gotten lost at the hospital. Booker remembered his child being born, screaming at a world that was too cold and too bright. The memory got sharper, deeper. He was there again, holding this fragile little thing for the very first time. Flash forward. Layla hugging him forever before the first day of school. He'd told her everything would be fine. God, how he hoped it was true. Flashback. The Prince concert where he met his wife. Happenstance. A bumped shoulder, spilled beer. A smile. It's the little things that shape a person's life.

...and again.

He was five years old, saying goodbye to his best friend at the orphanage in Mumbai. Being happy his friend was chosen. Wondering what he did wrong not to be. Stepping on the giant plane, watching everything he'd ever known get smaller and smaller. Waking up before the sun to milk the cows. A broken doll. Little Kenny Fisher. Gawd, he was gorgeous! Kissing Kenny Fisher behind school. Punching Kenny Fisher in front of the whole class. Morning crosswords with her first husband, hiking on the Potawatomi Trail. They were happy for a while; she'd forgotten about that. Opening the bakery. The place was so big, so empty, so scary. What if no one comes? What if?

...and again.

Being the only woman in medical school. Removing her teacher's hand from her thigh. Her father's hand on her mother's face. Holding that same hand when the bastard died. Children, lots of them. Other people's children she often wished were her own. His first wedding cake. Layla hugging him forever before the first day of school. He'd told her everything would be fine. God, how he hoped it was true.

...and again.

Booker remembered his child being born, screaming at a world that was too cold and too bright. The memory got dimmer, darker. Layla hugging him. When was that? He couldn't remember.

30
SHIVANSH–BOOKER–CAROLE–EVELYN

SHIVANSH WAS CATCHING up on corporate tax law when Booker was pulled over. His reading slowed a bit when he recognized the cop. This was the man who'd stopped Booker just the week before, the same asshole who'd cuffed Carole. Shivansh closed his law book when the argument began. Booker was right to speak up. Someone had to stand up to a bully like that, or he'd abuse his power forever. Still, there was a lot about this that made Shivansh uneasy. Booker had been stopped in the middle of nowhere. There were no cameras, no pedestrians, no witnesses whatsoever except for the occasional car passing by. If this ever went to court, it would be a classic case of 'he said, he said'. It didn't take a genius to know which *he* a jury would believe. When Frank took out his gun, Shivansh realized Booker might never make it to court. He got up so fast, his office chair rolled into the bookshelf behind him. Shivansh turned to look and saw a vase wobbling, the bookshelf leaning forward ever so slightly.

There is a precise moment in certain situations when one realizes they've lost control, that there is absolutely nothing they can do to change the outcome. Everything else happens in slow motion after that. Newton's Third Law pushing the chair back towards him. The top shelf swinging back and forth, trying to choose between momentum and gravity. One book tilting forward, then two. The vase diving headfirst onto the floor. Wanting to run and stop everything from falling, but knowing it'll fall anyway.

Shivansh jumped over the cascading books and made for the door. He felt his shoulder pop while putting on his coat and nearly passed out. He grabbed his keys from the counter and ran to the car, but fell into the bushes when the kicking started. Shivansh was powerless. He was on the ground. He was in handcuffs. He wasn't there to help. He shat himself when he felt his ribs break. Blunt pain response often shuts down in fight-or-flight situations, but it only shuts down in one body and Shivansh felt every bit of pain there was to feel. He managed to get up and stumbled to the car. He'd just backed up onto the street when he suddenly lost his breath. Shivansh was driving as fast as he could, but he was panicking, gasping for air that was already in his lungs, breathing in, and in and in. He was afraid, so afraid, and in too much pain to focus on the road. He didn't see the red light. He didn't see the bus coming from the left. He saw his lives flash before his eyes when the bus hit. He was absolutely convinced he was going to die. The car spun like a record for what seemed like an eternity. Shivansh let go of the wheel. He let go of everything. He watched the world fly by and the blood pool under his face. Then everything stopped.

Shivansh turned the engine off and took a few deep breaths. He could smell the shit in his pants. His shoulder didn't hurt, neither did his ribs. That pain was… gone, and so was the fear. It took a minute for him to realize everything else about Booker was gone as well. He didn't remember Booker's youth, or how he met his wife. He didn't know how to make croissants, or how many brothers and sisters he had. He was short. Shivansh was three instead of four. Few people ever experience dying and live to tell the tale. He was confused, disoriented, somehow unsure of his own existence. He hit his head against the steering wheel a few times, just to prove to himself that he was still alive. There was time, he thought. Booker was just unconscious. All he had to do was get there and he could help. He could fix this. He tried to start the engine, but his SUV was nearly broken in half. He couldn't get out, because the doors wouldn't open. Shivansh undid his seatbelt and crawled all the way to the back. He dug out the jack and slammed it against the rear window until it broke. He managed to extricate himself, then left the car behind and hobbled for an hour all the way to the scene of Booker's arrest.

Booker's car was gone when Shivansh got there. So was Booker. The only trace he'd ever been there was a dark stain on the cracked pavement. Shivansh kept hoping. Carole had been yelling at hospital staff for a good five minutes, but they wouldn't tell her anything. He stayed there for God knew how long, just staring at the blood. When the doctor finally came and told Carole the news, Shivansh kneeled and screamed so loud he thought his chest might explode.

It's hard to cope with one's own death. Booker had died, and Shivansh had died *with* him. He'd lost a friend, if friendship was a million times deeper and more intimate. The loss was impossible to put into words, but his thoughts were about someone else. Shivansh never wanted children. He'd never been a father before Booker bit him. He wasn't a father then either, but all he could think about was Layla.

31
CAROLE–SHIVANSH–EVELYN

Carole didn't want Layla to hear it from strangers. She didn't want the cops to knock on the door and tell them their father was dead. She didn't want the cops to tell Layla it was their father's fault, that he resisted, that he *deserved* it. She didn't want the man who killed Booker to come and say all that. Carole had just lost a fourth of herself, but even she couldn't imagine what this would feel like for Layla. Booker was their father. He was their caregiver, the one person they could always come to. He was the one to feed them, to put a roof over their head. Booker was their everything. Without him, Layla had nothing. A few words from Carole wouldn't change any of that, and she wondered if it was even worth being there.

Of *course* it was. Being there is what she had to offer. Layla would hurt just the same, but they wouldn't hurt alone. Carole wasn't sure if she had the strength, but she would at least try. She waited in Booker's driveway for a good ten minutes, gathering enough courage to knock on the door.

—Carole! Hi! My dad's not here yet. I don't know where—Wait, you'd know that, right? You're…

—Can we sit down a minute? There's something I need to tell you.

—Yeah, sure. Come in! I was doing homework.

—Layla, there was… Booker was pulled over on the way back from work.

—Again? Is that why he's late?

—Yes. Well, something happened when they pulled him over. Things went terribly wrong, and… Your father's dead, Layla. They took him to the hospital, but he didn't make it.

—…

—I'm so, so sorry, Layla. I don't know what to say. I just—I wanted you to hear it from me.

'Your father's dead.' 'I wanted you to hear it from me.' Carole couldn't believe those were the words that came out of her mouth. She felt like the worst person on the planet for fumbling that conversation. If there was a right way to say it, a way to soften the blow somehow, that was a hundred percent not it. She braced herself for Layla to break down in tears, explode in anger, but there were no cries, no screams. Layla simply got up and left. Carole didn't know whether she should follow or give them their space. She chose the latter because it was harder to screw up. Layla came back a moment later with a glass of juice. They sat again and stared at Carole in the most awkward way. They opened their mouth a couple times, but the words wouldn't come out. Finally, they were able to say it.

—Are you… He's not gone, is he? You're still— You're still my father, right?

Oh, God. Carole had just told Layla their father was dead and now she had to make him dead again, for good this time. Layla hadn't reacted as expected, but the wound was there just the same. It was real. To twist the knife in it felt like unfathomable cruelty.

—I'm not. We're not. Not anymore. We lost him too.

—What do you mean? How—

—When he died, a part of us—the part that he brought, what he was—it just… vanished.

—Do you still…?

—Do I still what?

—Do you have his memories?

—Only the ones since Ca—since I bit him.

—Can I… Can I see them?

—I don't understand.

—If you bite me, like you bit him, will I—

—They're not your father's memories, Layla, not really. They're… ours. I'm sorry. Booker's gone.

That time Layla understood. They would never see their father again. He would never talk to them, or hug them, or smile, or laugh. Layla's mouth started trembling. Soon, their whole body followed suit. They were crying and shaking uncontrollably, stopping only to catch their breath when their lungs hurt too much. After about ten minutes, Layla looked at Carole, their eyes begging for anything that would make the pain go away. Carole felt more helpless than she ever had. There were no words she could say, nothing she could offer that would make things better. She gestured for Layla to come closer, and she hugged them, hard, for as long as she could. Layla was exhausted. They cried themselves to sleep in Carole's arms, then woke up two hours later wishing it had all been a dream.

—Was it the cops that killed him?

—One cop, yes.

—What's gonna happen to me now? They won't let me stay in the house, will they?

—Not at your age, no. Do you have family nearby? Someone who can take you in?

—I have an aunt in Wisconsin, but I don't wanna go there.

—It might not be up to you.

—You don't understand, she's, like, super religious. She thinks I'm going to hell for defying God's will. I'm not making this up, she told me! Like, a bunch of times!

—Is there anyone else?

—There's my mom in Portugal…

—I hear it's nice over there.

—I don't want to go anywhere. Can I just— Can I stay with you?

—Layla, I… I don't know how to say this in a nice way. I—*we* love you very much because we were Booker for a while and the love he had for you is still there inside us, but we don't really know you. Most importantly, you don't really know us. I don't think you'd want to live with people you've only met a few times.

—You said you have some of my dad's memories. You were him for a while. That makes you like him, a little bit still, no?

—I don't know.

—Could I stay with you? Please?

Inside Carole's house, Shivansh poured himself a tall glass of tequila. They knew full well what the next word to come out of Carole's mouth would mean to all of them. 'No' would mean more than breaking Layla's heart again.

It would break a promise they'd never made because they didn't have to. They *were* Booker, and even with him gone, they knew he'd want *them* to take care of Layla. As for 'Yes,' well, 'yes' was complicated. No judge would choose Carole and Shivansh over family, at least no judge in their right mind.

Or in their *own* mind…

32
LANA

It was the second time in as many weeks that Lana was in court. She wasn't there as a witness this time. She came with the rest of the station. 'To show her support,' the chief had said. She'd smiled. 'Of course!' What she really wanted was to see that asshole burn, but she knew it wouldn't happen.

There was something else about that hearing, though. That Frank had killed someone wasn't a huge surprise, but he hadn't killed just anyone. He'd killed Booker. It could have been, as things often are, pure coincidence. Just like Carole attacking the same Booker not long before, or Shivansh stabbing himself inside his home, or the doctor being bitten by some kid in a baseball cap. All of it could have been happenstance. It was also possible that she would grow wings, or that everyone would turn into a blueberry muffin. Lana was autistic, and human interactions often seemed cryptic and overly complex to her. But Lana was also a cop, and like all cops, she was a firm believer in the law, especially the law of probabilities. The husband did it. Most crimes are solved with Occam's razor. It's that easy. Lana's problem was that she didn't have a simple explanation for whatever Booker was involved in. All the explanations were convoluted, so much so that she'd lost track of all the theories she'd come up with along the way. That's what she was looking for, that eureka moment where one simple idea would make everything fall into place. Carole was having an affair with Booker, Booker was jealous and attacked Shivansh, Frank was exacting revenge for... No, this was already too complicated. Maybe Booker owed money—it's always sex or money—but money to whom? To Carole? No. It had to be something else and maybe, just maybe, Frank would say something during his testimony that would point her in the right direction.

Lana was still in a wheelchair and stuck in a corner of the courtroom. It would be another two months, at least, before she could begin rehab. The doctors were confident she'd walk again, but they weren't sure how long it would take. 'We'll just have to wait and see and... hope for the best!' That's what they'd said, awkwardly. That sounded very unscientific to Lana. Up until then, she'd always thought of medicine as hard science, but after interacting with lots of doctors and nurses, it felt more and more like guesswork. The doctors *were* impressed with how well she took the news. She didn't mind the wheelchair much. Walking would have been better, and she couldn't reach the shelves in her cabinets without a gripper, but that was just one more thing to compartmentalize. Eventually, *something* in her life would have to go the way she wanted or she might run out of compartments, but she wasn't quite there yet. Now, if only the hearing could start. She'd gotten there thirty minutes early to make sure there was enough room for her to get through. An hour later, the judge still hadn't shown up. Frank was telling dad jokes to his friends on the force while his union rep urged him not to laugh in front of the victim's family.

Finally. The judge burst into the room, still buttoning up his robe, and everyone stopped talking. The clerk introduced the case and the judge waved for Frank to come to the stand. Booker was dead and there were no witnesses, so Frank was the only one who *could* take the stand. He answered questions for less than twenty minutes. It was like a school play, obviously rehearsed and mediocrely acted. There was a list of things every cop knew they had to say, preferably in order, when use of force was an issue. Establish proper cause: 'The suspect was driving erratically.' Lana knew everything that came next. 'Based on my training and experience, I believed…' 'The suspect became violent.' 'I believed my life was in immediate danger.' 'I believe I acted with proper force under the circumstances.' 'I believed' was the important part. Qualified immunity does the rest. It's not even a question of what happened. What happened doesn't really matter. What matters is what the cops believed was happening. If a cop *believes* he's in danger, then he is. If he believes he has to shoot you, he can, and no one can do a thing about it. Not before. Not after. Frank believed in precisely the right things, and the judge sent everyone home after thanking Frank for putting his life on the line every day. He would be reinstated the next day.

The judge never used the buzzwords people had heard on TV, and there was some confusion in the courtroom after he closed the case. Lana heard Layla screaming behind her and turned to look. That's when she noticed Carole and Dr. Schlapp were also in the courtroom. Carole grabbed Layla to stop them from going after Frank, then she hugged them as hard as she could, whispering something in their ear. Lana wasn't the best at reading human emotions, but there was something so genuine, so heartfelt about the way Carole did it that even she couldn't miss it. Lana was touched and surprised by the depth of their connection. As far as she knew, these people barely knew each other before Carole bit Booker at his shop. Now she was consoling his child as if Layla was her own. Instead of finding answers, Lana would leave the courtroom with more questions than ever. She didn't think that was possible, but there she was. These people had, apparently, all attacked each other. Carole bit Booker, Booker stabbed Shivansh, Shivansh bit Dr. Schlapp. They all had plenty of reason to hate one another if they didn't before. Instead, they'd somehow formed a bond so deep, Lana could feel it a mile away. That made her even more curious, and a bit angry. She wasn't mad at them; she was mad at herself because she couldn't help but be jealous of what they so blatantly shared.

33

SHIVANSH–CAROLE–EVELYN

SHIVANSH MAY HAVE also *been* Carole and Evelyn, but he still looked like Shivansh. Shivansh had Shivansh's face, which everyone knew was not the most friendly-looking. He looked like someone constantly doing math in their head. Hard, angry math. If one had to make a list of people a child would be comfortable grieving with, his name would have come up right before J. Edgar Hoover and scary clowns. Nonetheless, Carole and the doctor had to work, so he was the one spending the day with Layla, who was still in no shape to return to school. The family court judge had agreed, at Layla's request, to let them live with Shivansh and Carole until the custody trial. It would be a few weeks before anything was decided and plans to 'recruit' the judge had been put on hold until further notice.

Shivansh wanted to be present for Layla, so he sat across from them while they did crossword puzzles. He also knew Layla needed to process everything that had happened at their own pace, and so he spoke as little as possible. Layla, on the other hand, was bursting with thoughts and questions, but didn't feel the same connection they had with Carole, or even Dr. Schlapp. Layla would periodically look up at

Shivansh, who by then had realized the awkwardness of the situation and attempted a warm and gentle look that only made the matter worse. They had both been practicing this routine all morning when, without warning, Layla got up, stuck a finger inside Shivansh's mouth and, with their other hand, hit him with the hardest uppercut they could muster.

—FUCK! Fuck! Fuck! Fuck!

—I'm sorry! I had to!

Shivansh jumped out of his chair and grabbed Layla's hand. There was a small cut on their index finger. He dragged Layla to the kitchen sink and ran some cold water over the wound.

—Fuck! Fuck! Fuck! Fuck! Fuck!

—I said I'm sorry! Did I hurt your chin? I didn't mean to hit you that hard.

He gestured for Layla to stay and ran to the bathroom. He came back with a bottle of rubbing alcohol and quickly poured the entire thing on Layla's finger.

—FUUUUUCK!

—I—

Shivansh put his index finger over Layla's mouth to stop them from talking and pointed at the chair. The two sat back where they had been and stared at each other in silence for a good twenty minutes. Shivansh broke first.

—That was… not a smart move, Layla. Really, really not smart.

—I'm sorry, I just—Are you mad at me?

—Yes… *Fuck!* Why'd you have to do that?

—I just… I wanted to feel what you feel. I wanted my dad's memories. And you wouldn't let me.

—You'll get a lot more than that if we didn't stop it in time.

—Do you think we did?

—I don't know! We never tried to stop it before.

—How long does it normally take?

—About an hour.

—That long?

They looked at the kitchen clock in unison. It would be another forty minutes at least before they knew if Layla's poorly-designed plan had worked. Might as well have been forty days. A watched kettle never boils, and Shivansh thought it best to keep the conversation going.

—That's how it was for me, and Booker.

—What's going to happen to him?

—Happen to whom?

—To that cop. The one who killed my dad.

—The truth?

—Yeah, the truth!

—I think that was it. There was an inquiry and… now he gets to go back to work.

—That's not right!

—I know.

—I want him to pay.

—I know you do, Layla, but I don't think there is anything we can do about it. Besides, revenge won't bring your father back, you know that.

—You can do it. You can hurt him like he hurt my dad. The three of you can.

—No, Layla! We can't. We've already taken too many risks, hurt too many people. We have to be smart. We have to be careful, all of us. That's what your father would want.

—So he just gets away with it?

—Yes. He does.

Shivansh could tell 'smart and careful' was not what Layla wanted to hear, but they'd asked for the truth and that was the truth. As awful as it felt, there was nothing they could do about Frank, and trying anything would just put everyone at risk. Neither Shivansh nor Layla said a word after that. Layla just looked at the clock every thirty seconds, visibly annoyed with the leisurely pace at which the hands were moving. Shivansh was just waiting for any sign of the merge. Blurred vision, confusion, anything.

Then—boom. His own face appeared in his field of view and he *really* needed to pee. Layla hadn't wanted whatever happened to happen in the bathroom and had been holding it in this whole time. Shivansh started moving his fifty fingers. Evelyn was the first to do that, and it had felt really cool, getting all that new sensory input at once. This time Shivansh did it without thinking. He was stunned at how fast the merge occurred this time. There was no transition like there'd been with Booker, no warning. Maybe it worked differently with someone younger. There was definitely something different about seeing through Layla's eyes. They were newer eyes, better eyes. Everything Layla saw was brighter, sharper. They also felt… *lighter;* Layla barely weighed eighty pounds, but it was more than that. Aside from a finger, there was no part of Layla that felt any pain or discomfort. They'd forgotten what it meant to be young, before every part of you starts to wear down. Being Layla was like driving a shiny new car after you've spent years driving a beat-up clunker. They still didn't think bringing a child into the fold was a good idea, but there was no denying how good it felt to be young again. It was very… potent, and fucking awesome. It also felt better to be old, somehow. With the years had come… acceptance.

The knowledge of who you are and the freeing realization that you'll never be anyone else, no matter how hard you try. That was new to a quarter of them, and the other three quarters had long stopped noticing.

What Layla had done was reckless and impulsive, but maybe some good could come of it. Shivansh also knew where Layla was coming from. If he'd been in their shoes… Oh, yeah, he'd have done the same. He'd want his dad's memories. He'd definitely want justice. Like, who wouldn't? You can't just let dirty cops get away with shit like that. It was really hard to know how much of that thinking they owed to Layla themselves, but what were they gonna do? This was who they were now. They couldn't think differently if they tried.

In hindsight, it was super clear they'd been too hasty in rejecting Layla's revenge idea. Shivansh understood that he was now partly a child, but being a child doesn't mean you're wrong all the time, right? And what had he meant when he'd said 'we have to be smart' earlier? That was totally uncalled for. Layla was smart. They were super smart! Who could blame them for wanting just a tiny bit of justice for their dad? No one, that's who! And yeah, maybe careful is what Booker would have wanted, but Booker wasn't there anymore because that cop had bashed his head in. Screw careful. Frank had to pay.

Layla was right. Frank had to pay, but he wasn't alone. The whole police stood by him and did nothing. The judge let him loose. Really, when you thought about it, the whole *world* was responsible. A world that let people like Frank thrive, a world that oppressed and discriminated, a world where cops could kill Booker and get away with it. White male supremacy was the name of the game and everyone with power just *played along* because it kept them safe. It propped them up, cleared the way for them so they could pursue their dreams at the expense of everyone else's. It propped their children up, gave them a head start in life so big you'd need a jetpack to catch up to them. Fuck yeah, Frank had to pay, but everyone else had to change and there was but one sure way to do it.

They had to get them all.

PART 4

OUTBREAK

34

EVELYN–SHIVANSH–CAROLE–LAYLA

THEY WERE GOING to turn Marquette into a better place, one where everyone was treated as equal, where racism, sexism, ableism and all the bad -isms were a thing of the past. 'Not without their consent' wasn't quite compatible with their newfound enthusiasm; 'For the greater good' sounded so much better anyway. They were aware one could rationalize all kinds of atrocities with that motto, but they weren't doing anything bad! They wanted to transform their town into what they'd always dreamed it could be. They were going to make things better, fairer. Technically, it would be all that because there would only be one person in Marquette, but that person would have a good twenty thousand bodies moving simultaneously. That was cool. That one person would also be happy. They would take care of themselves, and the planet, and the animals. Gosh, that was exciting. That's what Evelyn thought, anyway. Being an eleven-year-old sixty-one-year-old man-woman felt really, really good, and she imagined it would only get better from there. She felt privileged to be a part of what was coming. They were going to change a whole town, the four of them were. It was like being chosen for the first mission to the moon, signing the Declaration of

Independence, or some other thing where only a handful of people get to do something super important.

They weren't only going to change Marquette; they'd be getting some sweet revenge for Booker in the process. In theory, they could wait until everyone in town had been turned and prosecute Frank again, but they would be the cops, the judge, the jury. The whole trial would be one person playing pretend, and that felt like cheating, on top of being a huge waste of time. This was Michigan, though, and they'd seen all kinds of yahoos walking around their neighborhood with guns and baseball bats. Being a vigilante wasn't exactly something they aspired to be. Fortunately, dispensing justice on your own without any legal authority was also the purview of superheroes, and Evelyn wore a Batgirl costume for the occasion. She'd bought that for a party two or three decades ago and it had been sitting in a box ever since. It still fit, somehow. They knew which part of them was responsible for the costume idea, but the adult part of their brain didn't seem to mind. Evelyn was the only one who owned a good one and she ended up on superhero duty. She was psyched. Her job was to work the mall. She couldn't exactly go around and bite random people at Kohl's, so she'd filled an automatic syringe with her saliva. The idea was to surreptitiously jab as many people as she could before getting caught. They thought she could get away with a dozen or so before anyone stopped her. If she jabbed people in the right spot, they might not even notice. If they did, they'd think a nasty bug bit them or something like that. Common sense was working for her in this situation: short of catching Evelyn in the act, most people would likely favor a more plausible explanation than the old lady in a cape injecting them with her spit.

Evelyn saw herself in a shop mirror when she got to the mall and, for a split second, she wanted to turn back. She'd looked in the mirror at home, but hers didn't go all the way to the floor. She'd been in her thirties when she'd last worn this thing and, not to brag or anything, in pretty darn good shape. Back then, it would seem, she didn't mind that half of her ass was hanging out of the costume. Now, she minded a tad. And who had designed this cape? It was just short enough to be utterly useless at covering anything. This was kind of embarrassing. Why, though? Why should she be embarrassed? She may not have been thirty anymore, or forty, or fifty, but damn if she wasn't the hottest sixty-one-year-old in a Batgirl costume in that mall. Accepting who you are is a pretty rewarding thing and Evelyn felt a sudden and profound urge to sleep with Carole or Shivansh again, even if sex grossed her out a little.

It was time for decisions. Her first thought was to pick someone she didn't like, ideally some real asshole, because, well, she was going to stab them. Then she realized she'd *be* that person an hour later, and that would suck ass. It wouldn't be so bad if the asshole was like, the one-hundredth person they brought in, because they would only be one percent a jerk. One-fifth a jerk was too much, and Evelyn sketched a new plan. Find someone nice. That someone appeared almost instantly—for real, it was like magic—strolling out of Banana Republic with two large bags in hand. Myrtle Hannigan. No kids, though she'd been trying for years. Late thirties, if memory served. Myrtle organized a fundraiser and clothing donations for the poor every single year. She was more or less the definition of a nice person and Evelyn was absolutely thrilled to jam a needle in her thigh.

—OUCH! What the—Evelyn?

—Hi Myrtle! It's been a while!

—Did you—Did you see something? I felt this pain in my leg, like—

—Pins and needles?

—No, more like a pinch.

—Well, that might be a pinched nerve. If it happens often, you might want to rest that leg for a while.

—I—Okay. Can I ask what you're wearing?

—It's Batgirl.

—I know, but… why?

—I just felt like it. Have a good day, Myrtle!

One down, a dozen more to go.

35
LAYLA–SHIVANSH–CAROLE–EVELYN

LAYLA FELT BETTER about almost everything. They were still eleven, but also an adult, multiple adults at that, and a man, and a woman, and non-binary, and black, and white, and brown, and—*oh my gawd*—so smart. They'd kind of sucked at ratios before, but now it all seemed like child's play. They wished they could retake their exams, but there was really no point to it since they would soon be the teacher and every student would give the exact same answers.

All their pain was gone too, all but one. Well, they sometimes ached a bit in their Evelyn-knees, but were not counting that. The Booker pain was as strong as ever, and so was the rage that came with it. The rage came with hope, however, hope for a better place to live, hope for a better world, and yeah, hope for some justice for the man who killed their dad. Thinking about Booker was a strange experience. He was their father, but Layla could also see the man. His memories, what little was left of them, were filled with love for his child. They were also those of a person, a whole someone who existed outside of fatherhood, something Layla had never even considered.

Oddly, perhaps, they didn't know which of the two they missed the most, the man or the father.

Layla's job was to knock on doors and ask if they could come in and call their mom. No one would suspect an eleven-year-old was about to bite them and run the moment they closed the door. They'd mapped out the neighborhood, found the right house to start the spread. Young people, able-bodied, folks who could overpower just about everyone when the time came. The plan was for the four of them to bring in about a hundred people without alerting anyone. These new people would bring in their partners, children, roommates. They would be two or three hundred by then, which should be enough to just tear through town and get everyone else. Evelyn had started her syringe spree an hour earlier and Layla had second thoughts about the whole thing when she became Myrtle Hannigan. Myrtle may have been a little too nice, and if the first part of their plan involved a bit of violence, the second part involved a whole lot more. She was also diagnosed with hemophobia, an irrational fear of blood, which made the prospect of biting into strangers much less appealing for everyone. Perhaps if they talked to people first and explained, they could find a way to do this in a more peaceful manner.

Nah, fuck them. They were now Bob Grass, an old stoner with long grey hair who kept telling everyone: 'Love is punker than punk.' Bob's definition of love was rather fluid and taking over a town by chewing on people somehow fit right in. He did have a point. What better gift to give someone than to expand their mind? Right. This *was* love. They would get the justice they wanted and make the world better, for everyone. *Igne natura renovatur integra.* Oh cool, they spoke Latin now. They were Lamar Moore, aka

The Mountain. Absolutely everyone in Lamar's life had pressured him to play football. His parents, his friends, his teachers. He'd always said no. Lamar was getting a degree in Classics and was obsessed with Roman culture around 100 BCE. Layla noticed every hint of Rome in the houses around them. The shapes (there were arches, columns and vaults everywhere she looked), the materials (Romans used tiles, and concrete, and bricks). Some of the houses on that street even used the longer, flatter Roman bricks. Lamar really knew his shit. He was also very large, hence the nickname and the pressure to play ball. Walking in Lamar's body felt so different from walking in Layla's, they wondered how they could be the same species. Lamar saw the world from a higher perspective—everything looked so small from up there. He occupied three times more space than Layla and the mere fact of existing felt more impactful in his shoes. Lamar shook the fucking ground when he walked. Oh, and those hands. Layla had never seen hands like that—big wide paws with knuckles the size of walnuts. One could face anything with hands like that. Layla bestrode the Jacksons' front yard like a colossus before knocking on their door with renewed purpose.

—Hi! I'm sorry to bother you like this, but my bike got stolen. Do you mind if I come in and call my mom so she can pick me up?

—Oh, sure! Stealing kids' bikes... People are just terrible, aren't they? Happened to my friend too, just last week. Come in! Come in! ... AAARGH! What the hell?

—Sorry!

Layla ran all the way to the street corner and turned to see if the Jacksons were in pursuit. They weren't. That was another reason Layla was given door-to-door biting duty. A lot of folks won't touch other people's kids, especially parents. They certainly won't beat them up, but many won't touch them at all. Like, no pat on the shoulder, nothing. That gave people little incentive to run after Layla, since they'd have to physically stop them, to grab their arm hard or something. That's a big-ass deal with other people's kids. For the Jacksons, it seemed, it was bigger than a bite on the arm.

Things didn't go so well at the next house. Joe Lafleur—big guy, he worked construction—wasn't home, but his twenty-year-old son Carl was. Whatever, Layla decided Carl would do. Being mostly uninterested in anything but Nascar and girls, Carl was unaware of the unwritten rule about not touching kids. He could run too. Damn! Carl was fast. Layla had six or seven brains by then, and they had the good sense to scream for help before Carl caught up to them. A few neighbors came to the rescue, and *they* knew about the rule. 'But she bit me!' was not the selling point Carl thought it would be and he went back home in shame while Layla moved on to their next target.

By the fourth house, they were becoming a lot more people. One by one, new sceneries flashed before Layla's eyes. New knowledge was born, new ideas sprang to mind.

They knew kung fu. Billy Morgan, from White Street. He was gay, never told anyone. His father would have killed him, literally. Billy should have been a dancer.

They could design bridges. Lea Chlumsky was a genius. No relation to Anna, but she liked people asking every time she traveled. Before one considered weight, and tension, and shear, and everything else, building a bridge was a beautifully simple act: connecting two otherwise disconnected points, often providing the shortest distance between them. It was almost poetry, turning chaos into pure geometry. Lea almost never smiled. She suffered severe tooth decay after years of purging.

Layla's mind was expanding so fast, it was hard to imagine they'd once been only one.

They surprised themselves by having that thought in Mandarin. Maggie Chen, she worked the night shift at Blockbuster. The previous tenant in Maggie's apartment had left an old piano and she'd taught herself to play. She didn't know it, but she had real talent, and absolute pitch. Maggie had planned to kill herself that night.

The one constant, the one thing every person who joined with them had in common was some form of anxiety, some deep, often unnamed discomfort with life and the universe. Few if any could see their real strengths. Everyone wondered what was wrong with them and no one, not a single soul, was ever truly happy. They'd all had moments of happiness, seconds, minutes, a few hours of bliss. The only difference between people was how often these moments came along.

36
SHIVANSH–CAROLE–EVELYN–LAYLA–MYRTLE–BOB–LISA–CARL

SHIVANSH HAD THE easy job. It was a weird one, though. They'd bought a classified ad that just said *Will bite you for $20*, with a phone number. They'd done it mostly as a joke, but a dozen people called. Shivansh booked the appointments twenty minutes apart. People came, they chit-chatted for a short while, then he bit them. They gave him their twenty bucks and left. They were all fine with a bite on the shoulder, except for one guy who had a more unusual request. Shivansh refused and after some back and forth, the man agreed to be bit on the thigh. It was… kind of gross, but efficient.

By the time Shivansh had completed his foray into weird shit, he was about forty people. That's when things started to get ugly. They knew something like this would happen, but living it was a lot harder than what they'd imagined. Children crying because they couldn't understand why their mother was trying to hurt them. Wives locking themselves in the bathroom before the husband kicked the door in. Things didn't just get ugly, they got public. People called the cops; fights broke out after the neighbors heard screams and tried to intervene. One dude posted a video of his wife going berserk on Facebook. It was only a matter of time before that thing got viral.

Shivansh et al. were now about a hundred people. That was less than half of what they thought they needed. Giving up wasn't really an option. If they stopped, there would be consequences for a lot of them, families separated, people going to jail. The alternative wasn't much better. A hundred people taking over a town of twenty thousand was going to make a whole lot of noise, if it was even possible. By then, Layla's impulsiveness had been mostly drowned out by reasonable adults, and one might have assumed that the urge to 'get them all' would have dissipated as well. Hell, no. The more they became, the more they realized how messed up the world really was. Everyone carried trauma in one form or another. Some had stories so painful, they could never bear to tell. Now they didn't have to. That alone was worth the effort. Sure, there would be some temporary pain involved, but you can't make omelets without breaking some eggs. Shivansh put his jacket on, took a deep breath, and headed outside to break a fuckton of eggs.

By 1:00 PM, the local press was everywhere. People were biting friends, family, strangers, all over town for no apparent reason. This was, for all intents and purposes, the zombie apocalypse. Scary as shit, but a dream come true for any reporter. Unfortunately for them, they couldn't run fast with all their gear, and by 2:30 PM, the *press* was biting people all over town. It was mayhem. Once people got off the street and found shelter inside buildings, the violence turned up to eleven. Twenty people with guns and baseball bats rushed inside the bank and took down the guard. The teller who triggered the alarm had absolutely no clue what was in store for her. The few who managed to escape had nowhere to run to. The cops didn't know where to go either. People were leaping out from behind bushes to take them down and bite them. Soon, there were bloody cops chasing other cops, tasing them before sinking their teeth into them. Those who called for backup only brought more zombie cops to the scene. Not a single police officer opened fire on their colleagues. These people knew each other, they knew each other's families, had barbecues together over the weekend. People died, though, other people. There were a lot of guns in the Upper Peninsula, Michigan Militia types with enough firepower in their basement to invade Canada. Adam 'Toothless' Croft was one of them, and he didn't take kindly to the mailman, an agent of the state, bursting into his home with his mouth wide open. Adam blew the mailman's head right off with a shotgun, then took to the street to continue the revolution. Him, the police had zero qualms about taking down; he was shot twenty-two times in the chest.

Slowly but surely, they got organized. They could look at a situation from all kinds of angles. If one person was unable to subdue another, someone else would help them, and another someone, and another. Everyone was everyone's backup plan, hundreds, then thousands of people moving about in a coordinated fashion. Evelyn may have been the one wearing the costume, but everyone who'd merged had powers that would have made the real Batgirl jealous, even Supergirl. Forget batarangs or super senses, the collective had thousands of bodies trained in all forms of hand-to-hand combat. They could see everything, hear everything all over Marquette. They were unstoppable. There had been few protests in the town's recent history, always peaceful, and never more than a couple hundred people. This was an all-out civil war. Neither the police nor anyone else was remotely equipped to handle something of this magnitude. They didn't even know *what* they were up against. Those who turned violent were of all ages, from all walks of life. They had absolutely nothing in common. It was like *Invasion of the Body Snatchers.* There was no sure way to know whether the person standing next to you was on your side or not.

When dinnertime came around, most of the town had been converted. Half the mob was going door to door to catch people in hiding. Shivansh led the other half to the police station, where the few cops who hadn't been caught had all retreated.

37
CAROLE–MARQUETTE

EVELYN WAS ON her way to the mall in her fancy costume. Layla was getting ready to go knock on doors. Shivansh was removing valuables from his and Carole's house in case the weird people coming over to get bitten had criminal intentions. Carole, in some way, had the simplest job. It was also the hardest.

Carole did her hair, put on her best work suit, and drove to the other side of town. She got out of the car, walked up to the front door of a house that looked just like hers, and rang the doorbell, Frank's doorbell.

—Patricia?

—Yes? I'm sorry, I'm terrible with faces. Do I know you?

—You don't. My name's Carole. I—I wanted to talk to you about Frank. Can I come in?

—…Sure. Would you like some coffee?

Frank had a wife, Patricia, and two children: Alvin, six years old, and Beatrice, a very precocious four. Carole already knew Patricia had been through hell living with Frank all those years. She'd shown up to Evelyn's office with bruises or a black eye on several occasions. He'd broken her rib once during an argument. Patricia, of course, insisted she'd fallen down the stairs. The kids were another story. As far as Carole knew, Frank had never laid a hand on them. As righteous as Layla, Carole, Shivansh and Evelyn felt at first about their plan, it meant doing to those kids *exactly* what Frank had done to Layla, and they quickly recognized the hypocrisy. The four of them had been staunch opponents of the death penalty their whole lives, and yet they'd appointed themselves judge, jury, and executioner, just like Frank had when he'd pounded Booker's head on the road. This was—it would have to be—an *exception* to what they all firmly believed in. It had to be an exception to what they wanted the world to be. They realized very early on that they were bound to fail. They couldn't build a better world if they brought to it the very thing that had rotted this one. As painful as it was to lose their friend, their father, to lose part of themselves, they would have to heal without Frank getting the justice he so strongly deserved. They could get *some* justice, though. They could lock Frank up for the rest of his life—*they* would be the justice system in Marquette by the end of the day. They could exile him, away from his family. There were lots of things they could do to Frank besides killing him; they just had to decide. They chose not to. In their one mind, that choice belonged to the person who knew him best, Patricia. Soon, though, Patricia would be one of them and there would be no such thing as 'her choice.' She had to decide while she was still Patricia, and that meant telling her everything. *Almost* everything.

Carole did. She told Patricia everything that happened on the side of the road when Booker was killed. Every detail. Patricia was noticeably horrified by the account, but she let Carole get to the end before she said anything.

—I'm really sorry for what happened to your friend.

—Thank you.

—Do you have any proof it happened the way you say it did?

—I do.

—Okay, then why are you talking to me instead of the DA?

—Because it's not the kind of proof a jury will ever see.

—What kind of proof is it, then?

—That's… difficult to explain.

—… Can you show me?

—I can. But first, I need to tell you a story. Imagine a world where everyone is… connected, where you see what everyone sees, know what everyone knows. Imagine a world where the person you were… doesn't *disappear*, but is *replaced* by something larger than you, a collective mind made up of everyone's uniqueness, but always thinking as one. In that world, you would share everyone's knowledge, but also their strengths, their aspirations, because you would become everyone. Do you understand what I'm trying to describe?

—Not really, but it sounds wonderful. Why are you telling me this?

—Well, in that world, I wouldn't need to show you proof. You would know exactly what I know. You would have *been* my friend when Frank pulled him over and you'd have experienced everything he experienced. You'd have… You'd have died with him that day.

—Let me get you a tissue.

—Don't. It's okay. I guess my question to you is this. If you lived in that world, and you knew everything I said is true, what do you think should happen to your husband? What should be his punishment?

—... That's a really weird question. I don't think I can answer that.

—Try it.

—I can't! It doesn't make sense.

—I know it's make-believe, but—

—No, I mean... How do I put this? Does my husband also live in that make-believe world of yours? Because the way you describe it, if he did, he would never hurt a soul. He couldn't, because he'd be hurting himself, right? Wow. Now it's me who's not making any sense.

—You still love him, don't you?

—I married him. We were kids, really, but he had... something. I'd be lying if I said there aren't days where I wonder if that person ever existed or if I made him up in my mind. But I still see glimpses of that man sometimes. He's in there, somewhere. My point is we don't live in that make-believe world. We don't know what other people think, or feel, or do. If we did, I think we'd all be... better, all of us.

Carole felt her heart shatter. She'd been Patricia before, with her first husband. She'd wanted to change him, to save him. She'd wanted to keep the good part of him, the part she'd loved, and throw away the bad, like you would a bruised apple, to fix him like a broken watch. She hadn't been able to help it then, no more than Patricia could help it now. That was just human nature asserting itself. Carole was painfully wrong at the time. Patricia, through no fault of her own, was just as painfully right. That's what broke Carole's heart. Frank *could* be fixed. He could be saved. But to save him, they'd have to *become* him. *Layla* would have to become him. That was too much to ask of anyone. Nevertheless, Patricia had chosen, even if she didn't know it.

—Thank you, Patricia.

—You said you could show me proof.

—I did… Do you trust me?

—I…

Carole removed a brooch from her vest and pricked the tip of her index finger. She handed the brooch to Patricia, who waited for Carole to say more. When she didn't, Patricia pricked herself and handed the brooch back. Their fingers touched for a minute or so, then Carole removed her hand and smiled.

—You know what? I think I'll have that coffee after all.

38
LAYLA–MARQUETTE

LAYLA WAS WALKING to the police station to join Shivansh, every cop they'd brought into their fold, and about eight thousand other people. Layla didn't *have* to be there physically; they were there over eight thousand times already. Still, the station was the last piece of the puzzle, the last step in their plan to make Marquette everything it could be. They already had a sense of what that would be like. Being Layla, being anybody in town, was a very different thing now. They were thousands, of all ages, creeds, colors, cultures, sexual orientations. They knew... well, it seemed like they knew *everything*. They were poets and scientists, janitors, soldiers, engineers, cooks. They were even a cat and a couple of dogs—some people are very close to their pets and, in the thick of things, they had bit Louise, Spot and Fluffy without thinking.

Layla was just past the Ramada when one of the thousands of things they saw made them stop dead in their tracks. On a street Layla had never been to, inside a house they'd never seen, a young girl was crying on the floor, begging for the strange man in her room not to hurt her like he'd hurt her mom. Elizabeth fucking Kwan was begging

Layla for mercy. It wasn't clear if the city of Marquette simply couldn't have cared less about little Liz Kwan, or if Layla's emotions were so strong at that moment, they took over nearly twenty thousand brains, but the strange man left Liz's room without a word and closed the door behind him. Layla wanted Liz to like them, they'd wanted it from the moment they met. Layla didn't want to *be* Liz Kwan, and as much of a jerk as Liz had been, the last thing Layla wanted was to see her in pain. We have to get them all, that was Layla's rule. Liz would have to be the proverbial exception that proved it.

There were two, actually. Bhakthi Wijesinghe was ninety-seven and terminally ill. She was terminally *old* now, but she had been terminally ill for more than twenty years. Her doctors had absolutely no idea how she survived but she did. Bhakthi just… stuck around. Among the many things afflicting her was a rare and aggressive mix of frontotemporal and Lewy body dementia. Nerve cells in her right frontal lobe were breaking down and abnormal protein deposits were affecting her brain chemistry. She had ceased to communicate completely years ago and showed no reaction to external stimulus of any kind. Whatever world Bhakthi lived in all those years, it was one of her own creation. Bhakthi was a favorite subject of neurologists, who often brought med students to her room. What made Bhakthi so interesting wasn't the part of her brain that had stopped functioning, it was the parts that were still going. There were all kinds of activity in the right frontal cortex, the precuneus, the left amygdala, the left insula, et cetera, all the areas we know that are associated with pleasure. As far as science could tell, Bhakthi Wijesinghe was the happiest person who had ever lived. She experienced *every kind* of pleasure, all the time, from the most basic, like eating or sexual pleasure, to those of the highest order. She could have been making music, saving kittens, having an orgasm, and talking to God, all at the same time. No matter how good they felt after merging with one another, no one in Marquette was going to mess with that.

Layla's day had been one for the ages. Even by historical standards, this was important. It wasn't as big as, say, the French Revolution, or the Indian Revolution, or the Taiping Revolution, or pretty much any other revolution, but still. It was *huge* by Marquette standards. Technically, it couldn't be bigger because it involved every single person in town, or at least it would when they were finished. They were so close. Layla was sure they'd feel even better when the job was done, but with a job that big, they saw nothing wrong with feeling some satisfaction for *almost* getting the job done. Heck, they were eleven. It's not every day an eleven-year-old leads a rebellion. Maybe *lead* wasn't the right word, per se, and they were not *just* eleven, but whatever. They certainly deserved a tiny part of the credit.

All they had to do now was to gain control of a single building. There would be other holdouts for sure—they would be finding people hiding in broom closets or under beds for days—but this was the last castle to storm, the last fortress. Though everyone inside would be armed, there couldn't be that many people left. Layla was already the bulk of the Marquette police force. But none of the cops knew exactly who was still at the station.

There was one person Layla hoped would be there. Of the twenty thousand pairs of eyes they could see through, none had glimpsed Frank since mid-afternoon.

39
LANA

Lana was making coffee when the phone started ringing. She was making coffee for the whole station, as she had since she'd come back to work. Frank had found a tray that fit nicely over her wheelchair arms and told her she should go around and serve everyone. She'd protested, of course. The chief had even taken her side—'Oh, Come on, Frank. She's your partner, not some lowly waitress!'—though he'd somehow found a way to make that sound demeaning. Demeaning was as good as it would get. 'Then again,' he'd quickly added, 'what else are you going to do around here with those wheels? Might as well make yourself useful.' Lana had done her best to find satisfaction in the process. Making coffee for lots of people was almost a science. It was also very frustrating. Too strong. Too weak. One had to find the right balance to minimize the number of complaints, though they could not be eliminated. The obvious solution was to make two pots, but there was only one machine and making the 'strong' people wait while she served the 'weak' ones was not an option, nor would it fully resolve the issue. Some people would find the weak coffee too weak and the strong one too strong. There were, in theory, as many desired concentrations as there were people, and everyone had a different threshold for compromise. She usually made two batches about thirty minutes apart, but she would only get to press 'Start' once that morning.

The calls were coming in one after the other. Domestic disturbance. Domestic disturbance. Domestic disturbance. Domestic disturbance. It wasn't even ten and every patrol car was busy responding to incidents of violence at home. The chief even started sending out desk clerks and detectives. 'Who, me?' 'Well, you have a badge, don't you?' Anything to avoid calling people in on their days off and paying overtime. Frank, too, had to go, obviously. He was still putting his coat on when the first call for backup came in. Officer down. Jim Butcher, of all people. Butcher was a good friend of Frank's. They shared just about everything: worldview, pants size, false arrest complaints, and an ego with its own zip code. His partner sounded a bit shaken. He said Butcher had been putting the cuffs on the husband when the wife had jumped on his back and chewed his earlobe off. Husband had then taken Butcher in and locked the door behind him. The chief sent Frank and every person left in the station to the scene. Everyone but Lana. Frank, being the gentleman that he was, *had* to make sure everyone noticed.

—Well, Lana, looks like you just lost your last customer.

—It's okay, Frank. I'll just bake a few pies while you're gone.

Lana wasn't good at sarcasm. Every time she tried, she'd end up the butt of a joke for a few weeks and she generally refrained from trying. Still, she was reasonably convinced she'd nailed it that time. She got confirmation when Frank left without saying a word. What a day. Successful sarcasm, and a dozen calls by 11. Lana couldn't remember the department ever being that busy. Full moon, maybe? She wasn't sure if that was just a night thing or if the moon affected people during the day. She'd have to look that up the next time she went to the—Wait a minute! Butcher's partner said the wife had *bit* him. That sounded a hell of a lot like Carole's attack on Booker. She also remembered Shivansh having a bite mark on his lip at the hospital.

—Chief? Can I talk to you for a sec? I think something's going on.

—You think? I don't have time for this right now. I'm calling State for help. It looks like the whole town's gone mad.

The chief had a point. Reports were coming in faster than central dispatch could answer. There was another call for backup. This time, a dozen people had stormed out of the bushes and assaulted two cops before running away. She wondered what they meant by 'assaulted.' Had they been bitten or beaten? The chief left the station to go to the mayor's office before she could ask him. It was just her, now. The phones were all ringing off the hook and Lana didn't know what to do. She was about to call dispatch when Frank rushed inside the station, panting.

—You're back? What happened?

Frank tried to speak, but he couldn't. He put both hands on his knees, trying to catch his breath. It took him a good twenty seconds to decide whether to speak or have a heart attack.

—Butcher went crazy, that's what happened. Chief! You gotta call State for help, it's a fucking zoo out there.

—He already did. You said Butcher went crazy. What did he do? Did he bite you?

—Not me, his partner. How do you know?

That was it. That was the eureka moment Lana had been waiting for all along. Dr. Schlapp had said it was Lyme disease that made Carole violent. Lana had read up on it and found that explanation highly improbable, but it had to be an illness of some kind. It wasn't a conspiracy; it was a condition. That's why it made no sense whatsoever. It might have been a microbe, a virus, bacteria, microwaves. Lana didn't have the medical knowledge to form an opinion on that, but it was something contagious, and it was spreading rapidly. Exponential growth was a scary concept. Starting with only Carole, if every infected person bit just two people, the entire town could get sick in fifteen iterations.

—It's the same thing that happened to Carole, remember?

—Who?

—Over at Booker's, a few weeks ago. We—

—Shut up and turn the TV up!

It was on every channel. Large groups of people walking the streets and breaking into people's homes. News crews filming the scene before being chased by a rabid mob. *Rabid* was the wrong word, though. These people were all bloody, dishevelled, but they weren't out of control like Carole in the bakery. They all looked perfectly calm. Frank grabbed the remote from Lana's hand and switched channel a few times.

—Frank, wait! Go back!

Channel 10 had a clear view of the crowd breaking into city hall. There had to be five hundred people there, but it was the ten or so wearing blue that caught Lana's attention.

—Is that Butcher leading the crowd?

—It's half the department. Go up front and lock the doors. I'll close the back.

—…

—*Frank!* You need to lock the front doors!

It was the first time Frank took orders from Lana. He didn't object or make a joke out of it. He came back a minute later and dialed a number on speaker. The phone rang once, twice, three times…

—Fuck!

—Who are you calling, Frank?

—My wife.

Four times. Five times.

—Maybe you should go.

Frank waited another second then he hung up the phone.

—No. There's too many of them.

Lana didn't have to say it. Frank knew he was a coward. Hearing it from her wouldn't change anything. He sat on his chair and stared at the ceiling for a while, then he started looking around. Something had changed, Lana could feel it too. It took a minute for her to figure out what it was and turn the TV off. Silence. There wasn't a single phone ringing anywhere. The whole station had gone quiet, except for the wall clock, which was now loud as thunder.

Tick. Tock. Tick. Tock.

Their hearts skipped a beat when they heard banging at the door. Frank got up and went to check.

—Who's there, Frank?

—It's…

—Frank?

—It's…

—Frank! Who's at the door?

—Everyone.

—What?

—They're all here. It's fucking everybody.

Lana joined Frank in the lobby. He was right. There were people in front of the station as far as the eye could see. That door wouldn't last ten seconds if they decided to storm in. They weren't storming, though. They weren't pushing or pounding on the window. Thousands of people just standing there, calm as a clam.

The crowd up front spread open and out came Jim Butcher, missing a chunk of his right ear. He was smiling.

—Can you open the door for me, Frank?

—Not before you tell me what the fuck is happening out there.

—We'd like you to come with us, Frank.

—Come with you where?

—You'll see.

—I think I'm gonna pass. If you don't mind.

—I'm afraid I do, Frank.

Butcher took out his keys and unlocked the door before opening it. Frank backed away and pulled out his gun. So did Lana.

—STAY BACK! Stay the fuck back, Butcher! I swear I'll shoot you!

—It's me, Frank. Are you going to shoot your friend? Are you going to shoot your wife?

Butcher stepped aside and a woman emerged behind him with two kids in tow.

—Patricia? What the hell are you doing here? Why are the kids here?

—Put the gun down, Frank.

—Patricia, what's going on? It's okay, Beatrice, everything's gonna be fine.

—Just put the gun down before someone gets hurt.

The woman approached slowly. Frank let his arm drop as she did. She moved closer, closer still. She gently kissed Frank before biting his lower lip.

—FUCK!

Frank pushed the woman away and raised his gun again. Lana had never lowered hers and was still aiming at Butcher. Then… Then absolutely nothing happened. Frank's wife just stood there, half a grin on her face. The crowd behind her didn't move at all. It took a good ten minutes before anyone spoke again. Lana did the honors.

—Patricia, can I ask what you all want with Frank?

—We want him to come with us. You should leave, now, Lana.

—Come with you where? Where are you taking him?

—That's… not your concern, Lana, but we *are* taking him.

—I don't think I can let you do that.

—He'll *want* to come with us. Just wait. Look around, Lana. I'm offering you a chance to leave. You should take it.

Lana had to make a choice. She couldn't just let them take Frank. He was an asshole, but he was her partner, and police officers don't leave their partners behind. Never. There is a rule for that. On the other hand, there wasn't much she could do to stop it, and though she was pointing her gun at Patricia, she'd left the safety on. Lana wasn't about to shoot the entire town. Most importantly, whatever bug was tearing through Marquette would not stop there. Containing the spread was the number one priority, and she couldn't do that if she became infected herself. She'd sworn an oath, and at that moment, the best thing she could do to serve and protect was to get the hell out of Dodge while she still could.

—I'll bring back help, Frank. I promise.

—You fucking bitch! Don't you dare leave me here!

—I'm sorry, Frank.

—I'll find you! You're gonna pay for this. Trust me, you will.

Lana did not trust him. She wheeled herself down the access ramp and headed towards 7th Street to get to the highway.

40
FRANK

FRANK KEPT HIS gun pointed at his wife the whole time. He didn't *want* to kill her, but he was thinking about it. He knew he couldn't stop everyone. He had a gun, but there were over a dozen cops in that crowd, and *they* had guns too. He would certainly never hurt his kids—he loved them both very much—but if it came down to it, he was going to take Patricia with him. Justice, you know. She'd betrayed him and she'd fucking sworn before God. He wasn't always kind to her, Frank knew that, but for better for worse, richer, poorer, all that shit. He *did* wish he were a better man. He wasn't, so what? Patricia had signed up for worse as well. 'Worse' was in the fucking contract. Now she wanted to take him to God knows where to do God knows what. She was sick, that's what she was. Whatever was wrong with Butcher—and something was definitely wrong with him, biting people like that—she had it too. They all did.

The back of the crowd moved a little. The ripple moved closer and closer until someone else stepped out front. Some black kid. Short hair. Frank wasn't sure if it was a boy or a girl.

—Who the fuck are you?

—...

—What? You're not gonna say? It's a fucking secret?

—...

—Well, fuck you, then. Fuck every single one of you. I ain't going nowhere.

Frank was about to pull the trigger when he saw something that confused him. Himself. He saw himself, pointing a gun to his face. He saw himself pointing a gun to his right, to his left. Frank started turning and what he saw turned with him. Whatever kind of fucked-up magic that was, Frank wanted no part of it. He ran all the way to the back of the station and tried to open the door. That's when it hit. A rush of emotion so big, Frank collapsed to the floor like a sack of spuds.

Over the years, he'd found a way to live with his sins. Most days, he didn't give a single thought to the bad things he did. That was just the way he was, no sense pretending to be something else. He was more honest, in a way. The rest of the town wasn't as forgiving. They didn't take kindly to him being a bigot, a rapist, and a killer. It was them, their children that Frank had abused in the backseat of his patrol car, then laughed about it with his cop friends over beer. It was their loved ones he'd killed. Booker wasn't the first person Frank had murdered. The first three bodies, everyone in town had just learned at once, he'd dumped off the decommissioned ore docks after stuffing a couple bricks inside their coats. Frank had stood in front of these people's wives and children when they'd filled out a missing person report, then he'd gone for lunch like nothing had happened.

Suddenly being Layla wasn't easy either. His encounter with their dad was still very fresh in Frank's mind and everyone teared up when they remembered it in gruesome detail. Everyone did. Alvin remembered it. Beatrice remembered it. Frank would have given anything to stop that from happening. He *was* his children now, and he couldn't bear the sight of himself. The amount of loathing twenty thousand people could feel all at once was astounding, but it paled in comparison to that of a father knowing his children see him as a monster.

Most of who Frank was would have been happy to just dilute the old Frank in a sea of others. He'd wanted to be a good man his whole life, now was his chance. A tiny part of him, about one twenty thousandth to be precise, just couldn't live with himself. In the end, it was the tiny part that won. No one understood how he managed to act as one the whole time, but Frank stood up and went out through the front door. Everyone made way for him as he walked slowly all the way to the old docks, a half a mile away. Every person in town followed, moved by a mix of curiosity, hatred and pity. It looked like a pilgrimage or a procession.

It was nighttime when they reached the shore. Frank turned to look at the town one last time. He never said 'I'm sorry,' but everyone knew he *almost* meant to. He'd kept his free will, but he still shared a part of him with the rest of the town, and they followed his wishes. Alvin and Beatrice went back home. They'd still see what everyone else saw, but it mattered, somehow. Frank didn't want his children there. He also didn't want to be alone at the end, so Layla went with him.

They were the only ones to walk the flimsy wooden path and climb to the top of the abandoned structure. They held hands all the way to the end, their way to forgive and to make amends. Frank took two big rocks he'd picked up along the way and stuck them inside his coat pockets. He took one last look at Layla, then jumped without saying a word and disappeared into the darkness.

41

LAYLA—MARQUETTE

THEY HAD DONE it. The town of Marquette, Michigan had a population of one. That wasn't exactly true. There were *three,* counting the two people they hadn't brought in, but it was true enough. They had turned the small city into some kind of utopia. It was free of hate, violence, racism, sexism. Part of that was a trick, a logical sleight of hand—it takes at least two people for any of these things to exist—but the people of Marquette were genuinely accepting. What gave their one mind its uniqueness was precisely the differences between them. Their concept of the *other* wasn't based on sex, or gender, or religion, or looks, or wealth. It couldn't be. They were rich and poor, old and young. They had skin of every color and faces of every shape. They had, through Frank's one moment of strength, found some justice for all the suffering he'd caused.

There was still much to do before they could rest, but forty thousand hands can do a lot in a few hours. Layla was helping bandage a few wounds at the hospital. The place was busy. Several people had fought back during the takeover. Five were dead. A few dozen were injured seriously enough to require treatment. Luckily, every person in town was now a registered nurse and it didn't take long for everyone to be taken care of. Layla was making the rounds before going home when they looked at a young man lying alone in a room on the second floor. They couldn't tell what was different about him at first, but it soon became clear. He was looking at Layla, but they couldn't see themselves from his point of view. They'd been methodical, going from door to door, but they'd apparently missed this one patient in all the commotion. Layla approached the bed. They paused for a moment when they noticed the young man's tattoos. This was someone who was filled with hate, not exactly the kind of person one would want to bite into.

Layla went to the desk next to his bed and pushed his chart to the edge, then a little more, and a little more until it fell and made a clunky sound hitting the floor. Fucking Louise! Being a couple of dogs made little difference other than people being a bit happier to see each other. That cat, though, was an asshole, and whatever urges it had were hard to ignore, even for someone with twenty thousand brains. Layla leaned down and picked up the man's chart. William Willoughby had been diagnosed as quadriplegic after an unlucky fall just a few weeks before. Layla browsed through the notes several doctors had left. 'Patient in full denial, referred to psych.' 'WW grew angry, had to stop session.' Clearly, this man wasn't coping well. Maybe he deserved it, but whatever he'd done in the past, quadriplegia seemed like punishment enough. He *was* a bad man, one didn't need to know him well to figure that out, but as far as the town knew, he'd never killed anyone. Most importantly, William Willoughby had never had any power, and that made all the difference. Layla was already a bunch of neo-Nazis—ex-neo-Nazis—and their hatred had all been washed away by the collective. William Willoughby's mind would be no different, just another drop in their cognitive ocean.

Marquette felt good about bringing him in. Take a broken man who is alone and suffering and make him into someone better. They could already see it happening, they'd experienced it many times that day. He would resist, his mind would struggle, but after a while he'd begin to see everything. He'd know what it meant to be the very people he'd hated all his life. He would see what they saw, feel what they felt. He would *be* those people. The hate and fear would rush out of him like wasps from a kicked nest and he would feel their strength, and their love, maybe for the first time in his life. There was excitement in the air. Layla smiled gently at the man and slowly leaned over. William Willoughby didn't make a sound, but his eyes screamed all sorts of obscenities. His skin had a very different flavor for some reason. Layla knew what every person in town tasted like now. Everyone was different, of course, but in the way different brands of hot dogs are different. It's still hot dog in the end. William was like a chicken sausage wiener, or a veggie dog. Not necessarily bad, but certainly not what you were expecting. The man hadn't moved in weeks and was being fed the same paste every meal. Maybe that had something to do with it, like grass-fed beef tasting different from grain-fed. Whatever. When the deed was done, Layla sat back in the chair next to the man's bed and waited for an hour so they could reassure him when their thoughts began to flood his mind.

An hour passed and Layla still couldn't see through William Willoughby's eyes. Another hour passed. Nothing. She bit him again, twice, just to be sure. While Layla waited, the neurosurgeon that she now was wondered if it was his spinal injury that prevented the merge. When nothing happened the second time around, Layla settled on that hypothesis and left the man alone. They wrote it down—Evelyn did—thinking it might later help shed some light on what had happened to them. There were other things on the agenda, but at some point, they would want to continue their research, which should prove a lot easier without having to hide it from everyone.

By 2:00 AM, everyone at the hospital was cared for, and a few more strays had been added to the mix. They were all tired and looking forward to a good night's sleep, but their work wasn't over yet. What they'd done was anything but subtle. It was now on national television and, as much as they wanted to be left alone, the powers that be would not let it happen. People were coming, and they had to be ready.

PART 5
EPIDEMIC

42

JEREMIAH BRIGGS III

JEREMIAH BRIGGS III was fifth-generation military, and he had a small penis. These two unrelated facts had, in tandem, come to shape every single aspect of Jeremiah's life.

When he was fifteen, his father was stationed at Fort Richardson in Anchorage, Alaska. It was there that young Jeremiah met Crystal Thomson, one year his elder. She had never been outside Anchorage and was quickly taken with the well-travelled Jeremiah. Despite her lack of passport stamps, Crystal entered this relationship with a net advantage in street smarts and general life experience. When, for his sixteenth birthday, Jeremiah very politely asked for what would have been his first blow job, Crystal pulled his pants down and, well, she snorted a little. Jeremiah called it a giggle, but it was definitely a snort. Terminology aside, Crystal apologized profusely and rightly pointed out that she was willing to do the deed, but Jeremiah would have none of it. He would later come to regret that decision, but the important part is that, from that moment on, women became creatures to be feared, for they had the power to destroy a man with nothing but a giggle. (It was a snort.)

Jeremiah's unoriginal given name made most life

decisions a whole lot simpler. The Third sat across from Junior for breakfast every morning, while the portrait of Jeremiah *tout court* looked upon them with stern and judgmental eyes. *Pro Deo et patria* was the family motto and no Briggs boy would seriously entertain the possibility of being anything other than a good soldier.

It is often said that men sharing Jeremiah's minimal endowment tend to compensate with a more 'manly' demeanor. Pouting their lips to make their voice lower, standing taller than others to assert dominance, walking like they have oranges under their armpits. That was all true of Jeremiah, with one notable distinction. The man was gigantic to begin with. Six feet, four inches, barefoot. You could have built a house on his shoulders. Seriously, the dude was *huge*. To hear him speak like a pubescent teenager waiting for a moustache to grow, and see him walk like The Undertaker, was somewhat disturbing to most. That said, the attitude and the wrestler walk were perfect for the military. They really ate that shit up. Unbothered as he was by companionship, Jeremiah gave himself wholly to his training, then to his career. He rose through the ranks quicker than anyone and, in all likelihood, could have gotten whatever assignment he wanted, as long as it didn't involve any technical skills. He chose the National Guard. While the snort had made him terminally insecure, Jeremiah loathed violence. The last thing he wanted was to have to kill people, or to tell other people to kill people, or do anything that had to do with killing. Bossing people around, however, was a dream come true, and the Guard was the best place to do that on a regular basis without ever having to pull a trigger.

Jeremiah was at the gym near his home in Detroit when the rerun episode of *One Life to Live* on every television was interrupted by a special report. In the middle of a busy street, three people were holding down a priest while a fourth, a young girl, was biting into his arm. The girl raised her head and looked straight at the camera. She couldn't have been older than ten, her face angelic and innocent, except for the blood pooling along the silver line of her retainer. What sort of devil made children want to eat a servant of God? Up until then, there had been little room in Jeremiah's life for the metaphysical. He had never questioned the meaning of life, or his particular role in the universe. The images of the 'Marquette Mayhem' he saw on screen instantly changed all that. Jeremiah Briggs had been put on Earth for a reason and that was to quell the uprising in the U.P. He got up, wiped the butt sweat off the curl machine, and headed home without taking a shower to wait for the ineluctable phone call. The call came as God intended and twelve hours later, he was in command of about two thousand troops and establishing encampments in Negaunee and Harvey.

Jeremiah was *inspired*, pointing left and right like a conductor as he gave orders to set up a base of operations. His great opus came to an abrupt end when one of the sentries spotted a lone woman in a wheelchair rolling down the Forty-One. Within minutes, the woman was surrounded by soldiers in hazmat suits, restrained and brought for questioning inside a negative pressure tent. After Army doctors took blood samples and mouth swabs, Jeremiah grabbed a chair and sat on the other side of the plastic wall, hoping to determine whether he was looking at a prisoner or a refugee. That was the tricky part of the assignment. Most insurgencies involve a readily identifiable group, a coterie of combatants sharing similar attire and ideology. The

Marquette Mayhem pitted seemingly regular folks against other seemingly regular folks. Though he had never been, Jeremiah thought the situation was akin to Vietnam, where telling friend from foe was a complex affair. The North Vietnamese looked a whole lot like the South Vietnamese, and some South Vietnamese were sympathizing with the North Vietnamese while some North Vietnamese were on the side of the South Vietnamese, and whoever thought it was a good idea to split countries in half really should have known better. Marquette was even worse since there was no border to begin with, just a whole bunch of people who looked as innocent or guilty as anyone else.

The woman in the plastic tent looked exhausted. She'd apparently spent the night alone trying to find shelter along the highway. There was something about her Jeremiah found… endearing. She *was* a woman and certainly not to be trusted, yet he found her somewhat less threatening than other members of the opposite sex. It could have been the wheelchair, or the bubble tent, Jeremiah wasn't sure, but he chose to approach the conversation in a more friendly manner.

43
SHIVANSH–MARQUETTE

In less than twenty-four hours, the town had resumed functioning as a community. It had made some tweaks to its economy: Marquette had too many restaurants and not enough teachers, too much fancy soap and not enough fresh bread. They'd also closed the shop selling Spider-Man and Pikachu dreamcatchers. These once unmanageable issues were now controlled by the collective, as was poverty, housing and every other problem individuals had never cared to solve. No one in Marquette would go hungry again or spend a night without a bed. Despite these fundamental changes and the fact that it was mostly silent, the town, for the most part, *looked* as it always had. Though they were prepared for contingencies, Shivansh-Marquette hoped appearances alone would be enough to convince the armed forces gathering around town that their presence was no longer necessary.

Shivansh knew the first step in any military endeavor would be to gather intelligence. As expected, the helicopters started flying over town at sunrise, raising the curtain on the world's largest ever theatrical production. Slowly, the streets filled with cars and people. Lights were turned on, doors unlocked. Shop owners stood outside to greet their customers. Lots of people would have gone to work anyway, but the devil is in the details when it comes to emotional impact. Marquette had a lot of military experience, but it mostly owed its morning choreography to Basil Basset, now retired, who'd worked as a stage manager on Broadway for over thirty years. The 'town comes to life' part of the show was going for a '40s aesthetic, with all the uncanny congeniality of a Christmas movie. Exaggerated smiles, everyone waving at everyone. A few well timed two-kisses on the cheeks to give it that certain *je ne sais quoi*. This was a silent movie, as the audience sat two thousand feet above the stage. They would add dialogue later if and when the military made an in-person appearance. Controlling twenty thousand bodies was a relatively easy feat for their collective intellect, but talking to themselves with the right mouths posed something of a sensory challenge. Shivansh's job was to play the Indian stereotype and add a bit of Asian flair to the scene. No one in town owned a proper sherwani, so he'd borrowed a New York pink blazer from Martha Smith across the street. On the third helicopter pass, Shivansh strolled down Washington Street, namaskar-ing his way to the Babycakes Muffin Company. When the rotor noise grew louder again, he exited the premises holding a large box of mint chocolate-chip brownies—props had to be big enough to be seen from a distance—and handed them out to a group of overly enthusiastic children who passed by wearing bright matching schoolbags.

The town's performance was flawless. It would be very difficult, near impossible, for anyone to justify a military intervention in a peaceful town where everyone looked so happy and calm. Marquette TV reporters were on the streets commenting on mundane events: a great Little League baseball rivalry, a bake sale to raise funds for the Rotary Club, and three exciting projects at the school science fair, all perfect ways to forget the 'unpleasantness' of the previous day. The violent attacks everyone had seen on television would not be so easy to dismiss, but the victims of those attacks were now kissing their attackers on the cheeks. This would work—it had to—and the town would be free to live its life as it wanted.

By eleven, the helicopters had stopped coming and Shivansh drove out to Negaunee to see if the soldiers were preparing to leave. He hit the brakes hard just past Brookton Corners. Spike strips were laid out over two hundred feet, with three Humvees blocking the road ahead. There must have been three hundred men bustling about behind the vehicles. From the Menards' rooftop three hundred feet behind him, Shivansh could see soldiers setting up large quarantine tents in a nearby field, enough to hold hundreds of people. Whatever the Army was planning to do, leaving Marquette alone wasn't part of it. They had to go to plan B, or plan C. Most likely C, though they were hoping for B. There was no plan D.

The first backup plan was simple: wait for the armed forces to visit in person and perform act two of the Basil Basset production. That now seemed unlikely given what Shivansh was looking at. The Army covering the road with tire-puncturing strips meant they weren't planning on using said road any time soon.

Plan C was a *pis aller*, a last-resort attempt to avoid a violent confrontation. It involved a face-to-face meeting between the armed forces and a town representative. What face this representative would wear had yet to be determined, but for diplomacy to have a chance to succeed, that face had better be engaging. Shivansh turned the car around and parked at Walmart to wait for others to join him. He saw his sunglasses sitting on the dashboard and tapped them a little to the side. Again, and again, until they were *this* close to falling and—

Oh, for fuck's sake! Fucking Louise again!

44
LANA

The temperature had gone down to the low 40s on the highway that night. Lana was wearing nothing but her uniform shirt, but she wanted to put as much distance between her and the crowd as she could. She made it about five miles outside of town before she lost all feeling in her hands. Lana didn't want to break into a building in case Marquette police were called. She couldn't trust anyone coming from there anymore. She found refuge inside the cabin of a garbage truck in an isolated parking lot, woke up just before sunrise and kept going towards Negaunee. There wasn't a car or a truck going in or out of Marquette and the highway was deserted except for Lana's wheelchair. She'd just passed the M-35 when a tan Hummer came out of nowhere and almost ran her over before stopping. Three men in hazmat suits came out, guns pointing at her. There was a lot of yelling—people can't hear anything with these things on. Lana was pulled out of her wheelchair and onto the ground before being cuffed and shoved into the Hummer for a twenty-second drive into the Army camp.

Once there, she was sprayed with some chemical before being thrown into a plastic tent. More men in yellow suits came in to poke and probe her with no apparent regard for her well-being. Lana pleaded for them to stop, but no one would listen. It was only when she asked for her wheelchair back that one of the faceless men deigned to answer. He brought her chair in and helped her sit. She was left alone for a good hour after that. She was about to fall asleep when a very large man approached from afar. He walked like he was holding oranges under his armpits and Lana wondered if it was a medical condition. Regardless, Lana didn't waste any time and spoke the moment he sat down on the other side of the plastic wall.

—Sir! My name is Lana Lannister. I'm an officer with Marquette PD and I need to speak with the person in charge!

—I'm Colonel Jeremiah Briggs. I'm in command of this operation.

—There's something terribly wrong going on in the city. I think everyone may have been inf—

—Whoa, lady. Not so fast. Why don't you start by telling me who you are?

—I—My name is Lana Lannister.

—I see you're wearing a police uniform. Are you with Marquette PD?

—...Yes.

—Good. Now we're getting somewhere. What can you tell us about what's going on down there?

—There is a... I don't know if it's a virus, or a parasite or something else, but there's a disease infecting people that's making them hyper-violent. They—They attack other people for no apparent reason, and they *bite* them. I don't know what's happening exactly, but I think that's how the disease is spreading.

—Okay. Can you tell me more about this… biting?

—I'm not sure I understand. They bite other people and they infect them, with their saliva, I guess.

—Interesting. So, you said these people—the ones that are infected—they become violent. *Hyperviolent*, I think is the word you used.

—Yes. It was on television; you must have seen it.

—I did, but when we checked this morning, things looked pretty calm down there, very business as usual.

—That's because they're *all* infected now, all of them. It all started with Carole Veilleux a few weeks ago. She attacked someone in a store. She attacked me too, then—

—Wait, wait. You were also attacked? Does that mean you're—

—No, no. She didn't bite me. She tried, but—

—We'll just have to see about that.

—See about what?

—About you being bitten or not. We're running some tests right now. We'll know if you're lying to us.

—I don't think you're going to find anything. There's a doctor in town, she did some tests, and she didn't—Actually, she might have been infected by then, so I can't know for sure.

—So, you're saying this doctor is also infected now.

—Yes. They're all infected. Everyone in town is.

—"All… infected…" Anything else?

—No. Well, yes. I think they may have killed a police officer. Frank Meyer.

—Killed him how?

—I don't know. I was on my way to you when it happened, if it happened.

—Then how do you know they killed him?

—I don't. I just told you.

—Was anyone else killed, besides Officer… Meyer?

—No, not that I'm aware of. I don't know that they killed anyone.

—You just said—Never mind. You must be exhausted, I understand.

—I don't think the disease is airborne, but I wouldn't go back there without some sort of protection.

—We know what we're doing, ma'am.

—I'm just saying—

—Listen, why don't we wait for your tests to come back, then we'll talk some more.

—Whatever you do, don't let anyone in town get close to you.

—That's good thinking. We can talk more about that when your tests come back, maybe over coffee, or something.

—What?

—It's fine. Just stay right where you are. I'll be back before you know it.

Lana was puzzled, and tired, and scared. She'd left Marquette to get help, military help, hoping to stop the spread of whatever had infected her townmates. She'd found exactly what she was looking for, but she didn't feel relieved. To the contrary, she was just as worried about the disease as ever, and she now feared for her own safety. The negative pressure tent was looking smaller and smaller as the minutes went by. Lana had always been good at compartmentalizing, but she'd run out of compartments and couldn't ignore this rising claustrophobia. She screamed for the strange man to come back and let her out. She looked for her keys inside her pockets, anything to tear through the walls. She tried ripping through them with her hands. She couldn't think, couldn't breathe. She felt so trapped, her brain went into tilt mode. Lana lay on her back and screeched at the sky like a pterodactyl while hitting the ground until soldiers came in and knocked her out with a sedative.

45
JEREMIAH

Jeremiah had had plenty of training about containing the outbreak of a contagious disease. He'd been faced with countless scenarios, from airborne pathogens to things that spread through close contact and bodily fluids. The latter seemed to be what was afflicting the people of Marquette, but unlike, say, ebola, no one seemed to be dying from it. They didn't even look remotely impaired. More puzzling even was that folks didn't seem to mind being sick at all. If he hadn't known better, he'd have thought they were happy about it. Jeremiah's best guess was that they were the victims of a parasite that infected the brain and manipulated them. It wasn't exactly his guess, the woman in the wheelchair had already said all that, but she hadn't been sure if it was a virus or a parasite, and he'd guessed it was a parasite. When he was a kid, he'd seen a documentary on some kind of fungus that turned ants into zombies. Oh, and this other thing that lived in bird shit before being eaten by snails. Ewwww. He'd forgotten about that one. The parasite moved into the eyes of the snail and messed with its brain to make it walk around in the sun and die. That thing was really gross, and it had made quite the impression on young Jeremiah.

Thanks to Officer Lannister, Jeremiah also had a lot more intel about the town, and maybe a coffee date. In a nutshell, he was facing in the ballpark of twenty thousand hostiles who knew the terrain better than he did, who had access to weapons and could turn anyone into a violent maniac if they managed to infect them. That meant anyone setting foot in Marquette was in danger, and there was no way Jeremiah would risk his men being hurt or turned into shit-eating zombie snails.

Containing the spread while doctors figured out how to deal with the problem was the best he could do, though it was easier said than done with such a large population. Jeremiah had nonetheless formulated a plan to maintain control of the city with minimal risk and without casualties. The city stood on the shore of Lake Superior and Jeremiah already had dozens of boats on patrol. He'd also set up barricades on every road leading to town. That left two large swaths of forest and trails to cover, one due south and one to the north-west. Jeremiah stationed troops along highway 41, thus blocking any exit through the south, and purposely left the forests to the north-west unguarded, making it the only obvious escape route. That would be their hunting ground. About two dozen sharpshooters with tranquilizer guns were positioned half a mile inside the woods. Their job was to incapacitate anyone who attempted to leave and bring them to camp so doctors could do their thing. The plan would ensure no one contagious left the area and hopefully provide a constant supply of guinea pigs for the medical team. Jeremiah wasn't the kind of man who would call his own plan great, but if someone else had come up with that plan, he'd undoubtedly have said: 'Wow! That plan's *great!*'

They were still setting up quarantine tents when a corporal no one really liked spotted a group of people walking towards the roadblock on the 41. Jeremiah grabbed the binoculars from the shunned officer. He turned the focus knob when all he could see was a blur, wondering what the hell was wrong with corporal reject's eyesight. And then… Oh. My. God. Once in focus, the group of people wasn't so much a group as it was a crowd, a multitude, a drove. It was a fucking army, and it was heading straight for them. Jeremiah yelled orders left and right. Soldiers took up positions behind the Humvees, ready to shoot tear gas and rubber bullets. Everyone else grabbed shields and batons in case the crowd got too close. Firing live ammunition at US citizens was the last thing Jeremiah wanted to do—it was also definitely frowned upon—but he had a dozen M-16s loaded and ready, just in case the citizens of Marquette had lethal intentions.

As the mob grew closer, Jeremiah spotted a woman walking ahead of everyone. She was short, well-rounded. She walked with more assurance than any woman he had ever seen. Jeremiah thought it might simply be the result of having short legs, but it still scared the bejeezus out of him. He recognized her immediately for what she was: his nemesis. She was Lex Luthor to his Superman, the Peculiar Purple Pieman to his Strawberry Shortcake. Wait, why did he think of that? She was the Reverse Flash to his regular Flash. She was Megatron. If God had chosen him to quell this uprising, then the rotund woman was without doubt the envoy of Satan. As she moved closer, with thousands in tow, Jeremiah knew that his moment of glory was also drawing near. He climbed on top of the center vehicle, took a wide stance, and placed both hands on his hips. When the woman was about two hundred feet away, he raised his right hand high and spoke loudly.

—Alright, ma'am. That's close enough.

In hindsight, Jeremiah wished he'd opened with something more solemn than 'Alright, ma'am.' Still, he thought he'd nailed the tone and sounded very movie-like. Had Jeremiah Junior been there, he would have been impressed.

46
CAROLE–MARQUETTE

Carole walked with all the confidence being a town confers. Behind her, four thousand seven hundred and thirty-five people walked with similar assurance while the rest of Marquette kept the town functioning. This was their one chance to avoid an open conflict with the armed forces that were amassing around town. If things went south, and the wrong kind of people were in charge, it could easily turn into a bloodbath. There was, of course, no shortage of firearms in the Upper Peninsula, but Carole, all four thousand seven hundred and thirty-six of her walking on the highway, didn't want to exacerbate an already tense situation and had chosen to go unarmed. As she got closer to the Army roadblock, she saw a huge man climb on top of one of the trucks and take the Superman stance. Carole kept walking towards him until he gestured for her to stop.

—Alright, ma'am. That's close enough.

—Hi! My name is Carole Veilleux. Are you in charge here?

—I am. I'm Colonel Jeremiah Briggs. Who am I speaking with?

—My name is Carole, Carole Veilleux.

—Hello, Carole. Can you tell me if anyone in town is in need of medical attention?

—No one's injured. We're all fine here.

—Am I supposed to just take your word on that?

—Well, we have a hospital. It's full of doctors, and nurses, and beds. You can call them if you want, or you can visit. Other than doing that, then yeah, you kind of have to take my word for it.

—I can do that, but I need you to do something for me in return.

—What's that?

—I'd like you to send all these people home. It's making everyone here nervous.

—Then why don't *you* leave? These people live here, it's you who doesn't belong.

—I'm afraid I can't do that. I have orders.

—To do what?

—Well, folks in Washington—my boss thinks there might be some kind of disease affecting all of you.

—All of us? Do I look sick to you?

—You don't. But we still have to be careful. Now if you don't mind, send these folks home, then my people will lower their weapons and you and I can talk.

—Hmmm. I do mind, though, a little.

—Well, Carole. That was me asking. Now this is me giving you an order.

The colonel puffed his chest while saying it, pouted his lips as much as he could. He was a man, a rather large one at that, and Carole assumed he was trying to sound commanding. Despite the effort, Carole was… unimpressed. She too was a man, for whatever that was worth. In fact, she was about ten thousand of them. She was *two* colonels. She was also a botanist, a beer master, a Nobel prize in chemistry. She had an IQ that couldn't be measured.

—I don't want anyone to get hurt, colonel.

—Lots of people got hurt already. It was on the news, everyone saw it.

—That was… temporary. Everything's fine now. Even you can see that.

—What happened to Frank Meyer?

—What?

—You heard me. Officer Frank Meyer. What did you do to him?

—No one did anything to him. Sadly, Frank Meyer committed suicide last night. Now I *know* you won't just take my word for that, but you can ask anyone. You can ask his wife, she's here somewhere.

—Oh, Carole. I'm sure you'll understand how a dead police officer isn't making me feel any better about this whole situation.

—I don't think your well-being played much of a part in Frank's decision. I'm sorry.

The colonel was peeved by Carole's lack of cooperation. This was a man who clearly wasn't used to having his wishes denied. The fact that it was a woman doing it might have been a contributing factor. Either way, he unholstered his pistol and gestured for the soldiers behind him to raise their weapons. Carole immediately recognized the riot guns and tear-gas launchers from her days in law enforcement and the military. Still, she continued slowly moving forward.

—Stop right there, Carole! Take one more step and I'll give the order to fire. Is that what you want?

—No.

—Then turn around and go home.

—The thing is, I don't want that either. How about you just let us be?

—Listen, Carole. I'm going to be honest with you. I need a few dozen people to surrender to me so our doctors can run some tests. Those tests come back clean, they're going to send me home and all of us can go back to our lives. So how about you and some of your friends turn yourselves in right now and save us all some trouble?

—Hmmm. That's very tempting, but I'm gonna have to say no.

—"No" isn't really an option here, Carole. We could take you by force, but we don't even have to do that. At some point, all of you will beg for us to take you in.

—I wouldn't hold my breath if I were you.

—Are you sure about that? There's no way in or out of Marquette. No food coming in, no garbage going out. Whether it's now, or tomorrow, or next week, you're going to do as I say before your people starve to death.

—Colonel—it is "colonel," right?—I appreciate you doing your job and all, but I think you'll let the food come in, and the garbage go out.

—And why would I do that?

—Because I'm standing right behind you.

The colonel turned and saw the butt of a rifle coming for his head. Carole didn't know for sure what his last solo thought was, but she could guess it was something along the lines of 'fuck me.'

47
EVELYN-MARQUETTE

Evelyn had been a doctor for over thirty years. She was a whole *bunch* of doctors now, half a dozen biologists, and a world-renowned expert in blood-borne diseases. She'd also serendipitously received the results of the whole-genome sequencing she'd ordered after examining Carole. As expected, there was nothing clear-cut about the results. What brought all these people together as one might have been the result of a combination of factors, none of which might even be genetic in nature. There was, however, an interesting missense mutation in Carole's NRXN3 gene, which encodes proteins that function as receptors in the nervous system. There wasn't a lot of literature on the subject, but Evelyn found a lone study in which a similarly located mutation was shown to cause an increase in observational fear in mice, a process thought to involve empathy. There was, of course, quite a gap between feeling someone's emotions and literally mind-melding with them, but Evelyn thought this path of investigation was at least worth pursuing.

That pursuit would unfortunately have to wait as the town had more pressing matters to attend to. Soldiers were at their doorstep, and likely preparing for a siege or some kind of assault. Evelyn knew full well an armed confrontation wasn't to their advantage, nor was it in any way necessary. They didn't *have* to do anything. Their numbers would grow no matter what they did and there was nothing the Army or anyone else could do to stop it. What the town *could* do was to speed up the process to make sure none of them were used as lab rats by overeager military doctors.

It had all begun when they'd walked to the shore to watch Frank jump off the old docks. It was a reasonably warm night for October and, this being Michigan, the mosquitoes were still out in force. By morning, hundreds of flying blood suckers had been added to the collective, along with a few cats and dogs, some mice, a couple cows and half a dozen deer the mosquitoes had bitten after tasting the townspeople. The mosquitoes didn't add much to the hive mind, except for constant blood cravings and some blurry images. Fortunately, Marquette now had the brainpower to sort out which body was in need of what and no one had turned into a walking vampire. The much-loathed insects were also extremely easy to control, like tiny RC airplanes people could maneuver at will. When Shivansh ran into the National Guard on the highway, the town had immediately sent out its newly formed air force. Remote-biting people using mosquitoes wasn't an exact science—the little buggers can't see much—but as the hours went by, more and more of Marquette was standing behind the roadblocks wearing an Army uniform. By 4:00 PM, there were few soldiers whose eyes they couldn't see from, and they decided it was time to make their move.

Evelyn stayed behind to help prepare the hospital in case the plan went awry, while thousands followed Carole on foot to meet what was left of their clueless enemy. They were still getting used to their increased numbers and it took Evelyn-Marquette a good thirty minutes to realize her body had never left her office. They had inadvertently sent Julie Brown instead. Julie was a landscaper, but she was now a doctor as much as everyone else. She was also younger and in better shape than Evelyn, so they decided not to correct their mistake. Evelyn's body sat at her desk to get up to speed on the latest literature regarding NRXN3. Her knees were acting up again and she allowed herself a glass of Patrón Estate Release. Being thousands of people had several advantages, not the least of which was that she could drink a fair amount and still be able to read with complete focus. Her knees would benefit from the numbing effects while her twenty-thousand other brains would keep her mind sharp. That was the theory, at least. It had never been put into practice until then. The prospect of getting wasted without consequence was appealing enough to the collective and Evelyn was looking forward to the results of the experiment.

48
LANA

LANA WOKE UP drowsy and confused. The sedative they'd given her had done its job and stopped her panic attack, but it would be a while before she completely recovered. She looked around and saw no one near her tent. The colonel had left with roughly half the troops stationed on the edge of Negaunee, though not before maybe-asking-her-out. Lana wasn't sure if the man had zero interpersonal skills or if he was a sociopath. The invitation would be wildly inappropriate either way—he was holding her against her will at the time—but she could at least relate to a lack of social astuteness. Regardless of the answer, his presence would be avoided at all costs, but maybe he didn't need to be locked up for the rest of his natural life.

There was little to do inside her bubble tent, and Lana spent the afternoon observing the remaining soldiers from a distance. What she saw would have been the most peculiar thing she'd ever seen, had it not been for the zombie apocalypse of the previous day. One by one, soldiers had what could only be described as some sort of seizure. Their face would twitch like they'd just licked a car battery, they'd lose their balance and have to hold onto the nearest thing, then be totally fine a moment later. After their episodes, they all began to run around camp, removing magazines from every weapon in sight. When their colleagues asked what they were doing, they just said 'Orders' and kept at it. It wasn't long before the people asking questions had their own mini-seizure, then *they* started disarming everything. They stored all the ammo inside a locked container. When they were done, one of the soldiers walked by Lana's tent holding the key to the lock. He smiled at her like they were long-lost friends and winked. All the soldiers got into their trucks and left, some towards Marquette, some heading in the opposite direction.

Lana still didn't have her keys, or any sharp object to rip a hole through the wall. Even if she managed to get out, she wasn't sure what to do next. She could walk to wherever the colonel had gone, only to be locked up again, *or* she could go into Negaunee and call for help, preferably different help. But it wasn't clear to her who the government could send, if not the very people who had just left her behind, so she did nothing. She sat in her chair in the middle of her bubble tent and waited for someone to come. About an hour later, she noticed the road on the horizon getting darker and darker. It took her a minute to realize it was filled with people, thousands of them, slowly walking towards her.

She soon recognized Carole, leading the way like a one-woman marching band at the local parade. About a billion things were going through her mind. These people were all infected, and they would very likely infect her once they reached the encampment. Whatever they'd done to Frank, they might decide to do to her. On the other hand, no one in town had tried to harm her that night. They'd offered her a chance to leave, and she'd taken it. She wondered what would have happened if she'd stayed, then guessed she was about to find out. The group stopped about five hundred feet from the camp and Carole walked the rest of the way on her own.

—Hey, Lana. It's a nice place you got there.

—They—They thought I had whatever you have.

—I know. Would you like to get out of that thing? It's got to be getting warm in there.

—Where would you take me?

—Oh, I wouldn't take you anywhere. Unless you want me to. You're welcome to come back with us, though. You can go home.

—What is going on, Carole? I don't understand what happened to everyone, to you.

—I don't know how to say it, Lana. We're… together? In a good way, I swear. You'll be with us at some point—I couldn't stop that from happening if I tried—but it doesn't have to happen right now. There's time if you're not ready. You'd better stay in there if that's the case, though, or the bugs will get you.

—The bugs?

—The mosquitoes. It's everywhere now… God, Lana, you look so scared—I'm sorry about that—but there's nothing to be scared of.

—Does it hurt?

—I don't have to bite you. I can do it with a needle. Just one prick on the finger.

—I meant does it hurt when… when whatever happens happens?

—Oh, that! No, not at all. It's… disorienting at first, but that doesn't last.

—I think I saw it happening, here, with the soldiers.

—Oh, yeah. I winked at you!

—What?

—It's… hard to explain, Lana. Just let me know what you—

—Is it mind control? Will you be able to control my mind afterwards?

—No, Lana. You and I will share a mind. Well, you, me and everyone else in town.

—I don't understand.

—For what it's worth, I don't understand everything about it either. All I can say is it's a good thing.

—But I'll be… you afterwards. I'll be exactly like you.

—Not exactly, no. You'll be like all of us, plus you, and we'll all be a tiny bit different because you're one of us. It's a bit like cooking, I suppose. Imagine we're a big stew.

—Or cake.

—Or cake, yes. And let's say you're cinnamon.

—I don't like cinnamon.

—You can be whatever you like, Lana. Vanilla. Is vanilla okay? When you mix in with the rest of us, you won't just be vanilla anymore, you'll be cake. And the whole cake will taste a bit more like vanilla.

—What if I change my mind afterwards? Can I go back?

—I don't think that's possible.

—Have you tried?

—No. What I meant is I don't think it's possible for you to change your mind. When you become one of us, you won't want to be anything else. If you did, it would mean all of us do.

—That sounds like something a disease would do to survive, make sure people don't want to get rid of it.

—It does, doesn't it? I can't tell you if we're happy being one because it's made us that way. All I can say is we *are* happy. I am. And I have reason to be! I'm here, with you, but I'm also removing someone's appendix right now. I'm making bread at Booker's and—

—And cake?

—No, no cake. Maybe later, though. My point is I'm all these different things and it wouldn't occur to me to want to go back to just being Carole. Not in a million yea—

—I think I'm ready.

—Are you sure?

—Yes. I'm ready now.

She was. She was terrified, but she *was* ready. She thought she might die, suffer horribly, lose her mind, or every other bad thing she could imagine, but there was a good chance she would finally get some answers. That's all she wanted. That's all she'd wanted from the beginning, to understand. She wanted it so much, she was willing to die for it. Carole helped her out of the tent. They exchanged a bit of blood with their index fingers, then they sat and watched the sunset together.

—It won't be long, now. I can hold your hand if you—

—Oh, no, but thank you.

Lana didn't want to explain tactile defensiveness. She didn't like itchy sweaters, clothing tags, or the insides of jackets when you can feel the seams. She hated walking barefoot on grass, and she absolutely couldn't stand holding hands with anyone. Ewww, just thinking about it… Still, Carole's offer made Lana feel a whole lot better.

PART 6

PANDEMIC

49
GIRAFFE

WHAT THE FUCK? What the actual fuck? That's what the giraffe thought, in English. He had absolutely no clue what English was or what the words meant, but he thought it anyway. Giraffe was eating leaves off a high branch when he started seeing things. Weird-ass things, too, not like a gazelle, or the weird animals that move around on four wheels. It was like that one time giraffe ate the plant you're not supposed to eat and his sister had to kick hyenas away for an hour while he barfed in the bushes. Giraffe saw his hooves tapping on black and white rectangles, only his hooves were split in five and the rectangles made this amazing sound when you pushed on them. Giraffe was scared like he had just seen a lion, but he didn't want the sound to stop. What truly fascinated giraffe was that he knew which rectangle to press to make the right sound at the right time. He didn't even have to think about it, not really. It was like walking in mud. The act required a tiny bit more attention than walking through the high grass, but not much more. It also came with a feeling of satisfaction that none of the usual things giraffe did provided. It was impossible to put in giraffe thoughts, maybe something like… 'good giraffe.' He couldn't wait to tell his sister, but realized there was nothing he could do to explain, unless his sister knew some of that English thing. That seemed highly unlike—*Whoa. My. Gawd.*

Suddenly giraffe was under water, swimming fast and breathing liquid in and out like that was fucking normal. Hot damn he was fast, like those tiny gazelles with feathery arms that galloped way up in the air. He started moving his butt left and right to propel himself but his long legs weren't ready for it and he almost fell to the ground. Okay, this was way too intense. Could anyone make it stop? Please? Oh, finally, something familiar. Savannah, and a tree, and a giraffe moving its butt left and right. And left. And right. Wow, the other giraffe's butt was moving at the exact same time giraffe was moving *his* butt. Let's try forward. Backward. Could it be…? Nah, that made no sense at all. Also, giraffe had never seen his butt, but surely it looked nothing like that. This was entertaining, though, and it wasn't scary like the underwater thing. Butt to the left. Butt to the right. He definitely wasn't looking at himself because the grass was as high as a tree. Unless of course giraffe was now small, super small, like those mini antelopes that jumped around going: 'Dik! Dik! Dik!' all the time. Whoa. Trippy. Giraffe could still see the branch he was eating from and… yeah, shtill chew on shome leavesh. That was somewhat reassuring. He may have had hooves that were split in five and he might breathe in water and maybe he was a tiny dik-screaming thing but he was still giraffe, at the very least. Giraffe had never been more than one thing at once but he had only seen the wildebeest come through fourteen times, so it was possible being more than giraffe was something that happened when one got older.

He wished he could ask his mom. Giraffe hadn't thought about his mother in years but now missed her like the day she'd been eaten. He didn't know how he should feel about that. It was a sad giraffe thought, for sure, but there was something good about remembering his mother.

It took about an hour for giraffe to get used to the way things were. He could still see all sorts of things he didn't see before, but he felt compelled to keep doing giraffe things as he always had. Giraffe had too small a brain to fully comprehend what was happening, but a large enough one to experience self-consciousness for the first time. Why was his head so fucking far from the rest of his body? Most things' heads, he now knew, were super close to the rest of them. Heck, he was now a fish and, as far as he could tell, that thing didn't even *have* a neck. Giraffe's was as tall as a tree and his head felt like a quadcopter drone, whatever that was, hovering high above the rest of it. There was really nothing giraffe could do about his neck and he figured he would just have to live with it. At least he had spots. Lots of things didn't have spots and giraffe couldn't imagine going through life without them.

50
MARIBEL DE LA BÉDOYÈRE

Maribel's grandfather was an optometrist in a small Belgian town. Her father was in the transport business and had money coming out of his ears. When he died, Maribel decided to go back to her roots and used her inheritance to buy her grandfather's shop as well as a dozen eyewear stores near her home. She did reasonably well with those, then met a man who'd invented a machine that manufactured eyeglass lenses at a fraction of the cost. She bought one machine from the man, then ten. A year later, she acquired the man's entire company. Maribel liked buying things, so she kept going. She purchased an eyeglass frame company, then another, then she bought them all. Soon, Maribel owned every lens manufacturer there was, every eyeglass frame maker, every eyewear store where you could buy them, even the optometrists who wrote the prescriptions for the glasses her company would make and sell. The sheer scale at which she operated saved so much money. She could produce a pair of designer-quality prescription glasses for under twenty dollars. What had brought Maribel to eyewear was the knowledge that people needed glasses to function, to read, to drive, to work. She was providing an essential service, changing lives one pair of glasses at a time. It was with that in mind that Maribel had decided to sell her twenty-dollar designer glasses for a grand.

She didn't just gouge prices for the rich. When Sanvi Gupta, who fixed computers in Bangalore, spent a month's salary on a pair of prescription glasses for his son, Maribel's company made a 3900% profit on them. There was nothing anyone could do about it because Maribel owned absolutely everything. Her one hundred and fifty thousand underpaid employees made and sold over eighty percent of all the eyeglasses in the world. If you went to the mall to compare prices between eyewear stores, you were choosing between Maribel, Maribel, Maribel and Maribel. Like all billionaires worth their salt, Maribel was a sociopath.

She was also a new mother. The experience had not been as life-changing as she'd expected, but those two thirty-minute sessions she spent playing with her daughter Evita every day brought her tremendous pride and satisfaction. For the last couple of weeks, Maribel had noticed people in her entourage acting with more… *disdain* was the only word that came to mind, though that seemed a bit extreme. The nanny, in particular, had more or less stopped talking to her entirely and Maribel made a note in her calendar to address the issue at their next scheduled meeting. The nanny had been with them since the start and replacing her was not something Maribel considered lightly, but her negative attitude was beginning to spill over onto the child. Evita didn't gaga or googoo at her mother anymore and if she had not been too young for such a sentiment, Maribel would have sworn that her daughter looked at her with contempt. Maribel decided to tackle the issue head-on, like she would any business problem. She purchased a six-foot-tall teddy bear and presented it to Evita during their morning session. The child seemed relatively impressed by the plush animal and Maribel was confident she'd nipped the problem in the proverbial bud. Her confidence wouldn't last. Evita soon lost interest in the giant bear and turned her attention to a pacifier laying on the coffee table. Evita moved the binky a little closer to the edge of the table, a little closer still. She pushed it again until it started wobbling, trying to decide if it would fall to the floor or not. It fell. Maribel picked up her child and gave her a tentative hug before calmly explaining that throwing things on the floor was not something people did in this family.

Maribel would learn a great many things that day, beginning with the fact that toddlers have very sharp teeth.

51
LOTS AND LOTS OF THINGS

ONCE THE MOSQUITOES joined in, it was only a matter of time before they became everything and everyone.

It was slow at first. Mosquitoes don't travel that far. Milk from infected cows didn't do the trick. Meat did, but it would take a few weeks for enough chickens and cows to merge, then be slaughtered, packaged, sold and eaten. The soldiers had gone back home all over the Midwest, but they didn't want another town to make the news until their numbers were much larger. The real shift came when it hit the water. Maybe some animal tried to catch a fish and missed, maybe it was something else, but once it was in the lake, things started moving fast. Big fish, little fish, that sort of thing. The food chain is a wonderful vector for propagation. Plankton, fish, whales, birds, seals, more mosquitoes, and, inevitably, humans. The people of Marquette weren't just from Marquette anymore, nor were they just people. They thought they were diverse before. They were, in a homogeneous American small-town sort of way. Boy, did that change fast! Within two weeks, they were reindeer herders in Sápmi, Scandinavian furries with mixed fursonas. They were the Bajau Darat, forced out of the sea to live a sedentary life, they were Lego designers, Maasai, Kazakhs, Swiss bankers and snake milkers. They were David Bowie. That was really fucking cool.

Synesthesia took some getting used to. People who hear colors, smell sounds, folks who think beef tastes oval or that the act of waiting is shaped like the letter 'K.' Synesthetics learned to live with it because they didn't know anything else, but it's a lot weirder when only a handful of your billion bodies see bright pink when they hear a G sharp. Mirror-touch synesthesia was the hardest to deal with. These people experienced physical sensations just by looking at other people. If they saw someone hit their big toe on the chair leg, their big toe would hurt like hell. Part of the challenge of being a bazillion people at once was figuring out which body needed what, and that was a lot more difficult with random bodies feeling things they shouldn't. Being other people who were nearby had been a lot more straightforward. It was easy to tell if a schizophrenic was hallucinating, since they could also see through the eyes of everyone around them. One thing was for sure, they were a lot happier as one. Also, they were David Bowie. That was really fucking cool.

They were trees too. They'd been trees for a while, they just didn't know it. They had to become Jaako Hult, a Finnish urbanist now living in Minneapolis, to figure that out. Jakko had been monitoring city park usage for his PhD. and had noticed a sudden increase in traffic despite the temperature drop. Once he merged, the collective dug a little deeper and realized people were now seeking sunlight more than before and had a tendency to stand facing the sun.

For the most part, they let the bugs and the food chain do the work, but they targeted powerful people whenever they could. Politicians, community leaders, people who would calm things down if and when they decided to expand their mind in a more forceful manner. They were in no hurry. By January, they were about 70% of the world's population and had stopped pretending in front of the other 30%. These people were really freaked out. Some tried to hide. One dude in Brazil tried to single-handedly take back control of the entire world with a machete. Most people saved themselves the trouble and asked to be brought in. It made sense. If your wife and kids were part of the collective, all your friends, every single person you interacted with, you'd probably want to be like them. Humans want a lot of things, but more than anything, they just want to belong. Why else would half the world have chosen to wear cheap cotton jackets with shoulder pads in the '80s? Those things were ridiculous. Anyway, on March 18, 2015, the world said 'fuck it' one last time and hunted down the few human holdouts left on the planet. That took a few weeks. There weren't that many people to find, but some were hiding in really strange places. Animals and plants all joined in, naturally. Humans tend to isolate themselves from everything, the environment, other species, other humans. There's a lot more contact between non-human life forms, more interconnection. Symbiosis, mutualism, commensalism, parasitism, competition, predation; all imply interaction between multiple living things. Mess with one, and it doesn't take long before all of them are affected.

Being all life on Earth had its own learning curve. For starters, it was a *lot* of sensory input to sort through. Humans had the mental bandwidth, but it took some practice. The vast majority of things lived a relatively easy-to-manage existence, being driven entirely by physical reflexes.

'Smarter' animals—no offense to the rest of them—were a bit more confusing. As a whole, being a dolphin didn't feel like being an orangutan at all, or a human, or a dog, but *part* of being a dolphin was sometimes close enough to cause trouble. Take a deep breath from the wrong body and suddenly you have a dead dolphin on your hands, then self-loathing for killing your dolphin self. Lots of things were tough to swallow. For one, life is fucking violent, and that gets weird real fast when you're the entire food chain. Does the killer whale let the seal live because it's also the seal? Does the seal let itself be caught if the killer whale is starving? Whichever way you slice it, there's a lot of gore in the end. Limbs being ripped off, bodies stripped to the bone by a thousand living things, more blood spilled in a day than one person could ever imagine. That was tough to experience for some, especially children. There *was* some trauma, that's for sure, but everyone was also a shrink, so that helped. There were also plenty of human problems to deal with, problems that are much more evident when you're both a billionaire and some kid sorting through mountains of garbage to survive. Redistributing wealth was a lot easier with everyone on board, but even then, it was a painfully slow process. The system was so messed up, it was difficult to fix without tearing it down and inflicting even more harm on a massive scale.

Still, they tried. One would even say that they did pretty well for a species only a few months old. It wasn't perfect, but for about six months, planet Earth was a much better place to live on.

Then the spheres arrived.

52
LANA–EARTH

Everyone was busy trying to fix the world. Moving money around was easy, but they had to rethink *everything*. Giant swaths of land used to cultivate one thing only, robbing the planet of entire ecosystems. Trillions of gallons of precious freshwater wasted on fucking pistachios. There were so many useless or plain damaging companies out there. A couple of centuries of entrepreneurial worship had littered the world with things that shouldn't be. Society valued ideas over real work and creating any business was seen as a worthy endeavor, no matter how poorly conceived it was. People flipping houses were called entrepreneurs. A restaurant owner could, with a straight face, say things like, 'My business will have to close if I need to pay a living wage.' (They were *sooo close* to getting it, but nope. No one got it. People blamed the greedy workers asking for ten bucks an hour instead of coming to the obvious conclusion.) One could 'short' a company on the stock market. Companies were dumping toxic chemicals everywhere because safely disposing of them wasn't 'economically feasible.' There were entire industries producing nothing but declining wages and shittier service. There was *still* leaded gasoline.

Store shelves were filled with products that could not exist without slave labor or endangering workers. There were 'Sexy Indian Halloween Costumes.' There was Uber. There were puppy farms. So many things needed to change, it felt at times like an impossible task.

Then there were the spheres to think about.

Lana had looked at those things with trillions of eyes, eyes on the sides of her head, eyes in front. She'd seen them in 2D, in 3D. She'd even seen them in infrared through the eyes of a bullfrog. They looked more or less the same in infrared. One hundred and twenty-eight metal balls surrounding the Earth in equidistant positions about 200 kilometers above the surface, keeping pace with the Earth's rotation. At least one was visible from anywhere on the planet. They'd arrived at once, seemingly instantly.

There was still much the world didn't know about the spheres. Their arrival had cleared most of low Earth orbit, wiping every satellite, as well as the ISS, out of existence. That's what people thought, at least; all they knew for sure was that the satellites weren't there anymore. They could have been elsewhere, but the most plausible explanation was that they'd been destroyed. The spheres didn't move, didn't send out any detectable signal, nor did they emit any light. Still, their shape and configuration, plus the fact that they were keeping pace with the Earth's rotation, left little doubt about one thing. This was not a natural phenomenon. There was now undeniable proof that intelligent life existed elsewhere in the universe.

More thrilling even was the fact that this life form, wherever it was from, had sent things to this very planet, to us. Why? No one knew, but the spheres were here and that was exciting. It really was, for about a week, then people stopped paying attention. In their defense, they'd been through some serious shit in a very short amount of time. The spheres, as alien as they were, didn't *do* anything. They were just dots in the sky. After a while, they became just another part of the scenery.

There *were* people at NASA gathering as much information on these things as they could. Had the world not changed, these few would have been wildly passionate about it. Unfortunately, they were also everyone else and boredom was the sentiment that prevailed. Birds were *really* into the spheres, though. Whatever these things did, they somehow enhanced birds' geolocation abilities. They had a much more precise GPS to work with and that saved them a lot of bird heartache.

Lana thoroughly enjoyed being everyone at once. She enjoyed it exactly the same as everyone else. Like everyone else, she also had a myriad of questions. How? They still didn't know. They knew how to bring someone in, but they had no understanding of what actually happened to that person. Why? Lana knew there might not be a why. It could have been blind luck, chaos, nature doing its thing. Still, she wanted to know if there was a reason for this. She wanted to know everything, that's why she'd agreed to merge in the first place. There was no need for law enforcement anymore, so her body had been reassigned as a surgeon. Everyone had the same knowledge and, in theory, everyone could do just about anything, but physical limits still applied. Certain bodies were better suited for certain tasks: Jeremiah Briggs was huge and could lift heavy crates and reach the top shelves, and so he was working in a warehouse. Lana, for her part, had very precise hands. Before the merge, she'd always thought that was a brain thing. She was indeed a meticulous person, but exact work also required the right tools, and Lana had perfect surgeon hands.

She had just performed a triple bypass on a fifty-year-old man and had gone to the cafeteria for much-needed sustenance. She was watching birds fly by through the eyes of an orderly when she noticed—when everyone noticed—something odd happening above their heads. The dot over Marquette was getting bigger and bigger.

53
LANA–EARTH

THE SPHERE OVER Marquette came down from the sky and landed on the edge of Harlow Park. None of the other spheres moved. Perhaps whoever, or *whatever*, was controlling them sensed that this was where it had all begun. The whole town came out to see the device. Lana rolled her way to the front of the crowd, but kept a good distance between her and whatever this was. The sphere was smaller than she'd pictured. She knew exactly how big it was—they'd looked at the spheres with every ground telescope in the world—but 275 centimeters felt a lot bigger in her head. The sphere was visible from the ground and had come from some place very far away. All of that suggested it was a ship of some kind. Or maybe it didn't, and she just really wanted it to be a ship of some kind. Either way, what she was staring at wasn't 'shippy' at all. It was smaller than an Austin Mini, perhaps the size of a very fat bear. It looked more like a weapon or a probe than anything one could travel in. A weapon certainly made sense. The spheres were spread evenly across the globe; if they contained anything deadly, the whole surface of the planet could be covered with it in no time. Oddly, that thought made Lana bolder, and she moved closer to the metal ball. There would be little point in sending something halfway across the galaxy just to hurt one person, and if this *was* a doomsday device, standing twenty feet away wouldn't make much of a difference. Lana leaned forward in her wheelchair and extended her arm to touch it. She felt some sort of static a couple inches from the surface and removed her hand immediately. Then she heard a click. It was just a small click, like that of a ballpoint pen, but it scared the crap out of everyone on Earth. Her seven billion human heartbeats were just beginning to slow down when the sphere split in half. There was a loud *pshhhhhh,* then the top part slid back inside the bottom half. The bowl it made was filled with white smoke that sloooowly dissipated to reveal... some kind of animal. It was about the size of a naked mole rat, greyish pink. It also *looked* like a naked mole rat, with a tiny tail, like a—It *was* more or less a naked mole rat, except from space.

This was, without doubt, one of humanity's most significant moments, perhaps *the* most significant moment. They were making first contact with a sentient alien species. Well, they assumed it was sentient. It could have been the alien equivalent of an actual rat they'd thrown inside the ball, like we shot Laika, and fruit flies, and rabbits into space. Nah, that thing was sentient. Lana wasn't sure how she knew, but she knew. The alien mole rat wasn't exactly pretty, but it was small, and from space, and kind of cute compared to all the things it *could* have been (like a giant squid, or some blob with a thousand eyes, and teeth, *inside* its eyes—ewww). The rat was very much non-threatening, and it grew on you pretty quick. It certainly grew on Lana. She didn't dare touch the thing, but she moved her face within inches of it. It was much cuter from up close.

Its mouth was minuscule, and it curled up like that of a quokka. Maybe it *was* smiling. It was everyone's first space rat, so it was impossible to tell. Lana was wondering what they were supposed to do with it. It might have been hungry—it had been in that ball for months—but they couldn't just feed it kibble and hope it didn't die. Though it didn't look the part, space rat *was* the more advanced species and therefore the one who should dictate the terms of this close encounter, at least in theory. Lana backed off a bit to give the critter some space to think. She waited and waited. Maybe the kibble thing wasn't such a bad—*whoa!* Space rat stood up on its hind legs, like a hairless meerkat. It moved its head around to look at everyone, then it spoke. Well, not really. Its little mouth didn't move, but Lana heard it speak very clearly. She heard it everywhere, all at once, through forty billion billion ears… Okay, so some of those weren't *technically* ears. She heard it through her fruit fly antennas, through her grasshopper abdomen. She heard it through her cricket forelegs and her lacewing wings. Every human body of hers heard it in its own language, words spoken softly, like a secret.

—We wish to speak to the many.

The what? The ma—Oh, shit. Lana-Earth smiled the biggest smile as she, as *they all*, understood what the rat meant. Everything that had happened to them must have been this being's doing. The tick, Carole biting Booker, merging minds together until there was only one, it was all in preparation for this, a prelude to an introduction. Whatever this species was, wherever they were from, they would not speak to one. That made sense, for every *one* is different. *One* is self-interest, contradiction. *One* is looking at the world through a drinking straw. They could never understand us by talking to a person. They had to talk to everyone, and so they had *made* an everyone.

That was freakishly cool, and equally intimidating. How the hell is anyone supposed to answer that? Whatever, Lana had to give it a go. She leaned over the rat again, took a deep breath, and told it who she was.

—My name is Lana. I am woman, man, neither and everything in between. I am every shade of skin, every shape and size. I am the Anishinaabe, the Ainu, the Belgians. I am a hundred years old. I am a newborn in her mother's arms. I am joy hearing its first cry. I am pain hearing every other cry. I am mother, father, brother. I am hunger and desire. I am love. I am memories of the perfect sunrise. I am death, a mother lion eating her own cubs, the ant gnawing at the wolf's carcass. I am hope. I am the glass squid hiding in the far depths, a flock of birds crossing the wild sea. I am the oak tree mocking the wind, daisies turning their heads to face the light. I am Junko Tabei climbing Everest only because it is there. I'm a friggin' cosmonaut. I am a goldfish, a Bryde's whale eating sardines eating plankton eating other plankton. I am irony, seduction. I am war. I am the hummingbird fighting for dominance. I am friend, lover, stranger and enemy. I am an elephant. I am a two-thousand-year-old fungus spanning two thousand acres. I am smaller than the eye can see. I am disease, microbe, parasite. I am the cat headbutting a chair leg. I am the cat lady giving it a home. I am a lighthouse keeper, a paper pusher, a baker

> killed on the side of the road. I am injustice. I am mourning. I am forgiveness. My name is Lana, and I am the many.

Lana had forgotten to mention David Bowie, but thought she'd done pretty well under the circumstances. The rat paused for a second while looking at her, and then it spoke again.

—You are so much more than that.

54
LANA–EARTH

THE KNOWLEDGE RUSHED into Lana's head like a tsunami tearing through a coastal town. Even with all the brains in the world, it was more than she could handle. Too much and too fast. She collapsed to the ground. Her body started to seize. Lana was convulsing like a fish out of water, utterly blind and convinced she was about to die. She welcomed it. She'd have done anything to quiet the rumble in her head.

The rumble did quiet. The seizure stopped. Lana still couldn't process everything, but her mind felt like it had somehow come loose from her body. She wasn't Lana anymore; she wasn't the many. The world around her felt… it didn't feel at all. It was neither cold nor warm. She couldn't see, or hear, or touch or smell. The words themselves meant nothing anymore. She desperately wanted to speak, though, to ask the one question that was consuming her: *What am I?*

Slowly, bit by bit, the answer came into focus. She was… Was that a rock? Yes. A small brownish pebble stuck in the sole of her shoe, a larger rock, a few feet away, providing shade to a yellow-spotted millipede. She was a large chunk of sedimentary rock thirty feet below that. She was a tectonic plate, slowly moving for over three billion years. She was the Earth. Brittle crust, thick mantle. Molten metal violently churning around its solid iron core. She was petrichor, that earthy smell when it's about to rain. She was the rain, the river, the lake. She was a cold ocean below Europa's ice shell, constantly stirred by the moon's gravity. She was a red storm, a swirling mass of gas twice as big as the Earth, defacing Jupiter's surface. She was the rings of Saturn, myriad ice particles dancing around a huge ball of gas. She was the smaller rings around Uranus, she was its eleven moons. She was Kepler-16b orbiting its two suns, the sizzling 55 Cancri e, circling its star so close it does it every eighteen hours. Lana was rocks, planets and moons. She was asteroids and moonmoons.

She was a cloud of gas and dust collapsing on itself, pressure mounting, squeezing atoms until there was enough heat to ignite fusion. She was a newborn star. She was thousands upon thousands of them. She was the Orion nebula. She was a blindingly bright quasar powered by a supermassive black hole. She was a pulsar spinning beams of light like a galactic lighthouse. She was nuclear pasta, protons and neutrons in the husk of a dead star, squished together so hard that they formed the strongest substance in the universe.

She was primordial goo. She was a cluster of unicellular organisms the size of our solar system, eating asteroids for lunch and planets for supper. She was a giant snake in a methane ocean around Gliese 581. She was entire civilizations. Stick-figures building two-dimensional worlds, green gooey things that could bend space and time. She was the weird space rat. She was Junko Tabei climbing Everest only because it is there. She was a small pebble stuck under her shoe. Lana wasn't just the many, she was fucking *everything*.

Lana woke up gasping for air. Was this a dream? Was *all of it* a dream? For a second, she feared waking in her room, alone, watching the world through only one set of eyes. Slowly, she began to see. She saw herself lying on the ground, she saw the Eiffel Tower, tall buildings casting their shadows on a Taiwan alley. She saw the little rat's face looking down at her above the rim of his metal space bowl. Not a dream.

Lana and every living thing on Earth felt a warmth inside them they hadn't thought possible. There was an obvious connection between all of them—they were each other—but they'd always seen it as artificial, the side effect of whatever phenomenon had begun in Marquette. But not only was that connection real, it went beyond anything they'd ever imagined. They were one with the entire universe, because *every single thing* in there was made of the same stuff. The alien had come with just one simple message: there is only *one* thing.

That really put things in perspective. Not that being every living thing on Earth hadn't been effective, but being one with the *whole universe* will really do a number on your priorities. There was only one thing. The best people could do, then, the *only* thing they could do as a tiny, tiny part of the one thing, was to try and make it a tiny, tiny bit better. Save a tree. Pick up their trash. Make someone happy. Everything else, strangers they didn't trust, wars fought over dead plants that had fallen to the bottom of the sea before the dinosaurs were even born, millions slaughtered because they prayed to the wrong god, the right god, lines on a map, telling people who they were allowed to love, where they were allowed to sit, it was all bullshit. It was pixie dust thrown into the air to make the throwers feel like they mattered more, more than plants, animals, the Earth, more than other people. That's what the rat meant: 'You're not special. You're amazing! But so is everything else, so take care of each other.' Okay, that's *probably* what the rat meant. People weren't a hundred percent sure, but that's what they got out of it, anyway.

And that's all they *would* get out of it. The space rat disappeared under the top half of its ball-shaped ship. It had done what it had come to do and evidently wasn't interested in chit chat, or kibble. Lana watched the sphere rise into the sky, then vanish entirely. Within seconds, every sphere around Earth was gone and every artificial satellite returned from God knows where to its original orbit.

55

LAYLA–EARTH

Layla wanted to see the space rat again. They knew Earth and everything on it was one with the universe, but knowing it wasn't enough. For a split second, they had *been* the entire universe. But the space rat had taken that feeling with it when it left. Like a bunch of addicts chasing their first high, the people assumed the space rats could give the feeling back. Twelve hours after the spheres were gone, Earth was already planning for their next encounter. They would multiply humanity's efforts towards space exploration so that they could, someday, seek the rodents out. It was hard to tell how long that could take; humans weren't even sure they could land on the Moon again. They'd need to do that first, then go to Mars, then find a way to go a million times farther. That wouldn't be easy, for sure, but being seven billion times smarter than plain Jane or ordinary Joe was bound to make progress a lot quicker. In the six months before the spheres arrived, they'd managed to cure about half of cancers and prevented Alzheimer's entirely. They were also close to bringing quantum entanglement communication to the masses after discovering RF signals from too many cell phones were harmful to the brain. They were kicking ass, from a scientific perspective, and travelling beyond the realm of our solar system seemed well within reach.

Whatever technology would be needed for interstellar travel, the space rat obviously possessed. There was hope, however small, that it might have left something behind, either by mistake, or as a clue for humans to follow. It could have been anything: a piece of metal, a unique rock, or something invisible, maybe an electromagnetic signature they could use to track the space rodent back to its home world. They needed to act fast. Being absolutely everyone meant that no one would accidentally disturb the site where the sphere had touched down, but for all their brainpower, people still couldn't control the weather. Five minutes of rain might have been all it took to rob humanity of whatever precious gift still lay in Harlow Park.

The world decided to send Mark Bedford. Mark was an electrician with near-perfect eyesight, and he had a decent gauss meter at home. He also lived right next to the park and didn't need to work until evening. The plan was for him to do a preliminary survey while more sophisticated instruments were delivered to the landing site. Unfortunately, they couldn't find Mark, nor could they see through his eyes, so they figured he was still asleep. Sleep was an interesting phenomenon they had been studying for a few months. Folks disappeared from the hive mind when they lost consciousness, which suggested they slept, and most importantly dreamed, as individuals. The most likely hypothesis was that it allowed the mind to rest and lightened the load of being a whole planetful of living things all the time. Whatever the reason, Mark Bedford was in the land of Nod, and someone had to get him out of there so he could comb through Harlow Park. Layla just happened to be in the neighborhood. They were usually working at Booker's Bakery, but would switch tasks every now and then to spend time outside and get some exercise. On that day, Layla was delivering mail. That was mostly unnecessary since no one had any reason to send a letter to themselves, but they'd kept doing it for sentimental reasons. Layla adjusted their mail route to stop by Mark's house early. They knocked on the door, waited a few seconds, then rang when they still couldn't see through Mark's eyes. Nothing. They rang again, and again. Layla played the entire Imperial March on the doorbell and, when that didn't work, they remembered no one locked their doors anymore and went in.

Privacy had become a very vague notion, but entering someone's home uninvited still felt awkward somehow, especially when the person was asleep. Layla tiptoed their way to the bedroom, but found the bed empty. They began to consider the possibility that Mark might be dead. They'd have known if he'd been hit by a car or something—they'd have felt it—but they'd be none the wiser if he'd died in his sleep. Death didn't mean much to people anymore. Booker's murder had been a traumatizing experience, but they were only four at the time. They were dying millions of times every day by then, from a heart attack, squished by a pedestrian's foot, eaten by an orca. Death was part of the natural order of things and one being's death was no more noticeable than that of a cell in a larger organism. Still, Mark Bedford having kicked the bucket would have been an inconvenience—they had zero clue where he kept his gauss meter—and Layla kept on looking. They went to the guest room, the living room. They were about to try the garage—maybe Mark had fallen asleep in his car; people slept in the weirdest places—when they heard a very weak, high-pitched sound coming from the end of the corridor. It sounded like a puppy or someone with severe emphysema trying to play the flute.

Layla entered the bathroom and found Mark Bedford awake, curled up into a ball on the shower floor and moaning like a baby. Layla was confused as they still couldn't experience his point of view, so they did something they hadn't done in almost a year. They spoke.

—Ssss… Ahem. Sir? Are you… Okay?

Mark Bedford looked up at Layla. He opened his mouth to speak, but started crying again before he could say anything. Layla knelt down and put a hand on Mark's shoulder. He grabbed it with his and squeezed hard enough it hurt. He wouldn't let go. He also wouldn't speak, and Layla thought he might have gone mute. It happens! Finally, he managed to get a few words out.

—It's gone.

—What's that mean, sir?

—It's just me, now. I'm all alone.

56
EVELYN–EARTH

MARK BEDFORD WAS screwed. The poor guy was already traumatized by losing his connection to everyone else, and he would soon be the most poked and probed person in the history of poking and probing. The rest of the world didn't bear any ill will towards him, but his personal discomfort meant very little when weighed against the possibility that more people would suffer this fate. Still, it was thought that shipping him to a research center halfway across the world would be cruel and unusual. A nearby location meant he could see his wife and children during his ordeal. Technically, his wife and children were everyone and he could have talked to them anywhere, but having them physically present seemed important to him. Evelyn had been Mark's family doctor for years and she was chosen as the world's avatar, her office becoming the epicenter of the scientific world for the foreseeable future. They kept the office itself as cozy as possible and filled the rest of the building with every piece of technology known to man or woman.

The first avenue of research chosen was the missense variants in the NRXN3 gene first detected in Carole's blood samples. As expected, Mark's DNA didn't show the same mutation. The question was: had he had the mutation before, while he was part of the collective? Conversely, would adding the same mutation to his NRXN3 gene help him reconnect?

They analyzed the genomes of a hundred different people and found that each and every one of them had the same mutation, but that wasn't sufficient to establish causality. It could simply have been a side effect of the connection, or one of several factors working in conjunction.

The biggest problem was, of course, an ethical one. Editing genes in a living human was at least theoretically possible. Recombinant DNA had been around since the early '70s, and the discovery of zinc-finger nucleases in the '80s had allowed scientists to target specific DNA sequences more easily. A few years later the first genetically altered corn, containing genes from the bacteria *Bacillus thuringiensis*, had been seen on American fields. Then food scientists had discovered that a particular yoghurt-making bacteria was creating its own immune defense against viruses. When infected, the bacteria would take small chunks of the virus's DNA and insert them into their own in segments known as CRISPR arrays. This would revolutionize gene editing, but it was still in its infancy. Nothing close to what would be required had ever been attempted, let alone on a person.

Mark Bedford was not only alive but in perfect health. There was, in fact, an argument to be made that Mark Bedford was the only person on the planet who *was* well. In the end, and despite his insistence to the contrary, it was decided that messing with Mark's genes using experimental techniques with no predictable outcome was not a morally acceptable risk.

Other solutions were explored, including the most basic ones. No one would dare bite Mark in case whatever *he* had was contagious, but they injected him with every kind of body fluid. They tried saliva, blood, of course. They performed a bone-marrow transplant, a cerebrospinal fluid transfusion. When all that failed, they decided to give him a skin graft, to see if prolonged exposure would work. A surgeon removed a small square of skin from the butt of Mark's wife. He was about to close the wound when he paused and started shaking uncontrollably. Everyone in the world lost sight of Mark's wife's ass at once and they understood the surgeon wasn't one of them anymore. The disconnection was spreading. Perhaps Mark was indeed contagious, and his mere proximity was enough to affect the surgeon. Mark was placed in a negative pressure tent they'd gotten from the military, and everyone evacuated the building. They would return with disinfection equipment and sanitize the hell out of every place he'd been in the last few days. (The wife's *derriere* was also taken care of.)

It had been an exhausting and scary day for everyone, but some people sweated more than others. Evelyn desperately needed a bath. She headed home while people in hazmat suits set up ultraviolet disinfection units in the building. She was barely a block away when she felt something… odd in Africa. The continent felt different, somehow. The entire world focused on it to figure out what was wrong. There was indeed a young boy in Equatorial Guinea who'd lost his link to the collective, but a single person missing wouldn't have that effect on everyone. (It hadn't when Mark disappeared, nor had they felt anything when the butt surgeon did.) It had to be something else. Evelyn had time to walk another block before the planet figured it out. *There were no lions anymore.* The lions were gone, and so were the rest of the big five: rhinos, elephants, leopards and buffalos. Not just some, all of them. The planet let out a collective 'FUCK' that could have been heard light years away.

Evelyn made it to her place a few minutes later. She was running her bath when all the lights in the house went off. She looked through the window: power was out on the whole block. There was no one on the street with whose eyes to see through, so Evelyn got dressed and went back out to see what had happened. There'd been an accident at the corner: a car had knocked down an electric pole. The driver was walking around aimlessly. She looked completely lost, like she'd skipped the arrows and taken a shortcut at Ikea. Evelyn asked the woman for her address and took her there so she could be with her family. This was… bad. First it was Mark Bedford, then the surgeon, a kid in Africa, all the fucking lions. What were the odds it would stop there? Evelyn didn't want to think about the answer. She walked back home, got undressed and turned the water on. She really smelled like a gym locker, but it was the whole world who needed that bath.

57
ALMOST EVERYONE

(ALMOST) EVERYONE WAS working overtime to find a solution, but they were quickly running out of time. Animals and plants were all gone by sunrise. Only people were left, and they were dropping from the collective faster and faster by the hour. By noon, the world could no longer keep track of how many people it was losing. A good third of the population was gone from the hive mind when the other two-thirds finally accepted the obvious. There would be no stopping this. In less than twenty-four hours, every person on Earth would return to being just that, a person.

They should have seen it coming. If the merging of minds had been nothing but foreplay to the space rat encounter, there was no reason for it to survive its departure. It had served its purpose, like a mother's milk when the child is old enough, or those Cadbury commercials: 'Just until Easter, then they'll be gone.' Only it wasn't egg-shaped candy being removed from store shelves, it was the strength, the intelligence, the sheer presence of trillions of minds and bodies being yanked out of people. It didn't matter how well-adjusted, smart or confident one was beforehand, they were billions of times that as part of the collective. This was like an ant becoming Mozart, and then becoming an ant again. To some, it was unbearable. The first to be hit suffered the most—they lost more, all at once—and most of the suicides happened in the first few hours. The rest would go through it piecemeal, losing themselves bit by bit until their turn came and they were removed from whatever was left.

How people coped also depended on their situation before they'd joined. It was obviously easier to go back to being a movie star than it was to return to panhandling, but the return of billions of people in place of one also meant the return of prejudice and all sorts of injustice. There'd always been a possibility that this would happen eventually, and so they had fixed a few things along the way, just in case: multinational monopolies had been ground up into manageable pieces, social nets expanded, minimum wage was now a living wage, healthcare had been nationalized everywhere, and the right to clean air and water had been inserted into just about every constitution. Still, it would be a rude awakening for some more than others. Money meant something again and it was still quite markedly spread along geographical and racial lines. Poor neighborhoods had improved somewhat, but not enough to give residents the same opportunities others were afforded by birth. Lots of hard-working folks who had started businesses would find they no longer existed because they'd been deemed redundant or useless. That may have been true, but it was no less heartbreaking (except for the guy selling Pikachu dreamcatchers, that guy really deserved it). Schools didn't exist anymore, and neither did law enforcement, newspapers, etc. So many essential jobs were gone, there was bound to be chaos for a while. It would take years for things to settle down and for everyone to find their place in the new/old world.

That wasn't what scared people the most, though. No one on Earth had been *alone* since the merge, not even for a minute. The prospect of living by oneself in a one-bedroom apartment felt like a life sentence. Even those with families had a lot to worry about. They'd been in perfect harmony during their time as one because nothing ever went unsaid. Unspoken expectations, jealousy, self-pity. All these things were likely coming back, accumulating like sediment to build the same old walls between them. As terrifying as it was for everyone, dwelling on the inevitable was a huge waste of time, and the dwindling collective chose to work on the one thing they could control. They couldn't save people from sudden cognitive loneliness, but they could make sure no one was actually *alone* when it happened. People gathered in parks, in arenas, on the streets, large groups made up of smaller groups. They wanted the first thing people saw as individuals to be their loved ones, or at least someone they knew. They held hands, hoping the constant physical sensation would make the transition easier. Some people had had no one in their lives before the merge, so they were given a someone. It was easy to guess who they'd get along with, everyone had been everyone for some time.

Short of a few exceptions, like Mark Bedford, the last people to join were the first to leave. All of Asia went back to normal, followed by Africa, then Europe. The remaining North American hive mind rapidly shrunk inwards until all that remained were the people of Marquette. Everyone in town gathered on the Northern Michigan University campus, forming clusters of family and friends. One person would start crying and be consoled by those close to them. When everyone in their small group had lost their connection, they'd leave, and the remaining townspeople would tighten their ranks. Soon, more than half the town was gone. Those who were left assembled in the Yooper Dome. The connected sat in the stands together. When their turns came, they hugged the people next to them and went down on the field. They waved while everyone cheered them on, then they went home. Slowly, the crowd grew thinner, the cheers quieter. By midnight there were only four people left.

Layla, Shivansh, Carole and Evelyn waited and waited. The empty stadium was now cold as hell and, after an hour, they decided to move their goodbye party to Carole and Shivansh's place.

58

LAYLA–SHIVANSH–CAROLE–EVELYN

THEY'D STOPPED BY Evelyn's office on the way and grabbed the bottle of Barrique de Ponciano Porfidio Añejo she kept in her safe. She'd been saving it for years, waiting for a special occasion that never came. This seemed to qualify. It was also fitting. Only three thousand bottles had ever been produced and they assumed most of them had been consumed by then. This was one of the last few, just like them.

Layla sat on a chair next to Shivansh. Carole and Evelyn took the couch in front of them. They remembered how strong they'd felt when they were the only ones. Four was so much better than one, but nothing compared to a thousand, to a million, a billion. Four now felt incredibly puny. They were but an infinitesimal fraction of their former self. Their little circle was also full of questions. Layla had moved into that house not long after Booker died. The whole justice system had been put on pause since the merge, but, eventually, someone would decide what would happen to them. Would Shivansh and Carole still want to be their guardians if the judge allowed it? They all thought so, but they'd never made that decision as individuals. In 'real life,' these people had almost nothing in common. Would they even be friends? The answer to that question also seemed obvious, but they were still one person. Everything might change in a minute, or an hour. Layla was twelve. Almost thirteen, but that was still noticeably less than Evelyn's sixty-two. Carole and Shivansh were smack dab in the middle, twenty-plus years older and younger, and they were a couple. They might not want a kid or an old lady in their lives. As improbable as that seemed in the moment, they couldn't ignore one simple fact. They never had before.

Whoa. Vertigo. Suddenly, Evelyn was the only person they were looking at. They couldn't see what Evelyn saw. They felt younger in a very bad way, inexperienced, insecure. They couldn't remember the war. They didn't know how to dress a wound, or what the symptoms of porphyria were, or how to make her famous Kugel anymore. They'd forgotten the sheer joy of bringing a baby into the world and—ewwww—they fucking *hated* tequila. They felt so fucking empty. They couldn't begin to imagine what the doctor was going through. It was devastating for them, but Evelyn had just lost three quarters of herself. She was a tough cookie, though, or at least she played the part well. She just got up and grabbed her jacket.

—Well… It's been nice being you all. I better go,
now. I have a feeling my office will be packed in
the morning.

Evelyn hugged Layla, Carole and Shivansh, then smiled and left the house.

And then there were three. They'd done their best to act cool until Evelyn was gone, but they were fucking terrified. The simple fact of existing was unfamiliar. For one thing, they'd never been *these* three, and three felt so… Three felt like being three, on the soccer field, when the other team isn't eleven but the entire world. Three was horrible and yet it was two more than one. Layla grabbed Shivansh's hand to reassure themselves while Carole could still feel it. Who would go next was the big question. Part of them, two-thirds to be precise, hoped it would be Layla. At least, there'd be two people around to help them through it. The other third of them wanted to go last, not yet realizing that two would go last, and not one.

Layla felt Shivansh's hand stiffen and their four eyes turned to him. Layla's adoptive father/husband always had this intimidating stern look on his face, but at that moment, he looked like a lost puppy. Shivansh started crying and Layla wrapped him in their arms. After a second or two, Shivansh pushed Layla away and went to sit next to Carole. He knew they were the same person, but he couldn't help it. Layla wasn't his wife to him anymore, and hugging a twelve year-old who, under different circumstances, might want to jump your bones was way too much for him to handle at the time. He lay down on Carole's lap and did his best to stop crying while she brushed his hair with her fingers. He quickly fell asleep, exhausted by the day's events.

And then there were two. Layla took a moment to realize what they'd lost. They didn't see Carole the same way anymore, like, not at all. They didn't like themselves as much. Shivansh had a way of not loving his wife they were missing terribly. They couldn't remember Mumbai. Neither could Shivansh, really. What he remembered were the sensations, the heat, the smells, the thickness of the air. They'd lost so many memories that day, billions of lifetimes worth, but these memories belonged to someone they cared deeply for and losing them was—Oh, no. *No!* Layla and Carole grew angry, panicked. They were about to lose each other's memories, but also Booker's, the few he'd made after he'd merged with Carole. In a way, Booker had never fully died. Now, he was about to. They would always remember him, but what it felt to *be* him, if only in part, that would be lost forever. Layla would lose their father, again. They would just be a kid again, alone and unable to control most things in their life. They would have nothing, absolutely fucking nothing. They couldn't handle that, not then, not ever.

Layla sat on the carpet and laid their head on Carole's free leg. They both begged a God they didn't believe in for Layla to drift off before the inevitable happened. It probably wouldn't be easier to accept in the morning, but who knew? It certainly couldn't be harder. Their prayers were answered, and for the very last time, Layla fell asleep as more than just Layla.

And then there were none.

PART 7

RECOVERY

(THREE YEARS LATER)

59
CAROLE

THE SHOPPER ROUTE bus turned the corner and Carole stepped closer to the curb as it drew near. She raised her purse over her head when she walked under the tree—the ticks were out of control that summer. This was her last day at the ad agency. She'd only worked part-time the past three years; advertising hadn't gotten back to its old self yet. She'd used the opportunity to go back to school. Being the oldest person in her class was daunting, but she was motivated. She'd graduated in two years and had just passed the registered nurse exam. She was already moonlighting as a physical therapist and her friend Evelyn had gotten her an interview at the hospital. Dr. Schlapp had even promised to hire her if she didn't get the job, but Carole knew she was just being nice. Changing career at that age was a huge step, but Carole needed it. She'd known that the moment she'd woken up as Carole again.

There were lots of changes in Carole's life. Not long after losing her connection to Shivansh, she'd begun feeling… like she'd lost her connection to Shivansh. They didn't fight or anything. Their life together was more or less the same as it had ever been. That was the problem. Carole wanted things she'd never wanted before, and Shivansh couldn't or wouldn't keep up. She wanted to watch new movies, not the same ones they'd seen a million times. She wanted to go camping. They never, ever, went camping. She wanted to be on top. She wanted to eat spicy food. Okay, maybe camping wasn't that big of a deal. She couldn't stand bugs and she never could sleep on an inflatable mattress, let alone the tiny foam ones. This wasn't about camping, or spicy food. Carole just wanted… something else.

Over time, she'd realized she just wanted to be loved. She wanted to be *loved*, not liked or valued or appreciated. She didn't want to be comfortable like an old pair of jeans. Was that too much to ask? Carole was well aware that she wasn't particularly attractive, not in the magazine or TV sense of the word. She was in her mid-forties, short and a little chubby. There was nothing notably unique or endearing about her physique. Brown hair, brown eyes, a semi-flat nose and a semi-weak chin. Carole was all that, but she was fucking *stardust*. She was a bit *more* of it than she'd have liked, but she was a hundred percent stardust. That wasn't something you *like*, or value, or appreciate. That was something you love and adore and—Oh, fuck yeah, she needed a divorce. Shivansh was a good man and he'd been nothing but kind to her during all those years, but he was more of a friend than anything else. He *was* a friend, her best one at that, and God willing he'd still be that when the dust settled.

The dust hadn't settled yet. They'd sold the house and bought two small condos in the same building. Things had gone remarkably well between them until Carole met Joshua Adams in nursing school. Jo-shu-a… That had such a good ring to it. He was twelve years younger than her and absolutely gorgeous. No, really, he'd been a real model and everything. She'd been utterly convinced he was gay the first time he'd spoken to her. He wasn't, and he fell in love with her like a sack of bricks thrown out a tenth-floor window. He *worshipped* her. They were still in the sex-four-times-a-day part of their relationship and that was, understandably, a bit more than Shivansh could handle. Still, their coexistence was amicable. He was distant, though. That hurt her, but she knew she'd hurt him too. As weird and shallow as it sounded, that made her feel better. They weren't sharing a life anymore, but they still shared something, even if it was pain.

It wasn't just Carole who'd changed. The whole world was different, at least for Carole. She didn't know if it was like that for everyone, but she felt more respect, more kindness from the people around her, from strangers even. She didn't get catcalled by construction workers anymore. The cashier at the grocery store didn't *throw* the bag at her in furious anger. She… handed it out vigorously, with barely a glimmer of annoyance in her gaze. Every single person on the planet missed being part of the collective like crazy, and Carole was no exception. Still, maybe some good had come of it. Collective or not, they *were* part of something bigger, they just couldn't always feel it. It was like carrying an emerald in your pocket your whole life—Carole had never liked diamonds, but emeralds were okay. You might forget it was there after a while, but that didn't really matter, it was still in your pocket whether you remembered or not.

Carole laughed out loud when her phone buzzed for the third time on the bus ride. She'd told Joshua they wouldn't see each other that evening and he was texting like he'd never see her again. Carole had a meeting with Lana

Lannister that night. The new chief of police had started a community outreach program and was looking for volunteers to help set it up. Carole really wanted nothing to do with it—she was too busy having sex with Jo-shu-a—but Lana had roped her in during her physical therapy sessions. Lana was doing pretty good. She'd been walking without a cane for a while and could even jog a little. She was still giddy as hell, though. That was fucking annoying.

60
SHIVANSH

CAROLE HAD ASKED for a divorce. That hadn't come as a surprise, he'd seen it coming for a while. He was just glad it had taken her that long to get the courage to do it. That was petty, he knew, but he liked having her in his life, and he wanted to enjoy it for as long as he could even if he knew he'd lose her eventually. It was over now, and he was sad about it, but in a manageable way. The new guy was harder to digest. He'd been replaced by a child! Well, almost a child, a naive puppy who couldn't keep his hands off her and—Alright, alright. Fortunately for Shivansh, that feeling wouldn't last long. He wouldn't allow it to. Jealousy was *way* too strong an emotion for him to experience on a daily basis. Besides, Carole deserved it. She deserved whatever she wanted. If she'd wanted to be with a woman, he'd have just dealt with it. He wouldn't have felt smaller or hurt because he was less of a woman than her new lover was. The kid was no different. She wanted something new, and he was the same.

Well, not entirely the same. He had, through other people's eyes, come to realize that his life could, at times, be considered uninspiring. He recalled all the excitement he'd felt when he'd shared a mind with more daring people.

Part of him wished he could relive it, but that was a very small part of him. The bigger part had never had much appetite for strong emotions. Bold was just something he wasn't and there was no sense pretending otherwise. He did, however, remember fondly how much he, Carole and Booker enjoyed watching birds when they were only three. Shivansh constantly strived to better himself and push his limits. Birding, he thought, *was* a passion, and one he could give himself to without feeling lost all the time. He also had a near photographic memory and his spontaneous remarks about plumage and nesting habits made quite an impression in his new circle of friends. Little did he suspect that Martha Smith, who lived across the street, was also an avid bird-watcher. She hadn't been before the merge, but she'd since stopped spying on her neighbors, or calling the police whenever black people enjoyed a picnic at the park. That freed up her schedule quite a bit, and birding was a way to pass time and put her keen sense of observation to good use. She and Shivansh had hit it off right away. They'd recognized in each other the same brand of rigidity that had made both their social lives more challenging than most. They'd even had dinner a few times. Those weren't dates, they were simply hungry at the same time after walking in the woods together. He'd since reduced the frequency of their outings when he began experiencing mild flutters of apprehension, but he was confident the butterflies in his stomach would soon die… or fly away on their own.

He was filing taxes for a non-profit when he realized he was still missing W-3s from Booker's Bakery and—Oh, shit! What time was it? Oh, god, 4:30. He was in trouble now. He imagined Booker laughing from beyond the grave because he knew Shivansh was going to get an earful from his kid. The two of them volunteered together at the soup kitchen twice a week and they... oh, yeah, they were going to be late. Shivansh had always given money to charitable causes on principle, but had found cooking for and serving others to be much more fulfilling than he'd imagined. The space rat was right. The best people could do was to try and make the one thing a tiny bit better. He wasn't sure how much filing taxes really helped the one thing, but serving a hot meal to someone hungry most certainly did.

Shivansh petted Louise behind the ear and rushed out. Wait. Did we mention he'd gotten a cat? He had. Carole had suggested it when she'd filed for divorce. Shivansh thought it was ridiculous, but this *was* Carole's last act as his wife and, as such, deserved due consideration. He'd gone to the shelter after a few days and asked for the oldest cat they had—he was exhausted just looking at the kittens. Louise had had a rough life until then and both the cat and Shivansh entered their relationship with low expectations. They had now lived together for a few months and they regretted nothing. Shivansh never loved his cat. He liked it very much, which was exactly what Shivansh wanted. Louise was surprisingly intelligent for something with a brain the size of a walnut, fiercely independent. She slept for sixteen hours a day and didn't like to be petted for more than ten seconds at a time. For the most part, she just lay there and did nothing, yet provided a soothing presence he'd quickly grown accustomed to. The cat was perfect, in the least exciting sense of the term.

61
EVELYN

EVELYN HAD JUST returned to her office from the rabbi's funeral. Being in the same room as his wife was… awkward. The rabbi had spilled lots of secrets in twenty years. Both women had also shared a mind for a while and respected each other, in a somewhat spiteful way. There was an unspoken covenant between them that would not be broken. The wife would never mention the affair, and Evelyn would forget about the wife stealing from the temple. Tit for tat. Unfortunately, it wasn't just the wife, *everyone* had been the rabbi and knew of his feelings for Evelyn. She felt like she owed the man her presence, but the looks and whispers took their toll on her. She'd have killed for a shot of tequila, but she'd quit drinking entirely. It wasn't by choice. It was God finally handing her the punishment she'd always expected. Hepatitis B, from the rabbi of course. She'd always thought she was the worse sinner for corrupting a man of God, but God, if he existed, apparently held the man of God to a higher standard. The rabbi had died of liver cancer. Evelyn had gotten away with cirrhosis, a slap on the wrist by divine wrath standards.

She felt guilty for going to the funeral, which only left time for a handful of patients that afternoon. Evelyn was sixty-four, and well aware that every birthday brought her closer to professional obsolescence. She'd actually been looking forward to retirement before the merge, but the passion and satisfaction she'd felt when she began her career had somehow been rekindled. She realized people didn't really need a space rat to tell them anything. Deep down, everyone knew. She found being a doctor fulfilling because she was helping people. She was making the one thing a little better, and she would continue to do so for as long as she could. She was, overall, quite happy with her Dr. Schlapp persona.

Being *Evelyn* was a different story. She'd watched Evelyn Schlapp from every angle during the merge and some of what she'd seen wasn't all that pretty. She'd always thought of herself as warm and friendly, and kept company with people who thought the same. When she'd become others, she found a cold and distant woman, somewhat snobbish and often condescending. Meeting Mr. Hyde when she'd only known Dr. Jekyll was uncomfortable, but not nearly as much as realizing what those who'd experienced her dark side all had in common.

When her last patient left, she took off her lab coat and noticed she was still wearing her funeral gown. She changed into something more colorful, a polka-dot dress she'd bought in Spain and had worn only twice. She went to the mirror to check her hair and fix her makeup. She was fidgeting. Gawd, why was she so nervous? She was only going to see the architect in the office next to hers, the Mexican one… For three years, she and José Lopez—she'd finally learned his first name from the mailman—nodded at each in the corridor or going up and down the stairs, but she'd never talked to him, not once. That was about to change. Evelyn locked her office door and went to the next one over to formally introduce herself and, if the opportunity presented itself, invite the man for coffee. She hesitated before knocking and cursed her father silently. In many ways, she knew the man she was coming to see, she'd *been* him for more than a year, and still… Even the will of everyone on Earth wasn't enough to erase all the scars a father can leave. To hell with it. Evelyn Schlapp might never fully stop being a racist, but she'd be damned if she didn't at least try. She knocked on that door with the conviction of a woman who, at long last, was figuring out who she was.

José Lopez opened the door wearing a very nice grey-green suit and the loveliest tie. He smiled and asked Evelyn what he could do for her. Evelyn told him she just wanted to know how he was doing and make sure the noise from her office wasn't a bother and all sorts of other pointless things until she finally found the nerve to ask.

—… And if you're not too busy, I thought you and I could get a cup of coffee and get to know each other better.

José Lopez thought about it for a second, then answered with the thickest New York accent Evelyn had ever heard.

—Sorry, lady. I've got no time for this.

Evelyn felt like crying on the way back to her office. She cried a bit once inside her office. How dare he? She just wanted to be nice to the man and… and… and this had absolutely nothing to do with him. Evelyn had gone there because she wanted to feel better about herself. José Lopez didn't owe her anything, certainly not his time. Having an awkward cup of coffee with a complete stranger just so they could feel like less of an ass didn't sound like a real hoot to Evelyn either, now that she thought about it. Oh, well. Live and learn, she thought, live and learn. What was it they said, again? Oh yes, Rome wasn't built in a day.

62
SOFTY

—THAT WORD HERE, it's spelled c-o-l-o-n-e-l.

Softy moved his eyes around to type.

—KERNEL LIKE ARMY

—I know, but that's how it's spelled.

—THAT'S STUPID

The doctor laughed. Softy couldn't lift a muscle, but it was obvious that he was nervous. It was the first time anyone had read his book, story, whatever. He was getting pretty good at typing with his gaze, but a hundred and sixty pages was a fuck ton of letters. It had taken him a year and a half to write this thing with all the googling he had to do to get the words right. He still made tons of mistakes, though, like 'colonel'—Nah, that couldn't be right. The doc must have been wrong. Okay, so maybe having a real doctor read the book wasn't the best idea if he didn't want her to point out typos and shit, but the whole writing thing was her idea, so it felt right to have her read it.

Softy's first year in the hospital had been quite a ride. It had taken him a while to get used to things. He was depressed for a while. There'd been some sort of riot in town during that time, he could hear it through the window. Then out of nowhere, this black kid—boy or girl, he wasn't quite sure—had come into his room and bit the hell out of him for no good reason. Twice! Well, he knew the reason. It was the Nazi symbols on his skin, the 14/88s and all the rest. Still, normal people don't sink their teeth into quadriplegics, Nazi or not. That's just weird. What came next was even weirder. People in the hospital stopped talking altogether. At first, Softy had thought they'd just stopped talking to *him*, but no. The corridors were silent. He could usually hear folks on the floor below through the air vent; nothing there either, not for like a good six months. Softy wasn't exactly looking for company, but months without hearing a single human speak! By the end of it, he really thought he was losing his mind. Then, just like that, people started talking again.

When he'd asked what happened, Bushra—that was the doctor's name—had told him this ridiculous story about minds merging, and a tick and a space rat. He'd thought she was making fun of him, but she'd kept at it for weeks, telling him bits of the story every day, fifteen minutes at a time during her lunch break. He'd figured she was just trying to keep him entertained. It worked. Softy guessed that most things in that story were metaphors for something else and that it was all meant for him. Like, the tick was maybe his accident, and the rest of the folks in there were all parts of him learning to deal with shit. He could never figure out what the space rats were supposed to represent, though. It didn't matter, he really liked the story, especially the violent parts, people biting each other and all, the thing about the syringe with spit in it. That was cool. The mushy-feely parts were a bit much, though. Like, people changing and understanding each other because they'd been in their shoes? Come on! That was a little too obvious. He'd told Bushra how he felt, and she suggested he write his own story, one without 'all the mushy stuff'—she'd air-quoted him when she said it. She said she'd help him with it if he wanted, but she'd asked for something in return. He had to get his tattoos covered. The doc was paying for it, so Softy said: 'Why not?' Bushra was the only person he was spending time with, might as well make her happy. He got the swastikas turned into a whole bunch of windows. Windows into his soul, he thought that was pretty deep.

As for the story, he stole a bunch from the doctor's version, but in the end, there was a big war against the space rats, with lasers that made people's heads explode. It was epic, and people didn't get all righteous for no reason, 'cause that's not how things work in real life. People don't change.

Yeah, yeah, yeah. So, he got his tattoos covered. He liked Bushra, she was cool, and Sakari, the shrink. They were both nice, but that was just two people. He still had about seven billion others to hate.

63
LYLE

Lyle was a great many things. He was sixteen. He was black. He was wicked smart, except for math. He wasn't bad at it or anything, just not as good as with the other stuff. He was an author—no, for real. He'd written two awful books when he was younger and thrown them in the trash, but his first horror short story was about to get published in an online magazine. He was really, really, excited, and nervous, and scared, and nervous. Lyle had a sweet tooth he'd inherited from his dad. He lived in his late father's house with an aunt from Lakewood, Wisconsin. She was a very religious person and had once expressed her disapproval with Lyle's transition in no uncertain terms, terms she now very much regretted using. Her concept of a greater being had been profoundly shaken by the merge and she'd come to accept that, maybe, God wasn't what she'd always made it out to be. She was also a big fan of 'Both Sides Now' by Joni Mitchell. She'd never paid much attention to the lyrics, but in hindsight, she thought God might have been sending her a message. When Lyle's mother made it clear she didn't want custody, she saw it as a sign, her chance to make amends.

Lyle worked at Booker's Bakery. He was a cook, a really good one. His kouignettes were *soooo* good, oh-my-God-I-could-eat-a-million-of-these good. Folks lined up an hour before the shop opened to make sure they got one. The bakery was doing great. During the short time Marquette was only one person, the town had paid off Booker's debts and bought the building so that his child could someday inherit. Lyle's aunt was holding it in trust for now, but the bakery and the house would be his when he turned eighteen. Lyle also volunteered at the soup kitchen with his friend Shivansh. He liked that a lot. He didn't see Carole much since the divorce, but he understood. They didn't want their lives to overlap too much. He was a Shivansh-friend, now. He was okay with it. Lyle was sensitive—he cried a lot during movies, it was embarrassing, really. He was… well, many, many, many things.

There were also a great many things Lyle *wasn't*. He wasn't popular. Even with hormones, he still had very feminine traits. Mind merge or not, Marquette wasn't exactly the most progressive place in the world. Teenagers might have fantasized about androgynous rock stars, but they wouldn't be seen holding hands with anyone who looked like one. Parents were worse. They all wanted their kids to grow up open-minded, but the one thing they wanted more was for the neighbors not to talk about them. Things *were* a bit better, though—or at least he didn't care as much. Either way, Lyle wasn't hiding anymore.

Lyle wasn't in school. The whole education system was still a mess and he'd chosen to take a break. He wasn't mad at his parents anymore. They'd done their best, he knew that. Whether that was enough didn't really matter, it's what they'd had to give. What else? He wasn't into sports.

He'd quit soccer after his dad died. He liked walking, though. Whatever. He wasn't depressed. That was actually a rare thing since everyone lost their connection to one another. Like everyone else, Lyle was devastated when it happened, but he'd had lots of practice at being alone. Kids used to shun him in school. Although a lot of it had been his own doing, he saw that now. He'd isolated himself on purpose—for fear of being hurt, sure, but a small part of him felt right at home in that bubble. There was also something he'd missed during the merge, though he didn't know it at the time. He'd been *everybody*, and so had everyone else. That meant everyone was the same. He'd hated being different for most of his life, but he'd come to realize that different was also a good thing. Yes, everyone was billions of times smarter, and they were curing diseases and changing the world fast, and—okay, fine, things were better on the whole, but there was something freeing about being unique. Being *you*, with all your quirks, and your bumps and bruises, that also made the world more beautiful. It made the one thing a tiny bit better. That's what Lyle thought, anyway.

It had been literal hell at the bakery that day. It was a hundred degrees outside and the AC had broken down, again. There had been a billion customers, all extra-pissy because of the heat. Now the shop was finally closed, and Lyle took off his apron. He was daydreaming about a cold shower when Billy, the manager, came and told him there was someone up front waiting for him.

—At five o'clock? Seriously? I just wanna go
hoooome!

Lyle walked to the counter. There was a girl standing there looking at him with an awkward smile. Slim figure, long black hair, absolutely gorgeous. Lyle's first thought was: 'Holy shit!' That wasn't the girl's name, that would have been unfortunate. Her name was Elizabeth Kwan.

—Liz?

—Hi, Layla.

—Hi… It's Lyle, now.

—Oh. That's cool. Am I—Am I bothering you? Maybe I should go.

—What are you doing here, Liz?

—I heard you worked here now and—Well, my mom was going to Walmart and I asked if we could stop by, 'cause I thought—I thought maybe you and I could go for a pop some place, or coffee if you drink coffee. I don't, but maybe you do.

—Wh—What?

—I wasn't finished! I had this speech in my head for a while now and… This is harder than I thought, okay? Look, I know I wasn't always that nice to you. Like, at all. And I'm sorry for that. I'm really, really sorry.

—It's… fine. That was a long time ago.

—No, it wasn't. And it's not fine! I was an asshole, and you weren't. You were nice to me.

—I barely talked to you at all.

—It was you that day in my room, wasn't it?

—What do you mean?

—I think you know. I was so scared then. I was crying and… The way that man looked at me before he left, I knew it was you. That's not true, I didn't know then, but I thought about it afterwards and you were the only one who ever looked at me that way. Why'd you stop him? You must have known it wouldn't make a difference. I mean, the mosquitoes got me the next day.

—It made a difference to me.

—...Anyway, after that, well, you were me, I was you...

—We were lots of people.

—Okay, but my point is that I was you. I was you for a while, and I really liked being you and when it was all over, I thought, you know, maybe that meant I liked you? ... Wow. Okay, I've said it.

—...

—I know, right? It took me three years to figure that out, and maybe you never wanted to see me again, but—

—Do you like milkshakes?

—...

—I make a pretty good banana shake. We could drink it outside, somewhere.

—Yes! I'll just go tell my mom I'll walk home.

—Where will you say you're going?

—I'll just tell her I'm with a boy I like. Hurry up! It's really hot in here!

ACKNOWLEDGEMENTS

THIS WAS MY first stand-alone novel. It's weird to think I'll never spend more time with any of these characters. I'd grown quite fond of the folks in Marquette. This is also my seventh novel and I don't think I can put into words just how grateful I am to still be doing this. So thank you, *you* specifically, for always being on board for my crazy ideas. I want to thank David Thomas Moore at Rebellion for giving my weird-zombie-book-without-zombies a home. Big thanks also to Seth Fishman, agent extraordinaire, for finding my weird-zombie-book-without-zombies a home. I hope this one sells a billion copies so we can all buy a horse and retire in Spain. There's a whole collective of people involved in putting a book out into the world: designers, copy-editors, marketing, publicity, the audio team, etc. I'm super thankful for all your talent and I hope you get a horse as well. If we can't all get a horse, then maybe we can buy one as a group and share it. A time-share horse…

Until the next book. In the meantime, let's all do what we can to make the one thing just a tiny bit better.

ABOUT THE AUTHOR

Sylvain Neuvel dropped out of high school at age 15. Along the way, he has been a journalist, worked in soil decontamination, sold ice cream in California, and furniture across Canada. He received a Ph.D. in linguistics from the University of Chicago. He taught linguistics in India, and worked as a software engineer in Montreal. He is also a certified translator, though he wishes he were an astronaut. He absolutely loves toys; his girlfriend would have him believe that he has too many, so he writes about aliens and giant robots as a blatant excuse to build action figures (for his son, of course). His debut, *Sleeping Giants*, was described by NPR as "one of the most promising series kickoffs in recent memory."